# Under a Christmas Sky

## Cat McGowan

Published by Saron Publishing in 2024
Copyright © 2024

*Under a Christmas Sky* is a work of fiction. Names, characters, places, events and incidents are either the products of the author's imagination or used in a fictitious manner.

ISBN-13: paperback 978-1-913297-99-2
ISBN-13: ebook 978-1-913297-98-5
Saron Publishers
Pwllmeyrick House
Mamhilad Mon
NP4 8RG

saronpublishers.co.uk
Follow us on Facebook or Twitter

# Dedication

To my parents
For your unending love and unfailing support
xx

# Chapter One

I can feel the perspiration forming on my chest and unwind my scarf, allowing the chill breeze, which is still managing to traverse the station despite the hordes of people, flutter over my neck. I can't believe this is happening. Muttering curses under my breath I lean back against the wall, wedging my bag tightly in between my feet with my heel as my thumbs start skimming across my phone. A large sweaty man, in a novelty Christmas jumper, squeezes into the gap next to me and my peripheral vision sees him doing the same as me and hundreds of other people all around us. But I try and focus on my phone, even though deep down I know it'll be futile.

As page after page takes forever to load – I guess the networks are jammed – I tune in to some of the voices around me.

"Rail strike..."

"Blizzards coming in..."

"Bomb scare." That one gets my attention and I briefly look up from my phone.

"What?" shrieks a harassed-looking mum with a young girl clinging to her legs and her arms full of shopping.

"Don't panic, not here," replies the original voice, now I can see belonging to her partner. "On the tracks."

I shift focus back to my phone. I don't care why every single train leaving London is cancelled. I just need to do something about it. It's no good though, everywhere I look there are no vacancies. Anywhere. Unless I fancy shelling out a grand for a night at the Savoy, which I definitely do not. That'll teach me for not getting a news app on my phone and avoiding Twitter. Maybe if I'd known five minutes sooner, instead of once I was attempting to scurry down the platform, I might just have found somewhere in time. Instead, with my head in the clouds, it had taken until I was at the ticket barrier before I realised something was totally amiss.

My phone beeps in my hand. Ten percent battery left. Great, that's just what I need. I feel a swell of emotion in my throat. Oh, God, I'm not going to cry, am I? I never cry. But there's a tell-tale tingle in my nose. Nope, not going to happen. I look around the station seeking out the faces of strangers, knowing their stories will distract me.

The mum is now being comforted by the dad while their daughter is looking about her with wide blue eyes and stuffing chocolate buttons into her mouth. At least I only have myself to worry about, not a child too. Realising there'll be others who have it much worse than I do causes the tingle to recede.

I stab angrily at my phone again, this time going to contacts and clicking on Stu's number. As it did the last five times that I tried, it rings for a while before going to voicemail.

"Hi, it's me again," I holler, much louder than I would usually speak in public but it's chaos in here. "Look, I've tried to find a hotel but there's nothing here. Thousands of people are in the same boat. I know it's a long way, but please can you come and get me? I haven't much battery, but I'll try to find somewhere to charge it. Ring me when you get this, please, I know it's asking a lot but..." I sigh deeply, forcing myself to say the next bit, "there's no one else I can ask."

I stand for a moment, nibbling on the corner of my phone. There really isn't. I don't have any friends in London, no one I can call and ask to stay at their place. Jo's the only person I know who lives here and she excitedly told me this morning how, after our meeting, she was away to her place in the country for Christmas. Nice for some, I remember thinking a little bitterly, at the time. Even if I wasted my last precious bars of battery phoning her, I can't imagine her London apartment is the sort of place where she'd leave a key hidden under the mat for emergencies.

I know my dad would have come but he's on nights this week. For about a millisecond, I consider my mum and then, remembering it's six o'clock on a Friday night, almost laugh aloud that the thought even entered my head. The small handful of close friends I have all live miles away and they have young children. I could never ask them to drive to London at night two days before Christmas.

I shove my phone into my pocket where I should feel it vibrate if Stu rings me back and pick up my handbag and folder off the floor, not even bothering to dust them down. A bit of station floor grime is the least of my problems.

I start to weave between the throngs of people, the majority of whom are heading for the exits too. It reminds me of the mass exodus at the end of a concert. Not that I've been to one for a while. When did I stop caring about live music? It used to be such a passion. Probably when tickets became so extortionate. God, I'm starting to sound middle-aged. Even in my own head.

Suddenly my folder flies out of my hand, carried away between the legs of some young business-looking types excitedly talking in loud, 'ra ra', voices about how they can crash in the office and get smashed on the leftover party booze.

"Hey!" I shout trying to get their attention as I push through the crowds behind them. I can only watch helplessly as my folder slides down and then bounces around people's feet before mercifully skittering towards the less crowded doorway of WHSmith.

I dart between angry commuters and stressed-out shoppers until I break free of the swarm, almost falling over in these stupid high heels. Another bad choice today, as it turns out. I bend over to pick up the folder when suddenly it's lifted into the air.

"For fuc..."

Then all the breath leaves my body.

You know that bit in films when the camera zooms into the main character's face while the background seems to move away? I swear that is what's happening right now. The noise of the station a distant hum. The masses of people just a blur of movement.

When I was twelve, a bully punched me right in the diaphragm. That's kind of what this feels like.

I take a really deep breath, hoping it will alleviate the whooshing in my ears. Luckily, all this has happened in about a second, so I don't think he's noticed my world turning on its head. Hopefully, he just thinks I'm surprised. Which I am.

"Hi," he says, casually dusting down my folder where he's retrieved it from the floor and holding it out to me.

*Hi*? That's his opener? *Hi*? Like he just saw me the other day. I know I'm just staring at him mutely, but I can't... I don't... what do I say?

He looks the same. I mean, not really, of course, his hair is shorter, he has a dark, stubbly beard. I glance down his body, encased in a grey, nicely tailored suit. He's broadened out, become more manly, but still trim. No sign of a beer belly or moobs. He was always worried about getting moobs. But he's still him, the same green eyes, the same way of holding himself, the same easy confidence. Damn it, he's now smiling at me gently, possibly worried that I'm having some sort of seizure as I haven't said a word. His smile is still just how I remember it when I allow myself to think of him. Something I try to do as little as possible. Often unsuccessfully.

"Thanks," I finally manage to croak while taking the folder off him, being very careful not to actually touch him. And we're back to staring at each other.

"At least it didn't get too trampled." He finally breaks the silence but doesn't break his gaze. Never one for eye contact, I've started glancing around the station. It feels so weird that life is just going on as normal all around us while I feel like I could implode at any second. It would be so easy to run, to dart back into the crowd and be swallowed up by strangers, disappear into the dark London streets. Never see him again. But my feet won't move.

Right, I can't let him know how much seeing him is affecting me. I can be normal. Taking a deep breath and mentally as well as physically squaring my shoulders, I smile at him, hoping it's not a grimace.

"Well, thanks again, I'm lucky you were here."

"Honestly, it's not so much luck. I was following you."

"Oh, OK, that's not creepy at all." Check me out, even managing a bit of banter.

He smiles broadly. Still got nice teeth, I see. I was kind of hoping they'd turned yellow or started falling out or something. "I saw you from across the concourse and, once I was sure it was you, I just had to come and say hello."

"Oh."

"Still an artist then?" He nods at my folder.

"Yeah, I illustrate children's books. I was here having a meeting with my publisher."

"Oh, that's fantastic. I'm so glad your talent isn't going to waste."

"And what about you? What do you do?" I can't believe I asked that question, partly because it's so banal, but also because I know full well what he does as I have, occasionally, in my weaker moments, googled him.

"I'm an architect," he says as if it's obvious. Which it is.

"Oh, of course, like you always wanted. Are you based here in London?"

"No, I'm back in Cheltenham. But we do a lot of business with a couple of London firms so I'm back and forth quite often."

"So, you're stuck here too then?"

"Yep, looks like. I wasn't quick enough to get a hotel room."

"No, me neither."

"What are your plans?"

"I've left a message with my boyfriend - hopefully, he'll be able to come and get me. What about you?"

"I'll figure something out," he shrugs, in a relaxed way. I always envied how unflappable he was, how nothing used to get to him. "Look," he continues, "as we've got some time to kill, how about we grab a drink? For old times' sake?"

*Nooooooo!* screams my brain, but clearly not the part controlling my mouth because I just say, "OK."

# Chapter Two

## Then

Rose slouched into the canteen, the soles of her purple DMs squeaking on the recently bleached floor, the smell of chlorine battling with the rich aroma of bacon and baking wafting from the kitchen. She'd already had breakfast that morning though and the canteen was filling up fast, so she bypassed the queue, settling herself on one of the brightly coloured chairs next to the small, veneered tables which were scattered around the edges of the room in an attempt to make the space seem modern and friendly, rather than a utilitarian college canteen.

It was infinitely preferable to the horrible, prison-like canteen of her old high school where she'd sat her GCSEs that summer. Even if her parents hadn't moved house, Rose wouldn't have stayed there for Sixth Form. College was always going to be her preferred place to gain her A-Levels, the autonomy suited her.

Rose shrugged off her coat and scarf and checked her watch. She had twenty minutes before her first class of the day. For the third time this week, she wondered if she should just get the later bus and then she wouldn't have to wait around. But she was pathologically punctual and would always panic about the bus being delayed and having to run into one of her classes late, with all those people looking at her. Just thinking about it made her sweat. Besides, this way she got time to work on her doodles. Pulling her drawing pad and pencils out of her bag, she settled back into the seat and started to sketch. Soon, she was totally absorbed in her task.

The girl was back, drawing again. Adam had spotted her as soon as she walked in. He didn't know why she fascinated him so much as she wasn't his usual type. Well, more accurately the type he would admit to liking to his friends. With her dyed red hair, multiple ear piercings and tendency towards wearing dark clothes, she would be described as an emo girl. But there was something about her quiet reserve and the look of focused concentration on her face when she was drawing that he found compelling.

He attempted to tune back into his friend's conversation but as they were just discussing last night's *Big Brother* – a programme he had no interest in whatsoever - he tuned out again and taking a sip of his tea managed another surreptitious look in The Girl's direction.

She was looking up at the kitchen hatch with an intent expression on her face before a soft smile tickled the corner of her mouth and her head went down again as she sketched feverishly. That's it, Adam decided. He had to know what she was drawing. Luckily today The Girl had chosen a seat near to the cutlery station, where they also put the milk, sugar and other paraphernalia.

"I'm just going to put a bit more milk in my tea," he announced to his friends as he scraped his chair back and stood up. Jenny and Tom barely gave him a cursory glance in response as their *Big Brother* conversation had got a little heated, both in strong disagreement about one of the entrants.

Adam adopted a nonchalant saunter over to the other side of the room, although had anyone been paying him the slightest bit of attention, they may have noticed that his attempt at a saunter just made him look like he had something uncomfortable in his pants.

As he poured some milk into his already half-drunk tea, Adam glanced at the girl out of the corner of his eye. She was still absorbed in her drawing and hadn't even noticed him.

He turned and took a couple of steps towards her.

"Hey," he attempted, but it came out like more of a squeak. Feeling a flush of embarrassment - he'd hoped his days of embarrassing squeaks were over now puberty was well and truly behind him - he was relieved that The Girl, or anyone else, had not heard him.

He cleared his throat.

"Hey," he tried again. It came out a bit too loud that time but at least she heard as she swiftly looked up from her work.

"You're in my art class, aren't you?" he continued.

She stared at him, blinking, for what was only a second, but it felt like longer. For something to do, he took a sip of his gross, cold and very milky tea and tried not to grimace.

Rose looked up at The Boy in front of her. Possibly the first person to directly address her since she started at this college over a week ago. Rose had a very solemn resting face and was naturally quite shy but the two elements combined made her appear bad-tempered and unapproachable. Now, at the age of sixteen and having moved house once again, she protected herself behind this veneer of a bad attitude which couldn't be further from the truth. She acted as though she didn't need anyone and was too self-conscious to actively seek out friendships or start conversations.

She'd been so engrossed in her drawing that it took her a moment to register that he'd spoken at all. Realising that he had, in fact, asked her a question, she gathered her wits to respond.

"Um, possibly... Tuesday mornings and Friday afternoons, right?"

"Yeah, I thought I'd seen you in there. What do you think?"

"Of the class? All right, I guess, so far. Our teacher seems pretty passionate so that's always a plus." Rose attempted to smile at The Boy who had moved closer as they were talking and was now standing next to her table. She found that she didn't mind though.

"Have you seen any of her work?"

"Our teacher?"

"Yeah, she displays some paintings in a gallery in town. I called in there on Saturday. They're pretty impressive if you're into modern art. What are you drawing?"

It was such a sudden change in conversation that Rose didn't have time to close her sketch pad like she normally would as he slid into the seat beside her and picked up the pad.

"These are awesome," he said, smiling.

Blushing furiously, Rose snatched the pad back off him and pulled it to her chest.

"It's just doodles," she said defensively, scowling at him

Adam realised too late that he'd crossed a boundary by picking up her sketchbook like that and now she was scowling at him, although he did think she looked rather cute doing so.

"Sorry," he said, holding up his hands. "I shouldn't have just taken a look like that. I know that art is personal. It was rude of me."

The Boy looked so shamefaced, that Rose realised she'd possibly overreacted. Years of being teased and taunted by a group of bullies at her last school, who thought nothing of throwing her sketchbooks into puddles if they got hold of her bag, had made her suspicious. But he seemed genuine and sounded like he was into art himself, so she should give him a chance.

"Sorry," she said, lowering her shoulders from up around her ears and putting the pad gently back on the table. "I was being defensive. You can look if you want, but it's nothing special, just doodles, it's kind of a silly hobby of mine."

With a grateful smile, The Boy flicked open the pad and started looking through the pictures. It gave Rose a chance to study him. Wearing baggy jeans and a faded Muse hoody, he had a slight skater boy look about him and at least he had good taste in music. Unless he was one of those cretins who wore a band's top without the faintest idea who they were. He was quite absorbed looking at her pictures which made her warm to him; he wasn't just glancing and moving on. She'd been right to trust him. Watching him look through her work, she couldn't avoid the fact that he was rather cute. He had spiky brown hair and green eyes and reminded her a bit of Gary Barlow from Take That. Not that she'd ever admit to finding a member of Take That attractive, of course.

He looked up suddenly and caught her watching him. As their eyes met, he gave her a little grin. Rose quickly looked down at her hands, fiddling with one of the many silver rings she wore and trying to ignore the little gallop in her chest when he looked at her.

Adam had caught her looking at him but thought nothing of it. Of course you would study the stranger who has sat himself next to you, although he did find her slight blush sweet as she looked away. She was obviously not the hardened character her clothing and attitude could make her seem. One hell of an artist too. She'd done characterisations of the canteen staff, turning them into animals. Without even looking up, he knew exactly which ladies were which. The tall gangly one she'd made into a stork, the friendly, smiley one into a cow, the one that never smiled into a haughty-looking pig. But beyond the humour, there was a skill to the drawings that made them come to life.

"These are really good," he said decisively, closing the pad and handing it back.

"Like I said, it's just a silly hobby. A way to pass the time," she replied with a shrug, but the slight smile was back, so Adam took it as a sign that she was happy with the praise.

"Well, I wish I could draw like that."

"You're doing art, aren't you?"

"Yeah, but only because I want to be an architect. I'm more into graphics and lines and structures, although I really appreciate art in general. I'm just not very creative, I guess."

They lapsed into silence for a moment, Rose still fiddling with her rings. A burst of laughter nearby caused them to look up at the mixed group spread out oh-so-confidently across several tables. Rose felt a familiar pang of inadequacy as she watched the girls in the group, in their fashionable clothes, make-up flawlessly applied, seemingly so secure in their friendships and their place in the world. Rose never felt that way. She always hovered on the periphery of life, feeling like the little kid with their face squashed up against the bakery window, smelling the cakes, seeing the cakes but without the necessary pocket-money to actually enjoy the cakes.

"Is it just animals?" A voice broke into her thoughts. The Boy.

"Sorry?"

"Your pictures, do you just draw animals?"

"Oh, no, I just like turning things or people into caricatures. Animals are my favourite - I can see it, you know. But sometimes I just exaggerate certain features. It's just a bit of fun. My main passion is watercolours."

"Really?" Adam couldn't help but sound surprised. From her emo-style, he'd expected her to make weird avant-garde structures out of chicken wire or something.

Rose shrugged and opened her mouth to say more when suddenly up bounced a girl with beautiful mocha skin and a perfectly round afro held back from her face with a row of little butterfly clips. She had a bright, infectious smile, revealing very white, slightly crooked teeth.

"Here's where you got to," she exclaimed. "Hi, I'm Jenny." She turned her smile to Rose and held out her hand.

"Rose," she replied returning the handshake feebly, feeling a bit over-awed at the bundle of energy before her.

"Come on, Adam, we need to get to class. Ugh, why is your tea so milky," she cried, picking up his mug and peering at it as he slid out from his seat. Then, "Wow, I love your hair colour, what is it?"

"Um, red..." Rose answered meekly, realising that Jenny was now directing the conversation at her again — it was hard to keep up.

"I meant which brand, silly, I'm thinking of dyeing mine purple. What do you think? Never mind, you can tell me another time. See you later." And in a cloud of perfume and hairspray, she was off, calling, "Come on, Adam," over her shoulder.

Rose found she was smiling as Adam solemnly slid her sketchbook back across the table to her.

"I'll see you around, Rose."

He smiled at her and followed Jenny, weaving a path through the now packed canteen, to where another boy stood waiting with his bag and coat.

Adam. She would never have guessed that was his name, but it suited him. Rose wondered if Jenny was his girlfriend and was surprised at the jolt of disappointment she felt at the thought. Feeling cross with herself, she shoved her sketchbook into her bag and threw on her coat and scarf. Just because a decent-looking boy was nice to her didn't mean she should get all carried away and start crushing on him like some silly little girl. He'd probably never speak to her again anyway.

# Chapter Three

I'm trying not to stare at him, as he stands shoulder to shoulder with other people in the crush at the bar. He'd confidently led us to a little old-fashioned pub down a couple of backstreets near the station. I'd been grateful for the cold evening air cooling my flushed cheeks and the busy bustle of people on the pavements which prevented any real conversation except for the odd "this way". It gave me a bit of time to gather my thoughts, well, attempt to, anyway. I still feel bamboozled. I can't believe I'm actually here. With him.

Christ, it's hot in here. I slip my cardigan off, adding it to the pile of my belongings on the bench next to me. We're crammed onto a small table in the corner. London, already heaving thanks to it being the last Friday before Christmas, has taken on an extra air of wild exuberance. That low-level excitement that comes from a big incident or event has joined the Christmas buzz (all the better as no one has actually been hurt so far) and the atmosphere in here is more like New Year's Eve. I must've heard the phrase 'blitz spirit' used at least three times on our walk from the station.

To distract myself from looking at the bar, I gaze around the pub. It's what I would consider a proper old man's pub. Green velvet upholstered seats, wonky wooden tables with those funny swirled table legs. A blazing log fire, despite the intense heat already generated from all the bodies. Strung up across the ceiling (which from its weird yellow colour suggests it hasn't been painted since the smoking ban came into force - gross) are those colourful foil Christmas streamers that I didn't even know you could buy anymore. If I could see the carpet, I'm fairly confident that it would be a swirly Seventies monstrosity. Basically, it's like sitting in a time warp. Appropriate really.

I'm about to start people watching, my favourite pastime, when he returns, carefully placing our drinks on the wobbly table.

"Sorry to interrupt your people watching," he says with a grin.

"Actually, I was just wondering why on earth they have a fire lit," I reply, refusing to allow him to think that he still knows me. Even though he obviously does... a bit.

"Yeah, it's rather warm, isn't it?" he replies, slipping off his jacket and yanking at his tie. He hasn't sat down yet and I'm mesmerised by his throat and collarbone slowly being exposed as he manages to pull off his tie and open the top couple of buttons. I catch a glimpse of chest hair at the base of his neck. That's new. Of course it is. I give my head a little shake to dislodge the images that are attempting to crowd in.

"Sorry, they only had the little mixer bottles of orange juice so I got you a J20, hope that's OK?"

"Yes, great, thanks," I murmur, taking a long swig.

"I'm just nipping to the loo," he says. "Back in a sec."

Phew. A little more time to compose myself. At least I can blame my undoubtedly flushed cheeks on the heat in here. I need to get my shit together. I am better than this. I don't need to fall apart just because a face from my past reappears. Even if it's the face of an utter bastard. But hey, the past is the past, right? I can be mature. Maybe this will be good for me. Cathartic in some way.

He seems so relaxed. But then why shouldn't he be? He's probably barely given me a moment's thought. It's funny he recognised me, though. I think I look so different. Sometimes I look in the mirror and I don't recognise the person who looks out at me.

Gone are the radical hair colours of my youth and now I have my naturally dark hair lowlighted with chestnut tones. I use decent conditioner these days and it falls in soft, glossy waves landing just on my shoulders, when it's not scooped up into a messy bun with pencils sticking out of it.

Like most thirty-somethings, my make-up skills have matured too, leaning towards a sensible, pretending I'm-not-wearing-make-up-even-though-I'm-caked-in-the-stuff look. I'm still slightly bohemian in my dress sense, I suppose, but then it's not like I have to dress a certain way for work. Although, now I think of it, I do tend to wear the uniform of an artist: loose, floaty tops and lots of ethnic jewellery.

Today I'm in black skinny jeans, a loose cream vest and a long, thick, maroon cardigan. I'm wearing a large silver pendant in the shape of a starfish hanging low over my chest. My only concession to the publishing meeting that I had with Jo this morning is my heeled shoes instead of my usual flat boots. At least it means that I look pretty decent for this surprise encounter. I even redid my make-up before heading for the train. How awful it would have been bumping into him looking like a shit show.

Not that it matters what I look like. I don't care what he thinks. I suppose I just wouldn't want him to look down at me. At least today I can be the part. The modern, successful artist and teacher with her crap together. If I'm honest with myself, most days I feel like I'm just acting a part. Maybe that's why I never recognise myself in the mirror? Maybe I don't even know who I am anymore?

But hey, I've played this part for over a decade, I should be able to pull off an hour in the pub. I take another fortifying sip of my J20, feeling grateful that he didn't push me to have something alcoholic, even though he's gone for a pint of bitter, it seems. Damn, there I am already thinking of him as thoughtful. I must not give in to his charms. I must remember at all times who he really is.

A rowdy group in the corner has just started singing along - well, wailing would be more appropriate - to a song that can faintly be heard coming through the pub speakers under the cacophony of drunken voices. The group's all decked out in ugly Christmas jumpers – they must be roasting – and a few are wearing reindeer antlers, glittery teenyboppers, 'comedy' glasses or flashing red noses. They've stood up and are now swaying en masse as they sing.

First off, what is it about this song? Why is everyone so obsessed with it? It's the most depressing and dirgy of all the Christmas tat. If I had to choose a Christmas song, which would be done under duress as they're all a load of crap, I'd probably choose Mariah Carey as at least there's a bit of fun and pop to that one.

And second, why does Christmas turn people into insufferable morons? I'm sure this group of blokes, when they don't look like a one-pound Christmas shop has thrown up on them, probably all hold sensible, respectable jobs and have a bunch of responsibility. And now look at them. I suppress a shudder.

I bloody hate Christmas.

Oh, and here comes one of the reasons for my particularly fractious mood, weaving his way through the revellers, grinning at the singing group despite the fact that the one on the end just partially body slammed him due to over-exuberant swaying.

He slides into the seat opposite me, still grinning, reminding me so strongly of the boy I knew it's like a punch in the gut. I seem to be getting those a lot this evening. I sip my drink.

"A bit mad in here, isn't it?" He grins. "But then, I suppose it's probably like this everywhere tonight."

I give him a tight smile and start fiddling with a coaster, tearing little strips of paper off and letting them pile on the table.

"Any news?" he asks.

I look at him with a questioning expression. He nods to my phone, sat on the corner of the table.

"Oh, no. I didn't think to check."

He stands up suddenly, peering at something over my head. His crotch is now only about a foot from my face. I'm not sure where to look. So, I crane my head around to see what he's looking at. Oh, there's a TV in the corner, showing BBC news, but I can't see over people's heads to read the subtitles.

"They're still saying trains won't be running till early hours tomorrow. Then they plan on running an extended service to get people home," he says, mercifully returning to his seat and putting his crotch way out of sight.

"Was it a bomb threat?" I ask, pleased that my voice sounds level.

"Seems like it. Either on the tracks or on one of the trains or something. They have to search all the tracks and trains, I guess. It must be a pretty legitimate threat for them to be willing to create all this chaos."

"So, you said at the station that you were back in Cheltenham?" I ask. See, I can converse like a normal person.

"Yeah, I have a flat in Clarence Square now. Do you remember it? We had a few picnics there."

I nod my head stiffly, trying to keep my expression impassive as my mind is assaulted with memories of bright blue skies, soft grass and a feeling of pure contentment. Of course I bloody remember, but I can't let it affect me. My impassive expression might be coming off as steely though, as he shifts uncomfortably on his stool before continuing.

"Anyway, I moved to London just after I graduated and worked here for a few years but then moved back to be closer to the family." He takes a gulp of his pint and once again my eye is drawn to his neck as he swallows.

"How are your family?" I say, without thinking. My plan on the walk here was to avoid any talk of the past and yet here I am with all these openers. But then I always loved his family.

"Good, thanks," he replies, his eyes drawn to the window.

I can't resist, I have to ask. "And how is Damien?"

"Oh, you know, Damien will always be Damien," he replies with a faint smile that doesn't quite reach his eyes. Of course, he must be upset about not being home for Christmas Eve. He was always so close to his family.

"What about you?" he asks, suddenly turning back to me with his smile at full charm. "Where are you living these days?"

"I'm in Bristol," I reply.

"Oh, really? How come you ended up there?"

I shrug, "I just did, I suppose. A job came up teaching art part-time and Bristol is a nice place. It's quite busy and buzzing with lots to do, but not too big. It made sense to move there."

"So, you teach as well as illustrate?"

"Yeah, it gets me out of the house, otherwise I'd go days without seeing humans."

"Oh, I'd have thought you'd love that," he says with a broad smile, that I can't help but smile back to.

"True," I acquiesce, "but it's not the healthiest way to live."

I catch his eye, and something passes between us. A million unspoken things. His face turns serious and I know, really know, what he's about to say. I need to speak first, but my mind goes blank.

In a moment of perfect timing, my phone starts to vibrate angrily across the table. I snatch it up and with a rush of relief see it's Stu calling.

"Excuse me a sec. Hello," I answer loudly, putting my finger in my other ear, but it's no use, it's too loud in here. "Hold on," I holler, "I just need to go outside."

I push my way through the sweaty, tinselled masses and swing through the doors out onto the street. The cold air hits me like a blast but it's welcome after the heat from inside. It acts as a bit of a slap in the face too. What was I doing asking about his family and stuff? Too personal. I need to keep things formal.

I step around a couple smoking just outside the door and tuck myself up against the brick wall of the pub. The streets seem a little quieter now that the station crowds have dispersed but it's still lively and buzzing out here under the coloured flashing lights adorning the pub.

"Hi, Stu? Can you hear me now?"

"All right, gorgeous?" he responds.

Biting down my annoyance at the term (it's such a fake affectation, he calls all women gorgeous like some sort of title and it winds me right up. I've asked him not to do it several times), I ask, "Did you get my message?"

"Oh, yeah, I did just now, but that's the problem, gorgeous, see, I'm already out and I've had a few. I can't drive now is the thing. All the lads are the same way or I'd ask one of them to get you."

"But it's only just gone seven, how can you already have had a few drinks?"

"Ah, well, I went out straight from work, see."

The fucking liar.

"You never go out straight from work, you always want a shower first."

"Yeah, well, it's Christmas, isn't it, a bit different, you know," he mutters.

I can picture him there, pint in hand, probably rolling his eyes at his stupid friends about the 'little woman giving him grief'. He always acts differently in front of his mates.

"OK, so you went straight from work but didn't hear or see your phone ring, even though you're on it constantly."

"I'm sorry, OK," he says, not sounding sorry at all. "We were playing pool and I didn't hear it ring."

"Here's what I think happened," I continue. "I think it's been all over the news, I think you'd have seen all my calls, probably listened to my messages but you didn't want to come and get me. You didn't want to miss your precious

Friday night with the boys." I put as much vitriol into my voice as I can manage. "So, you waited until you were in the pub and legitimately drinking before calling me back. Sound about right?"

"Oh, come on, Babe." It's 'Babe' now he's in full wheedle. "It's Black Friday, it's always a cracking night out."

"I'm stuck in London. On my own. Until morning. Aren't you even the slightest bit worried about me?"

"You're all independent and that, you'll be fine. Just find a twenty-four-hour café or something. Trains will be on again in the morning. I'll meet you at the station and we can go for brunch if you like? As long as it's not too early."

"You have got to be kidding me?"

"Oh, come on, don't be like that. You've never been the clingy sort, that's why I like you."

"Oh, that's why you like me? Well, do you know what, at this moment, I have no idea why I ever liked you! You're a selfish, ignorant prick. We're done."

Just as he starts to respond, in another display of perfect timing, my battery dies.

I manage to resist hurling the phone under the wheels of a passing London cab and lean back against the wall, shutting my eyes and taking a deep lungful of chilled air. I can feel the cold spreading through my chest.

I can't believe I wasted four months of my life dating that loser. Actually, I can believe it. I don't have the best track record with men. I knew deep down he was a bit of a tosser, what my dad would call a bit of a Del Boy, not that I ever let my dad meet any of my boyfriends. But, for some reason, I ignored all his tosser-ness and the fact that we were totally unsuited and just went along with it. I think out of sheer inertia. I suppose he was quite funny sometimes and I think I kind of fed off his confidence, as I don't have much of my own. When we first started dating, he was very charming and he managed to sweep me along, making it easy to forgive the more annoying aspects of his personality.

25

Still, Stu was a real low, even for me. I just seem incapable of holding down a decent relationship ever since, well, ever since I became an adult. I just can't seem to find love. I know it exists, I know I can feel it. I don't know whether I just choose badly or something in me just doesn't work anymore. Maybe I'm broken? Christ, there's a depressing thought.

As I watch commuters rushing home, navigating their way past partygoers in various states of inebriation, it's like I can see a parade of my exes in my mind's eye.

There was Mark who lasted about nine months; we had zero in common, but he was amazing in bed, so honestly, our whole relationship was just based on sex. I can't even remember his last name.

Then there was Alex, my longest relationship to date. He was nice, we both liked art, had the same taste in music; he was completely inoffensive. But he never made me laugh. He never quite got my sarcastic sense of humour either. There was no passion. We bumbled along for over two years until he got offered a job in America. He didn't even bother asking me to go with him, not that I'd have said yes. We just agreed that we'd come to a natural conclusion. Two years of my life and I don't think I even cried when it ended.

Then there was a string of vaguely unsuitable men that just didn't work out. The most memorable of which was Rob who I finally thought might be a keeper, I definitely felt a spark with him. Until I found out he was also seeing two other girls.

"Argh!" I let out a groan of frustration. I'd been focusing on entirely the wrong thing. Stu and I would have ended soon enough anyway, but now what am I going to do? I'm stuck in London, in midwinter, potentially for another twelve hours. At least for now, I'm not alone, although to be honest, I'm not sure if that's a good or bad thing considering the company I'm in. And now I'm freezing my tits off too, out here in this flimsy vest, I must have turned blue.

With a bone-weary sigh, I brace myself for the heat and masses and push my way back into the pub.

"Everything OK? You must be freezing!" He moves to rub my arm, but I manage to shrug him off as I sit down. Still, the slight touch of his warm hand on my ice-cold skin feels like a brand.

"I'll warm up in a minute," I reply, suppressing a shiver and giving playing it cool a whole new meaning.

"So, is your boyfriend on his way?"

"No, he can't come." Why the hell did I just say that? I should've said he was already at Reading or something. It would've been the perfect excuse to leave soon. The cold must have slowed my brain.

"It's OK though, I'll find a twenty-four-hour café and sit it out. I can catch up on my sketching; I'll just have to find an art shop or somewhere I can buy some pencils and paper from." I know I'm babbling, but I can't stop. "You seem to know the area; do you know of anywhere?"

"Not offhand, but I'll help you find somewhere," he says, draining the remains of his pint decisively.

"Are you sure? Haven't you got to try to get home?"

"I've got time," is his somewhat elusive answer, but he's already up and shrugging into his jacket while other customers are beginning to circle our table like sharks. So I stand and do the same.

"Do you think there'll be a scrum for our table when we move?" he says in a low voice close to my ear. "My money is on Asian Boris Johnson there."

A giggle escapes me. I'd had exactly the same thought about the strange-looking character edging closer to our table every second.

"Shall we sit back down, just to keep them on their toes?" I say back, getting a whiff of his subtle cologne as I lean closer. He chuckles in response but in unspoken agreement, we turn and leave. I can't help but look over my shoulder as we reach the door to see that Asian Boris Johnson was indeed victorious.

"Told you," says a velvety voice in my ear.

Outside, I zip up my jacket and tuck my hands into the pockets, nuzzling my chin into my scarf. A thin leather jacket also turned out to be a poor fashion choice today. Fine for hopping on and off the Tube but not for walking around at night in the middle of winter.

"This way," he says, guiding me across the road by the elbow. "There's bound to be somewhere along here. Although, I have to say I'm sceptical about your café plan. They're all going to be rammed."

"I'm sure I'll find somewhere; I'll maybe just have to go further from the stations."

"Oh, look at that."

He stops suddenly and points his finger to a shop front. An ornately decorated tree sits in the middle of the window display. Running around it on a circular track is a miniature old-fashioned train, puffing out steam. Tiny, glittering, snow-covered wooden houses are assembled around the track like a little village. Some even have lights in the windows. The whole scene is softly lit and a laser light somewhere gives the effect of snow falling.

"Isn't that awesome?" he says, his voice filled with childlike wonder.

"Yeah, the attention to detail is pretty impressive," I reply blandly.

"But it's so Christmassy."

"Ugh, Christmas. I hate Christmas."

"What?" He turns to me looking so shocked I might as well have said I was married to Elvis. "You don't hate Christmas!"

"Yes, I do." I start ticking things off on my fingers. "It's an over-marketed nightmare. People are forced to spend money they don't have to buy gifts for people out of a sense of duty or peer pressure. It's all over the TV and the shops from September. 'But it's Christmas' is the lamest and most overused excuse in history. There's all the forced jollity, all the guilt and pressure if, like me, you don't want to join in with the enforced festivities. I got a stroppy anonymous letter from one of my neighbours the other day just because I don't have Christmas lights up or a tree in the window. Apparently, I was letting the street down."

"You don't have a tree?"

"That's your takeaway? No, I don't really enjoy dragging dead flora, which is a huge fire hazard by the way, into my living room and throwing tinsel at it while constantly hoovering up pine needles."

"You can get a fake one, you know," he grins, humouring me.

I narrow my eyes at him.

"But," he says, looking like a little boy again. "How can you not like Christmas, you used—" I cut him off before he can get any further.

"I just don't like it, OK? And I bet there are tons of other people over the age of twelve who don't like it either and just pretend they do so they don't get called Grinch or Scrooge. Let's just move on, shall we?"

I turn and start walking down the street but as I look back over my shoulder, he's just standing there.

"Are you coming or not?" I ask, sounding stroppier than I intended.

"I've had an idea," he says, finally catching me up. "Let's spend the night in London."

"Don't be stupid."

"Hear me out. We're stuck here. All the twenty-four-hour places will be as full as the hotels by now but I'm sure we can find other places to entertain ourselves and, when we can't, we can explore the city at night. My favourite lecturer always encouraged us to look up but I've stopped doing that recently. I get to enjoy all the old buildings, lit up at night, you get to… I don't know… do whatever artists do. See life or something?" He shrugs but his enthusiasm for this crazy idea is almost infectious.

"Look," he continues, "I know we have a… complicated history."

Ha! That's putting it mildly. I look down at the ground, but he carries on regardless. "But I'm sure we can put all that aside for tonight and just have an adventure."

Easy for him to say. I can't look at him. I'm tempted, so tempted, but is it the stupidest idea ever?

"Come on, we're boring adults now. When was the last time you had an adventure?"

His feet enter my field of vision, which means he's standing a foot from me now.

"I dare you."

My head snaps up at that. His eyes, cool and challenging bore into mine. Every emotion I've ever had for the man before me rushes through my mind in a split second and before I can stop myself, I'm saying, "Deal."

# Chapter Four

## Then

Despite her efforts to the contrary, Rose couldn't stop thinking about Adam. She became hyper-aware of him; it was like she could sense him. Her eye was drawn to him in the distance, across campus. Immediately, she'd know if he was in the canteen. Just a glimpse of him would cause her to tingle and her pulse to quicken. Annoyed with herself for what she considered a pathetic reaction to a touch of kindness, she tried to avoid him, hoping it would pass. If she spotted him in the canteen, she just wouldn't go in. If he was walking towards her, she would subtly change direction, taking a more laborious route to her next class.

They'd had two art classes together and both days she'd arrived early and sat in her usual seat near the front. Even with her back to the door, she knew when he'd come in. She'd caught his eye at one point while picking up some supplies and he'd smiled and waved which she'd returned with a slight smile and nod before scurrying back to her seat and absorbing herself in her work.

She was settling into her college routine now, although still hadn't made any proper friends, not that she was really expecting to. This was her sixth educational establishment and rather than getting used to it and becoming the plucky, confident new girl, with each move she had retreated more into herself. Instead, she'd learnt to hide her natural shyness and lack of self-confidence behind a mask of indifference and contempt. People left her alone.

It meant that she was no longer bullied like she had been in previous schools, but it also meant that no one approached her to be friendly either. Well, until Adam last week and look how her awkwardness was messing that up.

She liked to tell herself that she enjoyed being a loner, but actually it was getting a bit tedious, and, late at night when she couldn't sleep, it confirmed her worse thoughts about herself: that she was worthless and unlikeable.

In sociology, they were about to embark on a group project and she'd been put with a few people who seemed nice enough. Except for one boy who constantly stank of weed, causing whatever room he was in to smell too. She could tell straight away he would be pathologically lazy and they'd all end up having to do his share of the work if they wanted a good grade. Which she did. They were all supposed to be meeting up that afternoon and Rose was allowing herself the slight hope that it might lead to more socialising.

For now, though, she was ensconced at a small table at the back of the canteen, half-heartedly picking at a plate of chips and cheese while sketching. This time her attention had been taken by a group of Jocks – she hated the Americanism but didn't know what else to call them – who were being loud and attention-seeky in the middle of the room, preening and showing off to a group of girls at a nearby table who were pretending to ignore them yet clearly delighted at the attention.

Rose was drawing the Jocks as crows and was quite pleased with how she'd managed to capture their arrogant expressions and silly, over-styled haircuts.

Then she knew he was there. A movement in her peripheral vision which her subconscious correctly identified as Adam. How else would she have known that he'd entered the canteen? But she did.

Head still bowed over her drawing, she watched him under her eyelashes as he queued up for food, looking very relaxed, his fingers drumming along on his tray to whatever song was pumping through his headphones. Dressed today in baggy jeans and a Converse hoody he looked even more attractive than when she pictured him in her head, which was far too often.

Adam started scanning the canteen, probably looking for his friends, so Rose dropped her gaze and concentrated on her sketching. But she kept stealing glances his way, watching him pay, noting where he sat. Suddenly the crows weren't so easy to draw. She couldn't focus.

Adam was chuffed. She was here. He'd hoped to catch Rose again. Since their brief conversation last week, he'd become even more fascinated by her. But she was proving quite elusive. Not usually prone to introspection or over-thinking, Adam had started to worry that perhaps she was avoiding him. Whenever he saw her in the distance, thinking they'd cross paths, she seemed to disappear. He hadn't seen her in the canteen again, despite being there early most mornings. He'd looked forward to art class, but she was already absorbed in her work when he'd arrived, and he hadn't wanted to disturb her. Then on Tuesday, when he had caught her eye and waved at her to join him, she'd given him a stiff smile and retreated. Maybe he'd been too forward looking at her pictures and he'd irritated her? But she'd seemed OK with him at the time.

Generally a happy-go-lucky kind of person, Adam would usually just go with the flow and if a girl didn't show any interest, then he wouldn't go out of his way to pursue her. So why had he spent the last few days coming up with excuses to talk to Rose again when she'd made no effort to seek him out? There was just something about her that called to him. He wanted to know her more. Thankfully, he'd come up with a plan and it was fool proof. He hoped.

Rose knew he was approaching her before he arrived—that peripheral vision thing at play again. She took some subtle deep breaths to calm her nerves and coolly selected another pencil to start shading her crows. It wasn't until he was standing right next to the table that she looked up.

"Hey," he said, smiling down at her.

"Hey," she replied and, despite her efforts to be aloof, she couldn't contain the shy smile that broke across her face.

"Can I sit?" Adam indicated the empty chair with her scarf draped on it.

"Yeah sure." She scooped the scarf off and Adam sat down, his attention straight away going to the sketch that she was working on. This time she made no attempt to stop him. He looked up, scanning the room until his eyes alighted on the table of jocks and he smiled broadly.

"Brilliant," he grinned, his eyes sparkling with mirth.

Rose felt herself colour at his praise. It felt nice.

"How've you been?" he asked.

"Good, thanks. I found that art gallery on the weekend, you know with Miss Pheasant's art in?"

"Oh yeah; what did you think?"

"Well, modern art isn't really my thing, but I did think hers was excellent."

"Makes you feel good about being taught by her, huh?"

"Definitely. Like, imagine they were really shit, it would be hard to take on anything she said in class."

"Totally, you'd constantly be thinking, Yeah, but your stuff is shit though."

"Exactly." Rose giggled; a sweet genuine bubble of laughter that made Adam instantly want to make her laugh again.

They smiled at each other, the ice further broken.

"So," continued Adam. "I have a huge favour to ask. Feel free to say no, like no pressure at all or anything. But I wondered if you might be able to make a poster for me?"

"What kind of poster?" Rose asked, instantly suspicious. Adam seemed genuine but something seemed off, he looked a bit uncomfortable.

"Well, it's for my little brother. It's his birthday soon and he loves comic books and stuff. I don't know what to get him and I thought, well... I hoped, maybe you could do a picture of him like a superhero? I thought if I brought you in a picture?"

"Oh, I don't think I can, sorry," she said regretfully.

"I can pay you if that helps."

"No, it's not that," she replied with a sigh. "I think it's a lovely idea but, this sounds wanky, it's just I can't do this sort of thing," she gestured to her sketchbook, "from a picture. I have to see the person in the flesh. I don't know why. I've tried before with celebrities in magazines and stuff and it just looks crap."

Rose looked up at Adam who seemed deflated and she felt instantly guilty. It was a very sweet idea, wanting to do something for his little brother.

"I know," she brightened. "Why don't I just meet him? Like, over the weekend or something, if he goes to a park or whatever, I could meet you there and get a look at him?"

"Oh, I don't know." Adam didn't look too pleased with the idea and Rose instantly felt like an idiot. Why would he want to see her on the weekend? He'd probably realise she has a crush on him now. She would never normally put herself forward like that.

"Just an idea," she muttered, scooping her pencils back into their case and wishing she could crawl in there with them.

Adam studied her, suddenly retreating into herself, the tip of her ear turning pink and clashing with the bright red hair tucked behind it. Was he overreacting? She seemed genuine and as he glanced again at her sketch, he confirmed that she definitely had talent. And, despite the humour in her drawings, it never felt like it was done with any malice or cruelty. Maybe he should trust her?

"Look, the park won't work but why don't you come to my house to meet him?"

Rose looked up into his eyes and smiled. It was like the sun coming out

Adam looked at his watch and picked up his pace. She was early! He could just make out her flash of red hair in the distance as she sat on the wall, her boots drumming against the bricks.

As he got closer, he instinctively slowed down to watch her. She hadn't seen him yet as her focus was drawn by a toddler chasing a pigeon around, getting under shoppers' feet. It was a particularly warm day for September and along with black tights and a denim skirt she was wearing a loose charcoal T-shirt which was slipping off one shoulder. He'd only seen her in long sleeves before now and he felt an unexpected twitch in his groin at the sight of the creamy, smooth skin of her shoulder and collarbone. Shocked by his body's response to a bit of skin – it's not like this was the 1920s, for God's sake – he paused for a moment to take a deep breath.

The sun took the opportunity to pop out from behind a cloud and Rose turned her face to the warmth, smiling softly. She really was beautiful. Her features were sweet and elfin, and he knew that, behind the heavy eyeshadow and thick black eyeliner, her eyes were a bright blue. What made her stand out though was that she seemingly had no idea of just how pretty she was.

She must have sensed him watching her because she opened her eyes and looked straight at him. Gathering his wits, Adam smiled back and waved as she hopped down off the wall and, swinging her tatty rucksack over her shoulder, walked towards him.

They'd agreed to meet in the centre of town as she'd only moved to Cheltenham a few weeks previously and didn't know her way around yet. Luckily, it was only a ten-minute walk from the centre to his house.

While they walked conversation flowed easily, and she seemed to relax in his company as they discovered a similar taste in music and films. He was very relieved to hear that she hated Big Brother just as much as he did and they both enjoyed a rant about the many ways it was awful while they strolled.

When they turned into Saint Paul's Road, she suddenly giggled.

"What's so funny?"

"Do you live far?"

"No, just two minutes up here, then my road is off on the left. Why?"

"I live up there." She pointed to the street they'd just passed.

"But when I said Saint Paul's Road, you didn't know it?"

"I don't know the name of any of the streets other than mine yet, and I keep forgetting that too." She giggled again, the sound tugging at Adam on a deep level.

"Sorry," she said meekly but still with a smile playing around her lips.

"What for?"

"Making you walk all the way into town for no reason."

"It's OK, it's been nice getting to know you a bit more," he said genuinely, smiling back at her. Their eyes locked and he felt something thud deep in his chest as a slight blush stole across her cheeks before she looked away.

"So, what's it like around here then?" she asked, and the conversation continued.

As they approached the house, Adam slowed slightly. He knew he should say something, give her some warning, but he didn't want to. He shouldn't have to explain anything or make apologies. Besides, deep down, he was curious. Curious to see how she'd react, whether she was the sort of person he thought she was. Maybe that was unfair on her and on everyone, but it was too late now anyway, he could see Damien's eager face in the window and his mum flinging open the door.

Rose was feeling incredibly nervous. It had been so lovely, walking here in the sunshine with Adam. There was something about him that made her relax and be herself. She shouldn't be able to; he was good-looking, confident, popular. He should make her want to retreat inside her shell, but he didn't. Something about the way he spoke to her, looked at her, made her feel... she didn't know. But it was different. She liked it.

And now, there was his mum looking like she had just stepped out of a Next catalogue: her hair perfectly cut into a choppy bob in classy honey-blonde tones, her boot cut jeans fitting her slim frame nicely and she wore a soft, patterned jumper (definitely Next). Rose was terrible at guessing adults' ages, but she figured her to be early forties at most.

Rose swallowed and clutched her bag closer to her side, instantly feeling lacking. They were probably some perfect Stepford family and she wouldn't fit in at all with all their perfection.

"Thank goodness you're here," called his mum. "Damien's been so excited to meet you. You must be Rose. Hi, I'm Karen, Adam's mum, obviously. Come on in."

She left the front door open and Rose instinctively hung back.

"After you," said Adam, closing in behind her.

With no escape, she took a deep breath and stepped into a bright and airy laminated hallway with a staircase and several doorways opening off it.

"Would you like a cuppa? Or would you prefer a soft drink?" Karen's head poked around the furthest door, probably the kitchen. "I have Coke or Diet Coke?"

"Diet Coke would be great, thanks," Rose replied, her nerves abating slightly at Karen's friendly welcome.

"You'd better go straight in, Ad, I'll bring you some drinks," Karen continued, disappearing into the kitchen.

"Sorry, Damien loves meeting new people so he's probably a bit overexcited. I haven't told him exactly why you're coming over, I just said you were drawing his picture."

Adam seemed strangely nervous which put Rose on edge again as she stepped into the room that he gestured to.

It was a large bay-windowed room that in a house like this would usually be the main family living room, but in this house, it was obviously Damien's bedroom. Within seconds, Rose had taken it all in and everything made sense: The Hulk bed cover on the hospital-style bed, the comic book posters on the walls and the oxygen tanks lined up like sentries in the corner and finally Damien, grinning at her, his eyes wide and excited in his pale, thin face as he wriggled impatiently in his wheelchair.

"Hi, you must be Damien; I'm so pleased to meet you," she said as she strode over to him and took his narrow little fingers in hers and shook his hand. "Cool posters. I love comics. Which are your favourites?"

That was the moment for Adam, right then. That's when with complete certainty he knew.

He sank down onto the small sofa in the corner of the room and watched rapt while Rose chatted with Damien about comics. Until they got to know him, people usually fell into two categories when they met his brother. Either they became all quiet and uncomfortable and didn't know what to say or they gushed and condescended to him, speaking too loudly or slowly. That really pissed Adam off. Yes, Damien looked different and he had problems but he was still just an eleven-year-old kid who deserved respect.

That's what Rose was giving him as she listened to his opinions while they flicked through one of his favourite comics. Karen entered the room carrying a tray of drinks and biscuits but stopped in the doorway when she saw Rose having what could only be described as banter with her youngest son, suddenly causing Damien to laugh aloud and bounce in his chair. She shot a look of pure admiration at Adam before speaking.

"OK guys, drinks and snacks."

Just over an hour later, Karen decreed that they needed to end the visit as Damien had to do physio. Rose had managed to do some simple sketches while they'd been chatting, so she felt confident that she'd be able to create the poster. Also, having seen the sort of comics that Damien favoured, she had a strong idea of how the poster could look.

"Come on, I'll walk you home," said Adam.

"It's OK, it's not far."

"Yes, but your grasp of the area isn't great; I don't want you to get lost." He grinned at her.

Rose gave Damien a high five and as she turned to leave, she was pulled into a fierce hug by Karen. The surprise of it made Rose stiffen but as she softened and relaxed into the hug, a lump formed in her throat. She wondered if Adam got to be held by his mum like this every day. Lucky bastard.

"You're welcome here any time," Karen said warmly, releasing her from the embrace.

Feeling a little dazed, Rose followed Adam out on to the street. It had cooled considerably while they'd been inside and she rummaged in her bag for her jacket. As she was pulling it on, she noticed Adam watching her intensely.

"What?" she asked, sounding huffier than she intended.

"Have you tried Black and White's yet?" he asked.

"I've no idea what you're on about."

"It's a café near here, they do amazing hot chocolate. Do you fancy it? It's on me, as a thank you."

The tingle that she'd felt all afternoon in his company intensified, making her feel warm and glowy.

"Sure, OK."

Doing her bag back up, she gave herself a mental talking to. She was becoming too infatuated with this boy with the gorgeous smile and lovely family and so far, he'd just been friendly. She needed to calm down. Maybe hot chocolate wasn't a good idea, but she couldn't find it in herself to refuse.

Falling into step beside Adam, they walked away from his house and she felt a little sad to be leaving the cosy, love-filled home.

"Your mum's nice," she said suddenly. "Pretty too."

"Yeah, she's awesome."

Rose was surprised, most sixteen-year-olds wouldn't say anything complimentary about their parents unless forced, but it was one of the things she liked about Adam: he wasn't afraid to be himself.

"Is it just you and Damien, or do you have any other siblings?"

"Just us, although I think Mum would have liked to have had a girl too. She's pretty girly and I reckon she gets a bit fed up of constant football, smelly shoes, comics and boy stuff," he said, smiling.

"Where's your dad?"

"One Sunday a month he goes fishing for the day. I just realised, I never checked whether you got enough sketching done to make the poster?"

"Oh yeah, definitely, and spending time with Damien gave me a real sense of his personality which really helps. I get why you thought of making him a superhero, like in his comics. I hope he likes it."

Adam paused on the pavement, causing Rose to turn and look at him inquisitively.

"You haven't asked," he said simply.

"Asked what?"

"Whenever people meet Damien, the first thing that they do is ask what is wrong with him, why he's in the wheelchair."

"Why does it matter?" She shrugged. "He's just Damien. I didn't want to define him by what's wrong with him, you know. I figured if he or you wanted to talk about it, you would."

Then suddenly Adam kissed her. She'd been about to speak and then his lips were there, warm, tender and delicious. She was so overwhelmed that she didn't kiss him back, just stood there, arms limply by her sides. Then, just as quickly as he did it, he stopped and stepped away.

"Sorry," he muttered, looking very uncomfortable. "I shouldn't have kissed you like that, I just..." He shrugged. "... Couldn't help myself."

A strange sensation started to sweep through Rose's body, starting from her feet, into her chest and out through her fingers. It had been a while since she'd felt it. She didn't recognise it as first. But then, as she couldn't stop the smile that felt like it was splitting her face in two, she realised it was happiness. With a courage that she didn't know she possessed, she whispered, "You can do it again if you like."

Adam looked into her face, his eyes twinkling as he stepped towards her, gently resting his hands on her waist. Then he tilted his head and placed his lips softly on hers. This time she returned the pressure, letting her bag drop to the floor as her arms looped around his neck.

Rose felt as if she were floating, she'd never been kissed like this before. This wasn't a clumsy snog behind the bike sheds while mates egged you on. This wasn't a White Lightning fuelled, washing machine style, facial assault in the park on a cold Friday night. This was magical and romantic. This was movie kissing.

# Chapter Five

"Hold on," I say, sense returning to me. "I can't do this, I'm already freezing, I'm hardly dressed to wander around London." I lift up one of my feet to demonstrate the unsuitability of my high heels.

"Hey, you said 'deal'," he replies while scrolling on his phone. "No backing out now. But it's OK, I have a solution. Come on, this way." And sliding his phone back into his pocket he turns back the way we'd just come. I have no choice but to totter after him.

He leads the way to, surprisingly, a bus stop, just as a bus approaches. I barely have time to get my debit card out of my bag when he's pulling me onto the bus, his hand on my wrist.

It's very cramped aboard, the windows thick with condensation. Unable to get a seat we're forced to stand holding onto the pole. We're pressed very close together and as the bus turns corners my body keeps leaning against his. I'm close enough to smell him; he smells of fabric softener and a touch of aftershave, it's nice and manly without being at all grandad-like. A bit like with the teeth, I'm kind of disappointed he smells so good, I would have preferred a bit of B.O. Although maybe not if I'm going to be spending the whole night in his company.

I can't believe I fell for it, that he managed to goad me into agreeing. What's wrong with me? Hmm... maybe I shouldn't pull at that thread! I can still say no, tell him it was a ridiculous idea and go on my own way. But... but something is stopping me. I don't know what it is, but I want to do this more than I want to run away.

I can't remember the last time I did something impulsive, and fun and daft. I don't know when I became so staid and boring. Is that why I don't recognise myself sometimes? Is the person I was still in here somewhere?

I think on some level I want to test myself. Prove that I can spend time with him. Closure, right? People are always banging on about it, maybe it's time I gave it a try?

The bus lurches around another corner and this time I'm thrown against him, my face pressed into his chest. His arms briefly tighten around me to steady me and for a second it feels nice, too nice. I pull away with a mumbled apology, not looking at his face.

Fortunately, it's only another minute or so until we're passing Marble Arch and stopping at the top of Oxford Street where I'm hustled off the bus and onto the thronging pavement. I know I said that I hate Christmas and I do, but even I can't help but feel a little childlike joy at the lights running up Oxford Street. It's gaudy and tacky and yet beautiful. I'm not really into shopping, sticking to the shops that I like and not really following fashion, but I still get a thrill from Oxford Street. It's always so busy and buzzing.

"OK, and we're here because...?"

"You'll see," he says with a smile. "This way."

We don't say much as we walk, dodging people laden down with festive carrier bags. It's close to closing time and so there's slightly less frantic energy than I expect I would have found an hour ago.

I love London, well, to visit anyway. I love the energy, the busyness, the obscurity, the mesh of cultures. One of my favourite things to do when I visit is to sit at an outdoor café somewhere busy - Camden is my preferred choice - and watch life roll past me. The minutiae of everyday life playing out in front of me. I love hearing snatched conversations, watching body language, making up people's stories, and London is the perfect place for it.

I've never had the guts to move here though. I fear I would be swallowed up by the city and disappear completely.

"We're here."

"Primark?" I say, unable to keep the shock out of my voice.

"Yep, come on, they close in a few minutes."

We hotfoot through the doors; it's quiet inside although the place looks recently ransacked. Weary-looking staff are dotted about, picking up clothes off the floor and restacking them on the shelves. I'm led over to the coats section. Large, tattered signs saying 'Up to 50% off' are dangling overhead and are stuck on the coat hangers in the corner. There isn't much to choose from. It reminds me of the remains of a jumble sale.

"Ah-ha, perfect," says the triumphant voice beside me.

"You are joking? That's hideous." He's holding up a gold, shiny, puffy, coat, kind of like a giant duvet just with a stretchy belt around the middle. It's long and has a fur-lined hood.

"It may be ugly, but it'll keep you warm and that's the idea, right?" Despite the smile, he says it with a challenge in his voice and eyes.

"Fine," I respond, taking it off him. I've never particularly cared about what I look like anyway and I don't want to give him the satisfaction of saying no. It really is hideous but he's right, it will be very warm. "But I'm choosing yours," I continue.

I lead the way this time, through to the Men's section where I'm disappointed to discover that the Men's coats are all a bit more tasteful. I do manage to choose a similar puffy style but in a colour that I'm calling snot green.

I then rush back to the shoe section grabbing a pair of copycat Ugg type boots. They look so cheap that I'm not sure they'll last much beyond tonight, but they seem very comfy and most importantly, warm.

We meet back at the tills where he insists on paying for everything and I don't bother arguing — this was all his idea after all. I see he's also picked up a dark blue V-necked jumper and some boots for himself too, as well as a matching pair of bobble hats, sets of gloves and a small, grey backpack.

Back outside, we huddle in the now closed entrance and switch our shoes over. My fake Uggs are so comfortable after rushing around in my heels that I let out a little groan of joy as I slip them on and wiggle my toes.

As I'm revelling in the comfort, he takes his coat and suit jacket off and puts the jumper on over his white shirt. He looks very preppy which makes me smile.

"What?" he asks.

"Nothing, you just look like such a grown-up."

"Wait till we're both in our puffas," he laughs, sidestepping the wistfulness behind my words. "Then we'll just look proper gangsta."

With trepidation I slide my arms into the gold monstrosity; it is very warm and cosy as I zip it up and tighten the belt. I almost don't mind the colour until a boom of laughter comes out of my companion.

"You look like you should be a character in a really bad rap video." He struggles to get the words out through his laughter.

"At least I don't look like a giant bogey," I retort, starting to giggle too. We both start laughing hard, the reality of our situation obviously sinking in. We must look so ridiculous. Two hours ago, this is the absolute last thing in the world that I thought I'd be doing. The realisation makes me laugh even harder.

Eventually, we calm down, wiping tears from our cheeks. We put everything we've taken off into the giant Primark brown paper bag and pop the gloves, hats and our scarves into the rucksack as our coats are so warm that we don't need them right now.

"Carrying this bag and my folder all night is going to be a pain," I realise and say it aloud.

"Ah, but I've thought of that. We've one more stop and then you can choose where we go next."

"I'm thinking of food actually," I say, my stomach rumbling in agreement.

"OK, this will only take a few minutes and then we can find somewhere to eat."

Once again following directions on his phone, we turn down a couple of streets, leaving the glittering lights of Oxford Street behind us until we come to a twenty-four-hour corner shop.

"What are we doing here?" I ask, flummoxed.

"Bag B&B," is the unhelpful response.

"What's Bag B&B?"

"It's like AirBnB but for luggage. Cities all around the world use it. Shops and hotels sign up for it, they just need a secure back room or lockers or something. Then you book in online and you can store your luggage there until you need it. I've used it when I've been on holiday and my flight is much later than checkout."

"Oh, clever," is my scintillating response as we step inside.

# Chapter Six

## Then

As a chill autumn wind whipped at them, sending crunchy brown leaves scurrying along the damp pavements Adam let go of Rose's hand, wrapping his arm around her shoulder instead and tucking her into his side.

Rose snuggled into him, grateful for the protection from the wind but mainly just loving being in his arms. It had been six weeks since they first kissed, and she still couldn't get over the fact that they were together.

At first, she'd held herself back, confused as to why he would be interested in someone like her. Despite being crazy about him, she'd acted aloof in his company, not out of some attempt to manipulate him but just out of sheer self-protection.

But Adam continued to be genuine, thoughtful, fun and his kisses just blew her away. Gradually she'd let her guard down. She no longer hesitated to initiate a kiss and didn't second guess texting him or seeking him out around campus.

Rose still felt people were judging them though; that they saw them together and wondered what a smart, good-looking lad like him was doing with a scruffy, Emo girl like her. Especially at college where there was a gaggle of bitchy girls who clearly thought Rose was out of line by hooking herself a boyfriend from their league.

The only place that she'd felt instantly accepted was with Adam's family. They'd all loved the poster that she'd made of Damien and had hung it in a prime position in Damien's room. The family all insisted that Adam invite Rose to join them for Damien's birthday tea, which she did, after some persuading, and had a lovely time.

Since then, she'd been to the house a few times to hang out with Adam or help him babysit Damien – not that they were allowed to call it that – when his parents were out. Each time, she'd been greeted so warmly, Karen always free and easy with her hugs, that she stopped feeling awkward or out of place.

Another strong gust of wind caused her to snuggle further into Adam, wrapping her arm around his waist. He dropped a soft kiss on her forehead as she did, the sweet, intimate gesture causing a warmth to bloom from her chest.

It scared her sometimes, how crazy she was about him. The more time she spent with him, the more she fell for him. Yes, he was very good-looking, but he was also funny, kind and intelligent and had a way of bringing out the best in her. She was scared that when the time came that he had enough of her, when he went off her and moved on, the sense of loss would be horrific. Like going back into a dark cave after being out in the sunshine.

She tried not to think of it and just enjoy being with him for now, for as long as it might last.

They reached the bus stop where there was already a large group of students huddled like penguins. Adam automatically turned his back against the wind and pulled Rose in front of him, wrapping his arms around her back.

Having always considered herself a feminist, it surprised Rose how much she loved these thoughtful gestures of his, like protecting her from the wind, or standing on the edge of the pavement so that he would get splashed by a passing car, not her, or giving her the last seat on the bus. It just made her feel cared for and nurtured, something she really wasn't used to.

She tucked her hands into the back pockets of his jeans and smiled up at him. He bent his head and kissed her softly.

She stepped closer to him, deepening the kiss, not caring that they were in public. The wind blew and the world carried on around them as they kissed, Rose revelling in the feel of his lips against hers, the butterflies in her stomach and the warm tingle in her chest. She still couldn't believe the way his kisses made her feel.

Instinctively her hands squeezed his bum, pulling him closer still. She felt something hard press against her stomach and Adam broke the kiss, stepping back from her slightly, his breath ragged and eyes glazed as he smiled at her.

Adam breathed deeply trying to regain his composure and wishing he had slightly more control over his body. He wasn't sure whether Rose had felt his erection and he didn't want her to feel uncomfortable. They'd done nothing more than kiss, amazing mind-blowing kisses, and he was more than happy to just stick to kissing for as long as she wanted, even though he fancied her more than any other girl he'd ever been with before. It was deeper than just fancying her though. He'd had girlfriends in the past, but he'd never connected with them the way that he had with Rose.

Adam was also aware that Rose had never had a boyfriend before. Part of what he loved about their relationship, as new as it was, was that they were honest and open with each other, there was no game playing or awkwardness. Well, once Rose had got over her initial reticence. She had been upfront about her lack of experience and had actually been surprised when he admitted that he wasn't as experienced as people assumed either.

He was so glad that he hadn't taken things further with any girls he'd dated in the past, despite the pushing from his school mates. He'd always been a bit of a romantic and now he was sure that once she was ready, Rose would be the one who would take his virginity. He just wished he could stop thinking about it so much.

"So," he said, clearing his throat. "Did you finish your latest sketches?"

"Yeah, during my free this afternoon. I also may have wasted a bit of time doing a drawing of Jenny," Rose replied with an abashed smile.

"Oh yeah? What do you see her as?"

"It just hit me at lunchtime; a cocker spaniel."

"Oh of course," Adam laughed. "I can't wait to see it. Are you going to show her?"

"Yeah, I think so, I mean, I think she'll like it, right?"

"I'm sure she'll love it. Jenny's good fun, she'll probably want it framed."

Rose was gradually starting to relax around Jenny and Tom, his friends from high school who had been some of the few who had chosen to go to college instead of staying at the school's sixth form. They'd been part of a wider group at school but since starting college had bandied together into a bit of a trio, even though they were all starting to make other friends too.

Jenny was scatty and a bit crazy, but a nice girl and Adam hoped that she and Rose would become good friends, not just because it would make life easier for him if everyone got on, but he wanted Rose to have a girly mate of her own. Having only moved to Cheltenham in time to start college, Rose didn't know many people and Adam sometimes felt bad that he had a wide social circle when she didn't. Not that she ever seemed bothered on the surface, but he was getting quite good at seeing the parts of Rose that she tried to keep hidden.

"Have you decided what I am yet?" he asked with a grin; it was a conversation they'd had a couple of times.

"Nope, I still can't see anything, I don't think I ever will, to be honest. You are just un-characteristicable," she grinned.

"I don't think that's a word," he laughed as she just shrugged, her eyes twinkling. "I've worked out what you are," he continued.

"Oh really? This should be good; you're rubbish at this game."

"You're a hedgehog."

"A hedgehog?" Rose sounded surprised but there was still a soft smile on her lips.

"Yep," he kissed her briefly. "You look a bit prickly on the outside," he kissed her again, "but behind the spikes, you're all cute and loveable." He kissed her again, more thoroughly this time.

"A hedgehog huh?" she said, smiling when they drew apart. "I'll take that."

Stepping off the bus, they briskly walked hand in hand towards their part of town. They'd fallen into the habit of Adam dropping Rose at the top of her street before continuing on to his own house a few streets over. When they first got together, he kept offering to walk her to her door, but she was insistent that there was no need.

"Shall I pick you up tonight and we can head into town together?" he asked as they neared her street.

"Or I can just call for you?" she replied.

"But my house is in the wrong direction."

"Oh true, I'll just meet you here then, shall I?"

"Rose," Adam said seriously, stopping and turning to face her. "Are you embarrassed about me or something?"

"No," she replied shocked. "Why on earth would you think that?"

"Well, it's just you've been to my house loads now and I've never even been to your front door. You always make excuses to avoid your house. What's going on?"

"Look, it's not you, it's just..." Rose tailed off and then sighed deeply. "My family, they're not like yours. My parents, I mean. They aren't horrible or anything, they love me and stuff, it's just... I don't know, after seeing your home and meeting your parents, my home just seems so... basic. But you're right, it's silly of me. My mum will want to meet you. I think she thinks I've made you up."

"Are you sure?"

"Yes," she replied, kissing him.

"OK, I'll just dump my stuff and get changed, then I'll be over. We ought to try to get into town quite early, I think it'll be rammed."

After one more lingering kiss, Rose turned and headed towards her house feeling strangely apprehensive. She didn't know why she'd been so reluctant for Adam to come over. She knew him well enough now to know he wasn't judgemental and it's not like her house was horrendous or anything, just a little neglected. Rather like her really. Deep down she knew that's what she didn't want him to see.

Adam knocked at the door feeling strangely nervous. Rose didn't talk about her family much. He knew her dad worked for the police force, which was nerve-wracking for a teenage lad, and that her mum worked part-time as a receptionist but that was about it.

The door swung open and seeing Rose's pretty face made Adam forget his nerves.

"Hello, beautiful," he smiled.

Rose leant forward and kissed him quickly before ushering him inside. Her terraced house appeared to be a slightly smaller version of his with a beige carpeted hallway leading to a staircase and a door to the rest of the house.

Rose seemed slightly agitated as she led him through a large but cluttered sitting room and into the small, dated kitchen at the back of the house. The back door was open, letting in the cold wind which was buffeting the blind over the window, causing a metallic clattering.

Rose's mum was standing in the doorway blowing a plume of smoke into the dark night.

"Mum, this is Adam," Rose muttered.

"Ooh, hello," she responded, stubbing her cigarette out against the brick of the doorway and flicking the stub into the garden. "Keith hates it when I do that, but it's too cold to be messing around with the outdoor bin. I'm Dawn, but you probably know that."

She stepped into the room, slamming the door behind her.

"Nice to meet you." Adam held out his hand which Dawn shook with a wry smile.

"Oh, you're polite, Keith will like that. That's Rosie's dad; he's rarely here but you might meet him at some point."

She flicked the kettle on and leant back against the worktop appraising Adam with slightly narrowed eyes. He took the chance to assess her back. She was slim, verging on skinny, with dyed bright blonde hair and piercing blue eyes. She had Rose's cheekbones and elfin features and was arguably very pretty but with a hard edge to her face somehow.

"Either of you want a cuppa?" Dawn said eventually.

"No thanks," replied Rose. "We're heading off in a bit."

"Oh, anywhere nice?"

"Yeah, remember I said, the lights switch on?"

"Oh yeah, bit old for that sort of thing, aren't you?" Dawn said dismissively setting about making her tea.

"It'll be nice," Adam responded, somewhat defensively, Rose had been excited about it all week. "There's a famous band playing."

"Oh, I heard about that, McFly isn't it? I like them. Apparently, it's already heaving down there."

"Yeah, we'd better go in a minute. Do you want to see my room?" Rose asked Adam.

"Sure."

"There's a euphemism if ever I heard one," cackled Dawn.

"Mum!" hissed Rose, embarrassed.

"I'm only joking, Rosie, I trust you to behave yourselves. You're practically an adult now anyway. I'm just glad you've finally brought a boyfriend home. To be honest, I was beginning to think you might be a lesbian."

Rolling her eyes, Rose grabbed Adam's hand and pulled him out of the room.

"Nice to meet you," he called over his shoulder, determined to make a good impression.

"You too," replied Dawn absentmindedly.

Rose ushered him into her room, slamming the door and throwing herself down on her bed.

"Sorry about that. Mum doesn't really have a filter, you know." Rose was fiddling with her rings, something Adam had learnt she did when she was uncomfortable.

"It's fine, I'm glad to have met her finally," he smiled sitting down next to her and threading his fingers through hers. She leant against him, resting her head on his shoulder as he took in the room.

It was spotlessly tidy and rather minimalist, at odds with the rest of the house that he'd seen as Rose had rushed him through. The walls were painted a deep plum colour with curtains and bedding in a similar but lighter shade and a silvery-grey carpet. He was surprised at first to see framed art prints rather than band posters lining the walls but as he thought about it, it made sense, her love of art did trump her love of music.

He wanted to go and nose at her CD collection, sure that they'd be alphabetised, but sensed Rose didn't want to let go of his hand just yet. Obviously having him here was a big deal to her. Adam had tried not to be too inquisitive when it came to Rose's home life as he'd wanted Rose to lower her defences and open up to him on her own terms, but there was definitely a weird vibe with her mum and he couldn't help but broach it.

"You and your mum seem quite different," he attempted as an opener.

"You're not wrong there," Rose scoffed bitterly. Adam could feel her shoulders tense, even though she remained still, her head resting on his shoulder.

"What do you mean?"

"Oh, just that Mum wishes I was more like her. You know, blonde, girly, outgoing."

"I think you're perfect the way you are," he responded loyally.

"Thanks," she replied flatly.

Adam shifted around, causing Rose to lift her head off his shoulder as he turned to face her. Taking both her hands in his, he kissed her knuckles. He'd obviously struck a nerve and he hated seeing her despondent.

"Seriously," he said, stroking her cheek, "you're the coolest person I know and I'm sure your mum is dead proud of you."

"She isn't actually," Rose muttered.

"All kids feel that way about their parents at some point or another," he replied, wishing he hadn't started this now as he suspected that he was just saying the wrong things.

"I heard her once, a few months ago," Rose continued in a low, flat voice. "She was talking to Dad about me, during one of their rows, they must've thought I was asleep. Anyway, she said all this stuff, like how it was no wonder I didn't have any friends and that I wasn't normal and a bunch of other stuff. Mum was nineteen when she had me and I always knew she resented me a bit, but it wasn't great to hear her say it, you know?"

"I'm sorry," Adam said, at a loss how to respond. How could anyone not think Rose was awesome, especially her own mum?

"It is what it is." Rose shrugged, visibly putting on a brave face, her shutters coming down. "We just don't have the sort of relationship you have with your parents is all."

Knowing Rose well enough to realise that she was trying to close the subject, Adam complied.

"I love your room," he said honestly. "It's very you; dark but pretty," he smiled.

Rose looked both relieved at the topic change and pleased at the compliment. Adam loved how he'd learnt to read the emotions on her face. Cupping her cheek in his hand, he leant in and kissed her.

Inevitably it turned into a make out session like it always did when they were alone in his room. He wondered if he'd ever tire of kissing her.

Suddenly, she pushed him away.

"Ah, look at the time, come on, we need to go."

She leapt from the bed and started putting eyeliner on in her dresser mirror. Unable to stand up until certain parts of his body calmed down, he leant back against the wall and watched her move around the room.

She reached into her wardrobe and pulled out a black, chunky roll neck jumper then pulled off her hoody revealing a thin little vest top. At the sight of her creamy skin and round, pert breasts peeping out of her vest, Adam had to look away. Not just to preserve Rose's modesty but because otherwise, he'd never be able to get up.

"I've got a surprise for you," Rose said suddenly, causing him to turn back. Thankfully, she was now in the chunky jumper, although she still looked gorgeous. Her hands were behind her back and she had a mischievous smile on her face, her previous despondence forgotten.

"I got us these." And with a flourish, she whipped out two pairs of light-up Christmas teeny boppers, in the shape of Santa hats, from behind her back. "Ta-da."

Adam burst into laughter, "Where did you get those from?"

"Poundland."

"OK, maybe the better question is, why did you get them?"

"Because they're funny and besides it's our first Christmas together, we have to do everything Christmassy." She came back over to him, kneeling beside him on the bed.

"But it's November."

She didn't respond but solemnly put the teeny boppers on her head and switched on the flashing lights. She looked like a little pixie.

It was one of the things that fascinated Adam about Rose, all her contradictions. She was often so self-conscious and lacking in confidence, but then didn't bother to try to blend in with the other girls her age, dyeing her hair bright colours and not giving a crap about fashion. And she thought nothing of wearing ugly light-up teeny boppers out in public. Most of the time she seemed quite serious and grown-up but then she had this fun, childish, adventurous side that was excited by fairground rides and, apparently, Christmas.

He loved her for it. Not that he'd said those words out loud yet. He didn't want to scare her off.

She was still looking at him with a perfectly serious expression on her face, although her eyes were twinkling. That could have been the glow of the flashing lights though.

"I dare you," she said holding out his pair.

"Fine," he said, with an exaggerated huff, "but you owe me." He put his teeny boppers on and copying Rose's serious expression, turned the lights on.

Rose giggled and clapped her hands together in delight, then bounded over to her wardrobe again to pull out a scarf and gloves.

"So, how come you love Christmas so much?" Adam asked as she wound the scarf around her neck.

"I don't know," she paused mid-wrap as if it was a question she'd never considered. "It's just a really lovely time of year. I love the frosty weather and being able to get all snuggly inside while it's cold out. I love all the pretty lights and Christmas songs and the whole goodwill thing. I just think it's nice that there's one time of year especially for letting people know they matter to you, you know. I guess," she continued thoughtfully while pulling her gloves on, "my family isn't particularly traditional, like we don't do much together, but Christmas has always been the time that we do. I always remember Dad taking me to meet Santa when I was younger, and Mum and I have always gone up to London for the day, Christmas shopping. Then 'cos he has a kid, Dad usually manages to get Christmas Day off and we just spend time together, the three of us, and Mum and Dad don't fight and it's just my favourite day."

Rose suddenly looked awkward, shifting on her feet, and a faint blush stole into her cheeks like she was embarrassed that she'd said so much. Sensing her vulnerability, Adam crossed the room to her and kissed her deeply.

"I love Christmas too," he murmured as he broke the kiss. "And I can't wait to do loads of Christmassy things with you."

"You don't have to wear the teeny boppers if you don't want to; I mean, I get they could be embarrassing, I just thought they were funny."

"Of course, I want to wear them. I'll treasure them forever," he replied, grinning. Although Adam was aware that he appeared quite vanilla compared to Rose, he actually didn't care what people thought. Years of putting up with rude people staring at his brother when they were out in public had given him a very thick skin and a very low opinion of anyone who judged others. Possibly why he hated the bitchy college girls who he knew sneered at Rose for being different. Although, he'd probably just hate anyone who thought Rose was anything but wonderful.

"Besides," he continued, "they might help us find each other if we get separated by hordes of screaming McFly fans."

"I can't believe Cheltenham actually got someone famous to turn on the lights. Back in Hertfordshire, we usually just had some bloke off local radio that nobody knew."

"Shame it's still just a pop band though, not someone cooler."

"Actually, don't tell anyone," Rose whispered seriously, "but I really like McFly. Their songs are catchy, and I love the singer's voice."

"Aww, you really are a little hedgehog, aren't you?" Adam laughed kindly as they made their way out of the room.

"Hold on," he said suddenly, grabbing Rose's hand before she got to the stairs. "Don't you want to take a pair of knickers, you know, to throw at the lead singer?"

"Shut up," Rose laughed, pushing him. "I should never have told you that, should I?"

"Nope," laughed Adam. And, teeny boppers flashing, they made their way out into the cold winter night.

# Chapter Seven

It's noticeably a few degrees colder when we leave the Chinese, having sated our appetites quite fully on their buffet. My initial awkwardness at being in his company has dissipated slightly; I've been able to not think about the past but concentrate on getting to know this new person that I've just met. That's how I'm compartmentalising it anyway. I'm sure it's super healthy.

We chatted easily about normal, trivial stuff over dinner; our jobs, where we live, TV programmes we both enjoy. We talked briefly about music although I veered the conversation away from that a bit sharpish as it seemed to be leading us down a nostalgic path which I'm keen to avoid.

We did discover that we were at the same Coldplay gig in 2011 though. It's made me wonder how many times we almost crossed paths in the past. Given what my meeting was about this morning,

I suppose it is a weird coincidence that this is the day that we should meet again. I didn't share that thought with him though.

Luckily, there was a plug socket just under the table in the restaurant, so I was able to charge my phone. I turned it on during our mango sorbets and received a barrage of messages; a couple from friends and Jo who were concerned about me, having realised that I might be stuck in London. And a few rather more unkind ones from Stu. I didn't bother reading them beyond the opening lines of 'You're a frigid bitch', etc.... and just deleted them.

This didn't go unnoticed, so I ended up spilling the whole story. Of course, it was only natural then to ask about his relationship status. I had been quite curious about why he didn't seem to need to rush home to a significant other.

Apparently, he was in a serious relationship for nearly five years which ended eighteen months ago and he's been casually dating (his words) since then. He didn't go into details about what happened in his relationship and I didn't want to seem interested enough to ask. I can't help but assume he did something to ruin it and his unwillingness to go into details just confirms it. Well, you know what they say about leopards…

Anyway, we agreed to avoid the Tube as much as possible and just walk, partly in order to 'look up' but also because the Tubes are probably manic. We'd decided to head back along Oxford Street and then cut down to Covent Garden—another favourite of mine despite, or in fact possibly because of, how touristy it is.

We fall into step alongside each other, our breath fogging in the crisp night air as we stroll along the now quiet Oxford Street. It's amazing the difference one hour can make. We don't talk much other than to point out a lovely building or interesting feature. The shop fronts are amazing and, without the hordes of shoppers blocking them, the buildings twinkle and shine.

"Your lecturer was right," I exclaim craning my neck. "We should remember to look up more. I've been down this road so many times but never really paid attention to the buildings above the shops, except Selfridges obviously, but some of the architecture is beautiful. Well, except for the horrible Sixties ones."

"I don't mind them actually. Yes, they could have been built to be more in keeping with the other buildings, but you know, every building tells a story. I mean, you can literally see where bombs landed. Obliterating one building and leaving its neighbour unscathed. And so, we just went on, whacked another building up, filling the space with the building style of the day. They didn't recreate what was there and pretend the Blitz didn't happen, but I think instead these buildings are indicative of the British mentality of picking ourselves up, dusting ourselves down and cracking on with it as best we can."

"I've never thought of it like that," I murmured.

"Nothing is ever just what it seems on the surface, surely you know that. Besides," he continued, a lighter tone creeping into his voice, "Britain was so skint after the war that shoving up a load of concrete with functionality over form was the sensible thing to do."

The atmosphere livens as we cut down through Soho towards Covent Garden, revelry once again the order of the day with the pubs and bars spilling their intoxicated clientele out onto the streets. There's almost a carnival atmosphere with the hubbub of chat, laughter and Christmas music creating a rich soundtrack for the different groups scattered about the place in varying degrees of normalcy. I didn't think I'd ever seen so many people dressed as Santa in one place! How on earth does a parent leaving one of the theatres with their children explain this? Especially sights like I'm witnessing right now: a Santa throwing up into a bin.

Things calm slightly as we enter Covent Garden itself, fewer drunk people and more tourists and amblers like us wandering around, soaking it up. I've always preferred Covent Garden at night, often getting the last train home after a meeting just so I can pay it a visit. The shops and stalls are closed now but I swear I can still smell mulled wine in the air. The up lights, which accentuate the yellow hue of the stone market walls, glow brightly, complemented by the strings of twinkling Christmas lights stretched across the cobbled square creating a sense of starlight.

Small, ornate Christmas trees are dotted around reminding me of excitable toddlers playing near their mother - the huge and heavily decorated Christmas tree that dominates the square. It must be at least twelve feet high and it's adorned with thousands of small, coloured, twinkling fairy lights. Despite my opinion of Christmas, I have to admit it's magnificent.

Most of the street performers have finished up for the night, bar a string quartet who have set up by the impressive Christmas tree and are playing Christmas carols. It's so sickeningly, perfectly Christmassy it's like something from a Hallmark movie and yet I kind of love it. I can feel it in my chest, a feeling I haven't had for so many years, I almost don't recognise it, but I think it's that Christmas feeling. The one I always used to get before - before it all went wrong.

By unspoken agreement we gravitate towards the buskers, their soulful music almost pulling us in like a magnet. There's quite a crowd around them and I'm a little surprised that people aren't attempting to sing along.

Standing here, surrounded by all this Christmas wonder I suddenly feel a bit emotional and a lump forms in my throat. After one more song, the quartet finishes and takes a little bow; I guess we caught them just at the end of their set. I clap as loudly as I can, my hands stinging in the cold but it helps the lump in my throat to subside. I ferret in my purse, only finding a fiver which I go and place in their bucket.

"Thank you so much," I gush. "That was really beautiful."

I turn back to see him watching me with a soft smile on his face which broadens as I walk back over to him, the Christmas lights behind him making him almost glow.

"See, you do love Christmas really. You're still a little hedgehog."

And just like that the Christmas goodwill that was beginning to unfurl within me evaporates. The use of that one little endearment reminds me in a millisecond of all that's gone before, all that I lost. A white-hot fury comes over me.

"Don't you dare say that to me," I rage. "You know nothing about me, who I am today. You think just cos you knew me, what? Well over a decade ago? That you can comment. I'm not some messed-up little kid anymore. I'm not the naive girl you knew, so cut it out."

His face pales slightly and he steps back, then his eyes seem to harden, his jaw tense.

"Right, message received. But you know, despite everything, I've been nothing but nice to you this evening. Let's just move on, shall we?"

He turns and starts walking away. Now I feel guilty. I did massively overreact. I guess he touched a nerve. So much for compartmentalising. He's right in a way, he has been good company, although he doesn't have the same axe to grind as I do.

But I can't accuse him of treating me like the girl from the past when I can't stop thinking the worst of him because of his past behaviour. I need to at least try to treat him with a clean slate.

"Adam, wait." It's the first time I've said his name out loud in ten years. It sounds strange to my ears and yet so familiar.

"I'm sorry," I sigh, catching up with him. "I overreacted. We said at the start of the night that we weren't going to think about our history, and I guess I haven't really been able to do that which hasn't been fair to you. Like I said, we're grown-up now and shouldn't be judged on the past." He looks a bit puzzled and opens his mouth to say something, but I'm not done. "You were right, actually, I was feeling the Christmas spirit, a bit." I look down sheepishly, "I think the emotion got to me, to be honest. But please don't call me hedgehog, OK?" I mutter.

"OK." He stares at me for a moment and I can't help but stare back, captivated by his eyes; he looks like he's about to say something serious but changes his mind.

"Well, if Covent Garden didn't do it for you, my next choice definitely will, we'll have you de-Scrooged by morning, mark my words," he grins instead. "Come on, this way."

"If I had a pound for every time I've heard 'this way' from you this evening, I could pay for a taxi back to Bristol," I tease, falling into step beside him.

"So, come on then, at the risk of you shouting at me again, what is it with you and Christmas? You used to love it so much."

"Yeah, well, things changed. A lot of things changed. Once my parents split up, Christmas stopped being about fun, family time and became bitter and depressing. The first Christmas after they split was the worst time in my life." I swallow, we're heading into dangerous territory, but I carry on. "I suppose Christmas was never nice for me after that and all I ever see now are the downsides. It's an awful time of year for so many and the pressure for this perfect experience just makes it worse."

"OK, Grinch, you don't need to start your tirade again," Adam says nudging me good-naturedly so I can't take offence. "Anyway, don't you want to know where we're going?"

"It's OK, I'm going with the flow. This is supposed to be an adventure, after all."

# Chapter Eight

## Then

Rose couldn't help but glare at the heavily pregnant woman standing in her slippers and dressing gown sucking furiously on a cigarette. What is wrong with people? The woman clocked Rose's look of disgust but just turned her head blowing a plume of silvery smoke into the air. Rose felt like stamping over to her and pulling the cigarette from her hand, grounding it into the floor with the heel of her DM and giving the woman a lecture about all the damage she's doing to the foetus.

The sad reality was though that the woman would already know the danger and the risk to her unborn child but just didn't care. *Selfish cow*, thought Rose venomously. Her mum was never going to win parent of the year or anything but at least she gave up smoking during her pregnancy and never smoked in the house. Rose couldn't wait for the promised smoking ban that should be coming in later in the year. To be able to go to pubs and restaurants without a constant fug of smoke in the air or leaving with the acrid smell sticking to your clothes and hair.

Rose checked her phone again; she'd been loitering outside the hospital for over an hour now and she couldn't feel her toes anymore. She'd known something was wrong when Adam wasn't there at lunchtime. He didn't have any classes until the afternoon on a Friday but usually came in a bit earlier than he needed to so that they could have lunch together. When she'd tried to ring him, it went straight to voicemail.

She hadn't been able to concentrate all through her sociology lesson until she became aware of an angry buzzing coming from her bag and excused herself to go to the loo, her sociology teacher being very strict about phones in the classroom.

Her heart had sunk when she'd realised that she'd missed a call from Adam and when she tried to ring him back, it went to voicemail again. But then a text from him had pinged through. Her heart sank even further to learn that Damien had been rushed to hospital and that's where Adam had been all day with his parents.

Rose had felt sick with worry for the rest of the afternoon and, although she understood that Adam couldn't keep his phone on, it was frustrating that she couldn't check if everyone was OK.

Restless and feeling impotent once she was at home, she did the only thing that she could think of and walked over to the hospital. She didn't want to impose on the family but just wanted to be close by in case Adam needed her.

Finally, it looked like her patience was paying off as she could make out a figure that looked like Adam walking through the lobby. She ventured closer to the entrance just as the doors swished open and Adam walked out. His face looked drawn and tired and there was a little crease of worry above his brow. He hadn't spotted her yet, as he was focusing on his phone.

Rose couldn't help but smile when, as he lifted his phone to his ear, hers started ringing in her bag. Adam turned to the sound and his look of surprise at seeing her there quickly turned to relief and then pleasure. She watched the different emotions play across his face as they drew together.

Rose wrapped her arms around him and he buried his head in her neck. She could feel the tension seeping from his body as she held him, the muscles in his back and shoulders relaxing into her embrace. She squeezed him tighter as if trying to absorb some of his stress and ease his burden.

"What are you doing here?" he mumbled into her hair without relaxing his hold on her.

"I was worried about you all and, I don't know, I just couldn't stay away. I wanted to be here for you."

"Thank you." Adam drew back then and kissed her gently.

"How is he?" Rose breathed, her forehead resting on his.

"Better than he was this morning but he's not out of the woods yet."

"What happened?"

"He had a seizure of some kind. It was awful." Tears sprang into Adam's eyes and he squeezed them shut.

"It's OK to cry, you know," Rose said gently, stroking his cheekbone with her thumb.

"Oh my God, your hands are freezing," he exclaimed, taking both her hands in his and starting to rub them. "How long have you been here?"

"I don't know." Rose shrugged nonchalantly. "An hour or so."

Adam stared at her so intently that Rose started to worry that she'd done the wrong thing. He opened his mouth to say something, but then seemed to change his mind and, cradling her face in his hands, kissed her fiercely.

Still reeling from the emotion-laced kiss, Rose barely heard Adam suggest that she go with him to get some food and just followed him meekly into the building.

The smell of cooking was instantly familiar and comforting, embracing them like a warm hug, as they entered the steamy interior of the canteen. While Rose grabbed them a table, Adam ordered four portions of shepherd's pie, two of which to be taken away and picked up some bottles of Diet Coke from the chiller.

Once sat with Rose at the table Adam tucked into his dinner with gusto. He hadn't eaten much all day. In between mouthfuls Rose chatted away about her day and filled him in on what he'd missed in art class that afternoon.

He knew he'd have to return to his parents soon and take them their much-needed supper and part of him was fretful about being away from his brother. What if something happened? But for these few minutes, he wanted to forget what a horrible day it had been and where he was and just be with his girlfriend like a normal sixteen-year-old.

Of course, over the years he'd been to the hospital with Damien a few times. When they were younger, there were big periods when his mum would stay in hospital for weeks at a time with Damien, and Adam and his dad would come and visit every day after school. It meant that Adam didn't have the same dislike of hospitals that a lot of people do and actually had fond memories of visiting.

Today had been different though. Today was scary. Adam knew that as Damien got older, they were actually always one year closer to losing him. That one day his fragile body will give up the fight. *Please God*, Adam thought, *don't let today be that day.*

At that speculation, the food turned to ash in his mouth and he closed his cutlery over the last few mouthfuls that remained on his plate.

Sensing the change in him, Rose put down her fork and held his hand over the table, smiling at him gently, the film of tears appearing over her eyes an indication of how much she was hurting for him. Adam gripped her fingers gratefully, rubbing his thumb over the soft skin of the back of her hand. Rose didn't say anything or offer platitudes, she was just there, understanding without him having to say a word. He was more grateful for that than he could ever express.

"I'd better get this food to my parents," Adam croaked, eventually, his voice thick with emotion.

They padded hand in hand down the quiet corridor towards the lifts, their footsteps, and the squeaking of the polystyrene food containers rubbing together, the only sounds. Adam was gripping Rose's hand so tightly it almost hurt, but he could have broken it for all she cared if it was comforting him.

At the lifts, Adam let go of her hand to press the call button. Before he could take it again, she handed over the two drinks that she'd been carrying in the crook of her free arm.

"Aren't you coming with me?" Adam asked, surprised.

"No, I wouldn't feel comfortable; you should just be a family."

"My parents won't mind."

"I know," Rose answered, although she strongly suspected that they would, "but I don't think it's right for me to be there. Look, I want to be here for you and there's no way I can go home until I know Damien is going to be all right, so I'm just going to be in here in the waiting area." She gestured down the corridor to where they had passed a selection of chairs clustered in a corner around a small Formica table.

"You can't sit there on your own for hours," Adam protested.

"Erm, have you met me?" Rose smiled. "I've got my music and my sketchbook, that's all I'd be doing at home anyway. Just if you need me, I'll be here, OK?" And she pressed a soft kiss against his lips to prevent any further discussion.

"If you're sure," Adam acquiesced, incredibly comforted that Rose would be there. If the clinical, sterile room got too much for him, he could escape into her arms.

The lift door pinged open and Adam wearily stepped inside, his shoulders hunched with worry. Rose hated seeing him like that, looking so dejected, no sign of his usual joie de vivre. She blew him a kiss as the doors started to close and he smiled at her gratefully, not breaking eye contact until the doors shut.

"I love you," Rose whispered into the empty corridor.

About five times in the last half an hour, she had wanted to blurt out those three words but had to stop herself. She knew weeks ago, months really, that she was unequivocally and completely in love with Adam. At first, she dismissed it as infatuation and that, after a while, those intense feelings would lessen but they didn't, they got stronger. The more time they spent together, the more they shared and the more their lives entwined, the more she loved him.

She'd seen him at his worst when he was grouchy with a stinking cold just before Christmas and still she'd loved him, snot and all.

They'd even had their first argument. Rose had pulled out of going to a party with Adam at the last minute because it was all his old school mates, and she was worried that she wouldn't know anyone and feel awkward. He'd been hurt and disappointed and ended up going without her.

Rose had spent the evening curled up in her room crying her eyes out, convinced that that was the end of the relationship and that he would find someone else at the party, someone prettier, trendier, more normal.

She'd eventually fallen asleep only to be woken by a thudding at her window. Adam was in her back garden throwing clumps of mud up at her room. She'd wrapped her dressing gown around herself and joined him in the garden, the cold air stinging her tear-swollen face.

"What are you doing?" she'd hissed at him.

"You weren't answering your phone."

"It's on silent, in my bag and I'd fallen asleep. But that doesn't explain why you're here." The fear that he was there to dump her caused a sharp pain to run through her chest.

"The house was dark, and I didn't want to wake your parents by knocking on the front door. I missed you, and I felt bad, and I wanted to check you were OK. You've been crying," he said, peering into her face in the dim light that filtered from her bedroom window.

She cried again then at his words which led to a very honest, intense and heated discussion about why she'd been so upset. He was very hurt that she didn't trust him, and she was upset that he didn't understand her reticence to go to the party and had made her feel bad about it. They made up pretty quickly, with a lot of passionate kissing, both full of remorse that they'd hurt each other.

But even when she'd been upset with him, she'd still loved him with all her heart. The fear of losing him had been so acute that it confirmed what she already knew: She was head over heels in love and it scared her beyond measure.

Sometimes Rose allowed herself to believe that he loved her too. It was almost impossible to comprehend loving someone so much but them not feeling the same. And, of course, there was the way he cared for her and treated her and the amazing connection that they shared.

Seeing him tonight she no longer cared whether he felt the same way, she just wanted to tell him, to pour her heart out to him, really let him know how wonderful she thought he was. But it wouldn't be right. Tonight wasn't about her or her feelings and she didn't want to put any more emotional pressure on him. She'd tell him one day.

Rose settled herself down on one of the hard, plastic chairs in the waiting room, wishing, not for the first time, that she had a little more padding on her bottom. She was in for an uncomfortable night.

She was just setting out her pencils when she heard footsteps approaching and looked up to see Adam. She leapt up from the seat, pencils scattering.

"Is everything OK?" she asked, the worry causing her voice to sound shrill.

"Yes, nothing's happened. I just..." Adam trailed off, running his fingers through his hair, making it stick up in little tufts. "I just thought of you down here and the fact that you came here for me and I've been wanting to say it for ages, but I haven't 'cos I didn't want to scare you off, or move too fast or anything, but I need to say it now. I love you, Rose."

Rose took a second to catch up with his garbled train of thought and realise what he'd just said. As she was processing it, Adam stepped closer, taking her hands in his.

"You don't have to say it back or anything, I just wanted to tell you that I love you, that's all."

"But I love you too," Rose whispered, tears of joy spilling from her eyelids. "I've wanted to say it for ages too, but I didn't have the guts."

Adam bent his head and kissed her long and hard and far too inappropriately for a hospital waiting room.

"I'd better get back," Adam said, finally breaking the kiss and leaving Rose's head spinning. "I pretty much just threw boxes of shepherd's pie at my parents and ran back out again. I haven't even told them you're here."

"OK," Rose murmured, unable to stop smiling, "but don't feel you have to keep coming out here to check on me, I'm here for you, not the other way round. I'll be fine."

"All right then." Adam gave her one more lingering kiss and turned to go.

Rose watched him walk back down the corridor, her heart feeling like it could burst with joy, despite the gnawing concern about Damien. He said he loved her. Just as Adam was about to turn the corner, she called out to him.

"Adam."

He turned and looked back at her.

"I love you!" Rose giggled.

Adam's face broke into a broad grin.

"I love you," he replied before blowing her a kiss and disappearing around the corner.

"Rose, wake up," Adam said gently, stroking her cheek. He'd watched her sleeping for a moment, curled up on the hard plastic chair, not unlike a cat, with her head resting on her balled-up coat. She'd looked so peaceful and so beautiful that his heart swelled. This funny, independent mess of contradictions whom he loved more than he thought was possible at his age.

He remembered scoffing at Romeo and Juliet when they had studied it in school. He had thought it was ridiculous that teenagers could feel that strongly. But now, he knew without a doubt that Rose was his 'one'. He would do anything for her.

It really saddened him that she had such a low opinion of herself and angered him when he thought about her parents' lack of interest in her being partially to blame for Rose's self-image. She deserved more. He'd vowed to himself as he watched her sleep on those uncomfortable chairs, like a little urchin, that he would never do anything to hurt her and never think the worst of her like her mum seemed to.

"Hey," Rose said blearily, pushing herself up. "I must've nodded off."

"No kidding," Adam smiled, smoothing down her hair where it had rubbed against her coat and was sticking up.

"Everything OK?" Rose asked, concern etched all over her features.

"Yes, thankfully," Adam sighed. "The doctor has just been in for a chat. Damien will have to stay in for a few days so they can adjust his medication and monitor him, but they're confident that he's out of the woods for now."

"Oh, thank God."

"So, Dad and I are going home and obviously we'll take you with us, but before we go, Damien wants to see you."

"Really?"

"Yeah, he's feeling so much better and is awake now and you know how much he loves you. Not as much as me though, of course," Adam said happily. The relief of being able to express his feelings was palpable. Rose jumped up from her seat and gathered her scattered belongings excitedly. The night had gone from awful to wonderful in just a few hours.

She and Adam had admitted their feelings to each other. He loved her! And, for now, Damien was going to be OK. She was so glad that he wanted to see her; she'd been incredibly worried and couldn't wait to give him a cuddle.

Rose had grown so fond of Damien in the last few months that he had really begun to feel like the little brother she never had but always wanted. She had hated the thought of him being ill. Although, of course, the whole experience had reminded her that despite his amazing energy and enthusiasm for life, Damien was very fragile and the thought of what could have happened made her blood run cold.

# Chapter Nine

As we walk through the twisting streets, the buildings becoming larger and grander with every corner we turn, I talk a little about my parents' split and how they are now. It's quite nice talking to someone from my past actually, someone who knows what they were like. All my friends only know me as an adult, and no one has met my mum.

She'd always been a bit too fond of a drink but since Dad left, it turned into a real problem. She just about manages to hold down a job but from Friday to Sunday she sinks into her bottles of wine and doesn't really come up for air until Monday morning.

I occasionally pay her a guilt visit. She still lives in Cheltenham and I usually aim for a Tuesday evening, when she's at her best. But we never leave the house. I have attempted over the years to get her to change her lifestyle, but she doesn't see anything wrong with how she lives, and I've grown tired of trying. It's such a waste, she's not even sixty yet and she could be so much more.

Dad met someone else, a mild-mannered widow called Jayne and seems happy enough. He retired from the force a few years ago which has made a big change in him. Like many ex-coppers, he works in private security now and without the pressure of the job, it's like he's a different person. He's even taken up golf and he and Jayne are usually found on the course on his days off.

Part of me wants to ask after Adam's family in return. As the night has gone on, despite my best efforts, I've thought about them more and more. I loved them all so much at one time but the pain of talking about them, of remembering, just about outweighs my curiosity.

Instead, I abruptly change the subject.

"How do you know where we're going?"

"Remember I said I used to live in London? I moved here straight from Uni and as a thirsty new architect I used to walk these streets endlessly studying the buildings and the city," Adam replies and then in a daft voice, "I know central Laandan like the back of me 'and innit."

"That's the worst London accent I've ever heard," I giggle. "Are you sure you really lived here?"

"Yep, for four years I shared a small, terraced house in Shepherd's Bush that had been horrendously reconfigured inside to squeeze in as many bedrooms as possible. But I got on with my housemates and liked the area, so it was a happy four years. Here we are, look up there."

We've come out onto the end of a curved tree-lined road and up ahead of us is a grand, light grey building, beautifully lit in purples and blues, vibrant against the dark night sky.

"What is it?"

"Somerset House, haven't you ever been here?" Adam asks, astonished.

"No." I shrug. "But I recognise that name. What's it known for?"

"You'll see," he says with a grin and consulting his watch grabs my arm and starts rushing towards the entrance. "We're a bit late, but it'll be OK."

"Late for what?"

But he doesn't answer, just leads me past the pillared front entrance and through an archway to the side.

We emerge into a huge courtyard and I can't help but gasp at the sight. In front of me is a large, heavily decorated Christmas tree, behind which is an ice rink full of happy skaters, their laughter frosting in the cold air. The walls of Somerset House envelop the square and the soft yellow lights beaming up onto the building highlight the features, windows and doors. It's breathtaking and like something off a postcard. Of course, I've seen this before, in pictures and films – I knew I recognised the name – but I've never actually been here.

I don't get to stand and gawp for long though as Adam is tugging me over to the ticket booth.

"We're not skating, are we?"

"Of course we are," he smiles.

"But you surely have to book?"

"I already have. I did it on my phone while you were listening to that quartet. We got the last two tickets in the last slot of the night. Come on."

Too shocked to respond I follow him mutely to pick up our skates. He remembered my shoe size, which is weird. I haven't skated for years; I hope I don't break my ankle.

We both take off our coats as they're too bulky to skate in and if memory serves, you can get pretty hot skating around. But Adam does take our gloves, hats and scarves out of his bag and once we're set, we wobble onto the ice. I nearly fall over straight away but Adam grabs my hand and helps steady me. I grip onto him tightly, not shying away from the physical contact like I usually would.

I feel like Bambi as we start to make our way around the rink. Adam, of course, is very confident on his skates and not flinching like I am every time other skaters rush past us. Due to the late hour, it's all adults on the ice and some of the more proficient are whizzing around at quite a speed, ice spraying from their blades as they pass. I notice Adam watching them with a slight look of envy.

"You can go off if you like?" I offer. "I'm starting to get the hang of it again... I think." Just as I say it, I wobble and nearly fall backwards. Adam swings around in front of me and takes my other hand too, to steady me. And then, like a smug bastard, starts to skate backwards, pulling me along with him.

"I take it you've done this a lot then?" I say trying not to stare into his eyes, which is hard as he's in my direct line of sight and all my concentration is going into moving forward.

"Yeah, I usually skate somewhere every year. This is my favourite place though, but I haven't been here for years."

I'm starting to find the rhythm of skating again and my balance feels better. Adam must be able to tell as he lets go of one of my hands and moves beside me again. Soon, we're skating relatively in sync and start to pick up speed.

Cheesy Christmas tunes are pouring out of discreet speakers and the lights shimmer and twinkle as we cruise around the rink, the cold air stinging my cheeks and lungs while the rest of me heats up. I stop thinking about the gloved hand holding tightly onto mine and just enjoy the sensations as I glide. All else is forgotten and I feel just pure joy in this moment.

It seems far too soon when our session ends, and we're ushered off the ice. I can't stop smiling.

"That was amazing, thank you," I gush, as we stumble onto the narrow wooden benches in the cloakroom and start untying our boots. "I haven't skated in such a long time and I'd forgotten how much fun it was."

"Not too Christmassy for you then?" Adam asks with a cock of his eyebrow.

"I think it's probably the Christmassiest place I've ever been to, but luckily it's so beautiful I can make my peace with it." I grin, wrestling with my skates to pull them off. I cannot get to grips with my left one at all.

"Need a hand?" Adam asks, his skates already neatly beside him on the bench. I'm about to say no when I realise how silly and futile it is to constantly be pushing him away.

"Oh, go on then, if you must."

I hold my foot out and he grips the boot tightly before yanking it so hard he almost pulls me off the bench.

"Sorry," he says, attempting to look abashed, but not quite managing it. "One more try, then we'll have to get professional help."

Fortunately, with a slightly gentler tug this time, the boot comes off with a pop and Adam nearly falls backwards, steadying himself just in time.

"Thanks," I laugh. "Do you think we have time for a hot chocolate? My treat. I kept smelling them as we skated past the bar area and now, I've got a real craving for one."

"Yeah, the bar stays open a bit longer." We make it over to the bar area, in a large marquee beside the rink, just in time for me to order two hot chocolates with cream and marshmallows. At the last minute, I give in to temptation and get them to pop a shot of Bailey's into them as well. It used to be my favourite way to have a festive hot chocolate.

The bar is full so, cradling our drinks, we step back outside and lean against the wall of the rink, in front of the Christmas tree, staring up at the stately walls of Somerset House, its many windows winking back at us.

"It's a fabulous building, isn't it?" I say, breaking the comfortable silence that had descended as we enjoyed our surroundings.

"I love it. It's a shame I didn't think to bring you here earlier in the night, we could have gone inside. Then again," he continues in a tone that lets me know he is teasing me, "there is a wonderful Christmas shop and lots of beautiful Christmas decorations, so you'd probably hate it."

I'm still buzzing from the skating, so I just laugh, "Yeah, probably." I take a sip of my drink, enjoying the little kick from the Baileys. I can't help but let out a satisfied sigh, causing Adam to grin at me.

"Do you remember when we took Damien skating?" I ask. It's the first time I've ever referenced our past and Adam looks at me a little surprised. But the memory is there and so strong that I can't help talking about it. "It was the rink in

Gloucester and your parents took us all after college one night. Remember you and your dad took it in turns to push Damien round on that... polar bear, was it?"

"A seal."

"That's right, it was a seal. Damien loved it so much, didn't he? He couldn't stop laughing."

Adam just smiled and continued staring at the building. Maybe talking like this upsets him, maybe he does feel guilty? But now I've mentioned his family I can't stop. Perhaps the Christmas stuff is finally getting to me and making me sentimental.

"How is Damien? He must be in his mid-twenties now?"

Adam says nothing, just stares ahead, tension in his jaw and his eyes glinting in the soft lights. And suddenly with a rush of dread sweeping across my shoulders and into my chest, I know what he's about to say.

"Damien died. Three years ago."

# Chapter Ten

Tears spring into my eyes and I'm overwhelmed by such a strong sense of grief that I clutch onto the barrier for support.

"But... but earlier you said..." I trail off.

Adam is still just staring ahead but I can see a silvery tear tracking down his cheek.

"I said Damien will always be Damien," he finally answers, his voice husky, "and he will be. I thought we'd only have that hour in the pub and... it sounds silly, but I wanted you to keep thinking of him how he was, you know?"

I nod, even though he's not looking at me. My mind fills with images of Damien, his happy, laughing face, how his head felt resting on my shoulder as we watched a film, his skinny little arms as he hugged me. How can he be gone? I put the remains of my hot chocolate on the ground, I can't stomach it now, and squeeze Adam's arm in what I hope is a sympathetic way.

"Do you want to tell me about it?" I ask gently.

"We always knew that we only had him for a limited time, that he would never be an old man. In a way, we were lucky that we had him as long as we did. It was a chest infection, in the end, it turned into pneumonia and his weak lungs couldn't fight it."

"I am so sorry."

Going purely on instinct, I pull Adam towards me and hug him, hard. I hear his paper cup clatter to the ground as he wraps his arms around me and buries his head in my neck. We cling to each other as hot tears streak down my face.

I'm crying for Damien, the wonderful boy I knew who was filled with love and joy and lust for life despite all he had to endure. I'm crying for Adam who loved his little brother with fierce devotion. And I'm crying for their mum and dad, the most loving parents I've ever known, and for the heartbreak that they've suffered. And, honestly, a few of those tears are for me too.

I'm not sure how long we stand, holding each other, my aversion to physical contact with him completely forgotten, but eventually, I pull away. I bend to retrieve our cups and take them over to a nearby bin, assuming Adam may want a second to compose himself.

I look back over at him, his strong profile silhouetted by the lights twinkling behind him. Now that he's told me about Damien, it would feel weird not telling him about the reason for the meeting I had today. Dishonest somehow. I know that I don't owe him anything, and it goes against all my plans to not reveal too much about myself or get too close, but my heart is over-ruling my head. It's suddenly so important to me that he knows, despite what happened between us, that I never forgot Damien. Deep down I suspect it's more complex than that, but I refuse to examine my feelings too closely. This just feels like the right thing to do in this moment.

"Come on," I say, grabbing Adam's hand when I return. "There's something I want to show you."

People are starting to drift out of the archway as the bar is closed now, but instead of going with the flow, I lead him to one of the closed doorways. Confident that neither animal nor human will have urinated on it in here, I sit myself down on the smooth, worn step. Adam towers over me, backlit by the lights of the Christmas tree.

"Sit," I instruct. Looking puzzled he does as I say and I shuffle up as close to him as our ridiculous coats allow while rummaging in my handbag and pulling out my iPad.

"You know how I said I had a meeting with my publisher, Jo, today? Well, up until now, I'd only illustrated things that I'd been asked to, stuff for other people, you know?"

Adam nods, clearly wondering where this is going as I tap on the screen.

"So, last year," I continue, "I approached Jo about an idea I had for a children's book. It was an idea I'd had for years and then finally I put it to paper. It comes out in the New Year, but I want to show you the mock-up."

"OK," he says slowly, understandably confused.

I show him my iPad, having opened the relevant file. It's the front page of the book, showing my main character, a superhero in a rocket-fuelled wheelchair, surrounded by his special superhero friends.

"But that's like the poster you did of Damien. Mum still has it up in the lounge."

Saying nothing, I flick the screen to the next page, it's blank except for the dedication.

*For Damien x*

"You see, after all this time, I still thought of him, of what an inspiration he was. I realised that kids who are different, or special or sick, don't have books that show them as the heroes they are. So, I've written one. The kids in this, all with special needs, are secretly superheroes who get up to adventures. Hopefully, it'll be a whole series. Here." I pass over the iPad and we sit in silence while he reads.

Adam hands the iPad back when he's done and, as I slip it back into my bag, he rests his face in his hands, his elbows propped on his knees. After a moment, with a deep sigh, he lifts his head and looks at me with a gentle smile.

"I don't know what to say."

"I'd always planned to post a copy of the finished book to your family. I drove past their house a few months ago and saw your dad going inside, so I knew they were still there."

"They'll never leave, there are too many good memories of Damien there. But they'll love it, your book. I mean, it's just fantastic. Damien would have been over the moon. He loved you, you know."

"I know," I whisper.

"Come on, you two," calls the brusque voice of a security guard, breaking our moment. "We're closing up now."

Adam stands as I zip up my bag and then pulls me to my feet. "I don't know about you, but I could do with a drink. Let's try and find a bar, shall we?"

# Chapter Eleven

I battle my way back from the toilets through the masses of people, spotting Adam tucked in by the stairway, holding our drinks and looking around the room at the merrymaking. Even from a few metres away and trying to be objective, I have to admit he's a very good-looking man.

He still has the Gary Barlow thing going on and just like Gary he's improved with age. His cheekbones are slightly more defined, his eyes wiser and his physique refined. In his white shirt, with the collar loose and the sleeves rolled up, I can see his body, always slim, has become firmer and more manly and well... pretty gorgeous, if I'm honest. I swallow, resisting the urge to fan my face.

I mustn't think that way, though. That way madness lies. A lot of the resentment I've felt has eased; knowing what he's been through, losing his brother, has softened my opinion of him. But I mustn't get carried away. I mustn't forget completely.

He sees me coming and smiles at me. My stomach does a little flip flop. Clearly, my body hasn't got the memo about him. It's probably like muscle memory or something. I reach him and he hands my drink over.

"Here you are, pink gin and lemonade. Not a drink I would have guessed for you in a million years."

"Oh no, what would you have gone for then?"

"Well, assuming you no longer like Cider and Black, probably... I don't know a Tia Maria or bourbon or something."

"Tia Maria?" I laugh, "Who drinks Tia Maria?"

"Yeah, but pink gin, though? Isn't that all trendy and hipster?"

"I know it is," I admit, "but like you say, I don't go for cider anymore and wine just makes me think of Mum. There's this gin bar I meet my colleagues in once a month and they have all these different flavours and, well, I just like it. So there." And I poke my tongue out at him before taking a sip and licking my lips dramatically. "Mmm, delicious."

Adam throws back his head and laughs, a rich, deep sound that carries above the noise of the bar and makes me tingle.

Just then, a rather large lady, in a very tight top, her boobs almost falling out, unsuccessfully squeezes past Adam, causing his pint to spill over his arm.

"It's a bit busy," I say, moving closer as the lady now tries to push past me, her breasts jiggling like pink blancmange as they press against my arm.

"Just a bit," he replies, "but it's doubtful we'd have got in anywhere else at this hour. Actually, can you do me a favour and put these in your handbag?" He reaches into his back pocket, retrieving his phone and slim wallet. "The last thing I need tonight is to be pickpocketed."

"Of course," I reply, popping them into my bag and doing up the zip firmly. Thankfully, this place has a cloakroom where we were able to stash the rucksack and all our other winter layers. I may not be dressed up to the nines like a lot of women in here but at least in my vest and necklace, I'm passable. I touched my make-up in the loos too, slapping on a bit of extra eyeliner for good measure.

We're jostled again as a group of shrieking women push past us.

"This is doing my head in," Adam says close to my ear. "I've got an idea, but you need to play along. Are you up for it?"

"That depends, what is it?"

"Look, up there," he points to the wide stairway leading up to the next floor which from the volume of stair traffic is probably as busy as this one. But then I see what he's pointing to. To the right of the stairs, there's a rope closing off that side with a sign on it saying, 'Private Party'.

"Fancy crashing it?"

"But we can't," I argue, "there's a bouncer." I gesture to the bull-like bald man, dressed all in black posted at the top of the stairs and perusing the crowds with a cold, hard stare.

"Confidence, my dear," Adam responds with a wink and, taking my hand, pulls me up the stairs. As we ascend, he puts his arm around my shoulders and starts to walk with a slouch as if he's drunk. When we're a couple of steps from the top, he turns suddenly to me, cradling my face in his hands, his nose and lips millimetres from mine. His eyes, however, are trained on the party area the other side of the banister. To the bouncer, it will look like we're kissing. I can feel myself starting to tremble at his proximity and try to regulate my breathing.

"Now," he mutters, and he turns and pulls me up the final few stairs. We reach the top just as a dishevelled looking trio are coming out of the party, the bouncer lifting the rope for them. Adam grabs the closest one in a firm handshake.

"Hey, man," he bellows, doing that manly back slap thing. "I didn't know you were here. Not leaving, are you?"

"No," hiccups the man, looking a bit confused but playing along, obviously too drunk to realise that he doesn't know Adam from, well, Adam. "Just going for a smoke."

"Ah, come and find me later, yeah?" Adam continues with a slur. "I'll buy you a pint."

And taking my hand, we pass the trio and swan into the private area, the bouncer closing the rope behind us. No questions asked.

"I can't believe that worked," I giggle into Adam's ear.

"I told you, it's all about confidence," he grins.

"But what if someone here realises that we're not supposed to be here?"

"Look around, everyone is too busy having a good time to care about us. I'd say it's definitely an office party. If anyone asks, just say you know Dave, there's always a Dave."

"Do you do this a lot?" I ask, shocked.

"Nope, first time, but it's going so well I might make a habit of it. Besides, what's the worst that can happen? They'll just ask us to leave."

He's right and I relax. It's much better up here. Everyone seems pretty hammered but there's a lot more space and we ensconce ourselves by a pillar without fear of being bashed into.

"So, what did you think of the bouncer?" he asks. "Definitely a rhino, right?"

I freeze for a moment, my drink halfway to my lips. Am I really able to do this? Play our old game, like we're eighteen again. I look at him sharply. There's a slight smile tugging at his mouth but there's no mistaking the challenge in his eyes again. After my reaction to the 'hedgehog' comment, I feel like he's testing me. Despite the prickling feeling in my shoulders, I refuse to show him that I'm bothered.

"No, with those nostrils, definitely a bull," I say coolly, then take a hopefully nonchalant sip of my drink. See, I can keep my head.

"Yeah, you're right," he laughs, "you were always better at this than me."

"Well durr; I was doing it way before you came along, remember?"

"I remember," he says softly.

Suddenly I can feel it again, the sense that he wants to talk about it. I've come on leaps this evening but that's a step too far.

"Oh, I love this song," I exclaim in an attempt to throw him off, realising a second too late that I don't even know it.

"You love Justin Timberlake?" Adam asks in disbelief.

"Yeah, he writes all his own stuff, you know."

Actually, I don't know that at all, but I think I maybe heard that somewhere. It sounds plausible anyway.

"Let's go dance then," says Adam, totally calling my bluff.

"Er..." I rack my brains for an excuse but it's too late. Adam has turned and is heading for the small dance floor in the corner of the room and I have no choice but to follow meekly.

Despite the multicoloured flashing lights, it's quite dark on the dance floor and just crowded enough that we blend in but not so crowded that everyone is crashing into each other.

To be fair to Justin Timberlake, this song has a good beat and even though I don't recognise it, I'm able to dance along quite happily. I have always enjoyed dancing, something people are often surprised about. Evidently, I don't seem like the dancing type. It does feel a bit weird though, just the two of us bopping around like this. I don't know where to look. Whenever I catch Adam's eye, which is frequently as we are facing each other, we just smile uncomfortably or sip our drinks.

I'm about to suggest that we go and sit somewhere when a Christmas song comes on. I can't say it now or it'll seem like a silly overreaction to Christmas music. Instead, I give Adam an exaggerated eye roll and he laughs.

Honestly, though, this is one of the few Christmas songs I can stomach and it's clearly a popular choice as the little dance floor suddenly becomes much more crowded and spirited. There's a lot of spinning and hopping going on around us. One group of ladies is performing some sort of high kick move. I'm glad my drink is almost empty or it would have been spilt five times by now. At least it's eased the tension, we're just being jostled around, laughing at the antics going on around us. I even join in with a couple of spins and kicks myself. As does Adam, which cracks me up.

The song ends and the lightweights shuffle off the dance floor, fanning their faces. It takes a couple of seconds before I recognise the relaxed tones of Chris Martin from Coldplay; I'd forgotten they had a Christmas song. The DJ obviously thought people needed to cool off after that last track. I love Coldplay, but this isn't exactly a bop-along-to-song. A few people are starting to couple up around us or get into swaying groups. Without a word, Adam takes my glass from me, putting it with his on a shelf to the right of us. Then he holds out his arms.

Before I know what I'm doing, we come together into a classic dance pose and start to move. I'm aware of his warm fingers as his hand chastely rests on my waist and I try not to grip his shoulder too hard. The tempo picks up and we really start to dance. Adam always was a strong lead and I move without thought, just following the music and Adam's strong hands leading me around the floor.

As he spins me away from him and then back into his body, the years melt away. The coloured lights flash and the world around us recedes. We're seventeen again.

# Chapter Twelve

## Then

"Come on, Birthday Boy," Karen instructed. "Dance with your mother."

As Rose had come to expect at Curtis family gatherings, Karen's disco light was on and music was pumping from the stereo while they waited for their curry to be delivered. This was the second family birthday that she'd been invited to and then there had been Christmas and New Year as well. Once presents have been opened, they all have a dance in the living room. Adam's grandparents resist for the first couple of songs before getting up and joining in good-naturedly.

Then once they had exhausted themselves, they would feast on the celebrant's takeaway of choice, all sat around the huge pine table in the kitchen where they would remain for the evening, playing board games and laughing.

Rose thought it was all brilliant fun and a far cry from birthdays in her family. She loved that Adam, on his seventeenth birthday, was still up for it. Of course, they would be doing something with friends on the weekend too, but this, his actual birthday, was family time.

She watched him spinning his mum around the room as she laughed girlishly and it hit Rose, as it often did, just how lucky she was that this gorgeous person loved her. Her. She also felt incredibly grateful that she'd been welcomed into this loving family.

Adam's grandparents were sat together, holding hands on the sofa, and Dan and Damien were dancing together by the fireplace – well, Damien was spinning about in his wheelchair giggling away. He caught Rose's eye from where she was perched on the corner of the armchair.

"Come and dance, Rose," he called.

Rose, who loved to dance, didn't need to be asked twice and she hopped up and joined Dan and Damien by the fireplace. Soon she'd felt Adam's arms around her and their little dance floor spread to include everyone, even Gran and Grandpa who, as normal, had only abstained for two songs.

When the song changed to a slow one, rather than ask for it to be changed, Adam surprised Rose by catching hold of his mum, and, as everyone else backed out of the way, mother and son gracefully waltzed around the living room.

Rose watched them, amazed. She knew Adam was a good dancer, she'd seen him at the lounge mini-discos and their college Christmas party. Unlike Dan who, bless him, only had classic bad dad moves, Adam could genuinely dance. But she didn't know that he could dance-dance, like with proper steps and everything.

Catching her open-mouthed gaze as they waltzed past, Adam winked at her, clearly pleased to have caught her by surprise. Karen saw her too and pulled away from Adam, walking over to her.

"Do you know how to waltz, Rose?" she asked kindly.

Rose just shook her head.

"I've been teaching Ad to dance since he was eight," Karen continued. "Well, his father is useless, and I figured I needed someone to partner me at weddings and stuff." She said this with a grin over at Dan who, far from being offended, just laughed.

"Hey, my dancing is legendary," he called over the music.

"Yes, but for all the wrong reasons, sweetie," countered Karen. "Come on, get up, Rose, I'll teach you. Just think how lovely it will be if you two can dance properly at your summer ball."

"Mum, I don't think Rose will want to," Adam interjected, coming to her rescue. But as Rose looked into Karen's kind smile and was aware of the eager faces of the family surrounding them, she felt that she couldn't be churlish and say no, despite her nerves at being the centre of attention.

"Actually," she said, taking Adam's hand, "I've always wanted to learn how to dance properly. Strictly is a bit of a guilty pleasure," she admitted with a blush.

"Yay!" Karen clapped her hands and pulling the pair of them into the middle of the room, placed Rose's hands onto Adam's body.

As Rose looked up into Adam's beautiful green eyes, her nerves dissipated and she started to feel a little bit excited. She loved being held by Adam and there would be nothing more romantic than being able to dance with him properly.

Karen was a good and patient teacher, having studied dance for years until a bad back and motherhood put an end to her career. She still taught aerobic dance classes three times a week, though. Adam was a strong lead and luckily Rose was naturally a good mover so soon they were confidently moving around the room as Karen called time. The only distraction came when, after much giggling, Damien persuaded his dad to pick him up and follow them around the room in an exaggerated tango. The whole family were in fits of laughter when the doorbell rang announcing their curry had arrived.

The casual lessons continued for months off and on until the night of their summer ball when, resembling James Bond, in a sophisticated tux, Adam led Rose in her flowing crimson dress around the crowded dance floor.

When recounting the night to Karen, they didn't tell her how all the other students were drunkenly wailing along to the slower songs or snogging messily on the dancefloor, so as not to disappoint her.

Instead, Rose told her of the sparkling chandelier and mirrored walls of the hotel function room and how she was like a princess dancing with her prince. Which was exactly how she'd felt.

# Chapter Thirteen

The song ends and I find myself pressed tightly against Adam's body, our faces inches apart and our eyes locked. My heart is beating so strongly I'm sure he can feel it. That was like an out of body experience, I forgot that I could ever dance like that.

I'm vaguely aware of other people around us; I think that some had moved out of the way to let us dance. I can't tear my gaze away from his, though. I can feel the rise and fall of his chest against my breasts and I'm conscious of their treacherous response.

Still, we stare. I'm not imagining it. I hadn't forgotten it; that connection between us, deeper than anything I could ever explain, is still there. He must feel it too.

My senses are on fire, every millimetre of my body tingling, yearning, so strongly I feel like I could faint. Everything in me is screaming to move my head an inch closer and bring my lips to his. How wonderful it would be to sink into him, lose myself in him again. I can only assume Adam feels the same as he hasn't moved away.

I almost do it, I almost give in. And then in that second, I remember. The pain. The grief.

I pull away, breaking the spell. I don't look at his face, I'm not sure what expression I'll see on it, is he upset or relieved? I'm not even sure which one I'd want to see.

"I need the loo," I mumble and stumble off to the toilets.

Once inside, I resist the urge to splash cold water on my face – far too dramatic – and instead, bolt myself into a cubicle and sit down heavily on the loo, grateful that the previous occupant had bothered to put the lid down.

"For fuck's sake," I mutter putting my head in my hands.

What I should be doing is giving myself a large slap. What the hell was that back there? It was exactly what I've been trying to avoid all night. I'd been determined to keep things light, not to get too close.

I'm just responding to the positive memories of us together, that's all.

I was right before, it's like muscle memory. Everyone reacts strongly to their first love; it's not about the person, it's about that time in your life when everything was fresh, new and exciting, and hormones were whizzing around. Life hadn't got to you by then, well, if you were lucky.

I remember reading an article about when Facebook first became popular; it was responsible for lots of relationships ending. People were able to get in touch with their old boyfriends and girlfriends again and, in some cases, they ended up rekindling.

Inevitably, once in the real world, these relationships didn't last. Rose-tinted-glasses syndrome or something. Nostalgia is a powerful force. Look how many crappy eighties and nineties films are considered classics, not because they're actually good – show them to a Gen Z and they'd laugh at you – but because they make you feel... something.

That's what is happening here. Adam is a crappy nineties film that I think I like because it reminds me of snuggling up on the sofa with a bag of sweets and not a care in the world.

I blame Christmas too. It always has a nostalgic air about it as a season. And, tonight, I've let myself get a little enchanted by it again, the twinkly lights, the frosty air, the music, the bloody ice skating. It all seduced me a bit.

I should give in to the bad memories, the ones trying to push their way in, like black smoke curling under a doorway. If I let myself remember, really remember, I could hate him again.

But I can't do it. Years of suppression means I can't help but push them away. It's like I'm in a room inside my brain yelling "No" at the top of my voice and frantically gaffer taping the bottom of the door, ignoring the fire raging behind it.

It doesn't help, of course that, history aside, Adam is a charming, fun, good-looking bloke. It's hard not to be drawn to him. If I'd met him for the first time tonight, I'd be flirting like crazy and possibly suggesting we shell out on that room at the Savoy just for a night of unbridled passion. Not that I make a habit of jumping into bed with people, well, not much, anyway.

Realising that I really do need to pee galvanises me out of introspection. I'd better get back out there quickly anyway, I don't want him to realise anything is wrong. I just need to act cool, calm and collected and deny that I almost kissed him.

When I return, he's hovering near the bar, staring into space with a rather grave expression. He looks all brooding and sexy. I'm pretty sure if I were pulling that face, I'd just look like a witch. His face softens as he sees me approach but the smile he gives me doesn't reach his eyes.

"Everything OK?" he asks when I reach him.

"Yeah, fine, sorry I was a while, there's always a queue in the ladies," I lie.

"I was going to get us another drink, then I realised you've got my wallet."

"Oh yeah, don't worry, it's my round anyway." I turn to the bar, propping my elbows on the shiny wood and taking a deep breath. I think I managed to seem casual and relaxed. Hopefully, we'll get back to the friendly rapport we developed at Somerset House. We just need to stay off the dance floor.

"I forgot to ask, what are you drinking?" I ask over my shoulder and catch him staring intently at me, the serious expression back on his face.

"Oh, IPA please," he mutters, forcing a smile as fake as the barmaid's boobs. There's definitely a weird vibe between us now. Come to think of it, maybe alcohol isn't the answer here? Oh well, one more can't hurt.

I'm feeling a little lightheaded by the time we emerge back onto the streets. I've never been a big drinker (thanks, Mum) so I'm feeling the impact of the three gins I've had. The icy air hits me like a bucket of cold water as we step out of the doors and I hurry to put my coat on. We decided to leave the bar ten minutes before it shut to beat the rush and I'm glad we did as it gives me time to layer up, this time going for the whole shebang with hat, gloves and scarf too. Adam does the same and once again I giggle when I get a look at him, we must look so ridiculous, especially with our matching bobble hats.

Things had normalised as we sat with our drinks. We ended up having a very in-depth discussion about which Marvel hero was the best and putting the films in order of preference. It was typical pub banter and just what we needed to regain our equilibrium.

"Where now then, boss?" Adam asks with a smile.

"I don't think at any point this evening I've been the boss," I smile back, "but right now, if I'm going to last until morning, I definitely need a coffee and possibly some chips. Then," I stop to consider for a moment, "I'd like to walk along the river, I think."

"Your wish is my command. This way."

Within minutes we find a McDonald's, the pale, harassed-looking staff struggling to deal with the swarms of drunk people seeking late-night munchies. Feeling a little shamefaced to be among them, we join the back of the queue. As I gaze around, I realise that not all the customers are people who've been out partying.

All the tables are full, mainly with bedraggled, tired-looking bodies tucked into their coats, leaning exhaustedly up against walls or snoozing softly, upright in their chairs, heads lolling at strange angles. Briefcases, shopping bags and, in some cases, suitcases are shoved under the metal tables and piles of empty tea and coffee cups litter the tops.

"You were right about all the twenty-four-hour places being full up," I say, suddenly feeling immensely glad that I have had company this evening, and actually had a lot of fun. I have the urge to give Adam's hand a squeeze of thanks, but I ignore my tingling fingers and give him a broad, genuine smile instead.

His eyes widen slightly in surprise, but he smiles back warmly. Then, I feel his hand give mine a squeeze of understanding. We always did think in sync and manage to converse without saying anything.

As we shuffle closer to the front of the queue, Adam nudges me and nods towards the corner of the room.

"Remind you of anyone?" he asks with a smile.

There sits a girl of about nineteen at a guess, her short hair dyed a deep purple. Her tired eyes are ringed with heavy eyeliner and dark eyeshadow which has smudged somewhat during the night. She looks particularly pale under the unforgiving fluorescent lights. She's turned away slightly from the rest of the room, a battered rucksack up on the table creating a barrier between her and the person sharing her space who is currently fast asleep on folded arms and snoring slightly. The girl is focused on a dog-eared paperback but is still managing to give off a 'don't talk or look at me' vibe. It's like she's behind a little forcefield created by her attitude.

It's like seeing a teenage me.

I can't stop staring at her as my feet automatically follow the queue forward.

"That's just what you looked like the day I approached you in the canteen," Adam murmurs.

"I still don't get why you ever bothered talking to me," I say lightly.

"You don't?" Adam sounds surprised. "You were just fascinating, and, you know, beautiful."

"Hardly," I scoff. I never could take compliments.

"I don't regret it, you know, despite everything," he says so softly I only just caught it.

I am floored. How do I respond to that? Do I regret it? I'm not sure. They were easily the best two years of my life. But was it worth the pain afterwards? I don't know.

Luckily, I'm saved from responding by reaching the counter, but then realise I haven't asked Adam what he wants.

"I'm going to have a burger instead of chips. As there's nowhere to sit, it's easier to walk and eat a burger. What about you?" I turn and ask Adam.

The server tuts impatiently, which is kind of fair enough.

"I'll have whatever you're having."

"OK, in that case, two double cheeseburgers, two black coffees and two chocolate doughnuts, please? For the sugar," I say to Adam in response to his raised eyebrow.

As we wait for the order, my eye is drawn to the girl again. I never did understand why Adam singled me out on that first day in the canteen. It used to bother me but once I felt secure in the relationship, once we bonded, I stopped questioning it. Romantic, teenage me just decided we were destined to be together and that was what happened.

Now, I can be more objective. Despite his ordinary outward appearance, Adam is drawn to the unique, the different, the quirky in all aspects of his life. With the wisdom of age, I can understand that the other girls who fawned around him, all versions of the same person, at least on the outside, wouldn't have captured his attention.

Plus, let's be honest, on some level, all men want what they can't have, don't they? I'm sure a lot of the appeal lay in my apparent indifference, the aloofness I wore like a shield to protect myself was actually what drew him to me. Ironic really, considering.

Oh dear, the girl has caught me staring at her and we've locked eyes. She gives me a look of pure contempt and I feel myself blush as I look away. I wish I could go over to her and say, 'I wasn't judging you, I used to be just like you.' Maybe even whip out a photo on my phone to show her. Except I don't have any old photos of me on my phone so that won't work. Besides, she would just think I was a weirdo. Which I suppose I am. Why does it bother me that some random girl thinks I don't like her? It doesn't matter... and yet somehow it does.

It's funny, isn't it? We spend our teenage years desperate to become an adult, to make our own decisions and forge our own way in the world. And yet we never realise how, good or bad, our teenage experiences shape our lives more than anything else. That the relationships we garner in our formative years set the foundations for all relationships that follow, either in an attempt to replicate or avoid.

Thinking about all the men I've dated over the years, none of them has resembled Adam at all, either physically or personality-wise. I've made no attempt to get to know their families or be involved in their lives beyond the confines of our relationship. I've never opened my heart and my innermost thoughts to any of these men to whom I've gladly given full access to my body.

God, when I think about it, all these years that I've mentally boxed everything away, that I thought I was better, I've still just been running away.

"Rose, are you OK?" Adam's voice pulls me out of my reflection. He's awkwardly holding a bag and a coffee in each hand. I hadn't even noticed our food was ready. "You were miles away then."

"Sorry, yeah, the late hour, I suppose," I mutter, relieving him of my share of the order.

We step out, blinking into the night, the muted glow of the streetlamps a little disorientating after the bright fluorescent lights. I'm aware of the faint tang of fried food emanating from our clothing and fervently hope that the cold soon blasts it away. The frosty air is crisp and fresh, stinging my cheeks slightly and no doubt instantly turning the end of my nose pink.

"Someone was giving you evils as we walked out," Adam says with a grin, wrestling his burger free from its packaging.

"Yeah, I know but to be fair, I started it. Inadvertently, anyway," I reply, doing the same. It's quite hard when you're also holding a coffee, the heat of which is beginning to burn the pads of my fingers. "Hold on a sec."

I put my coffee on the floor, fully unwrap my burger, then open it to pull out the pickles which I dispose of in the nearest bin. Licking a stray bit of ketchup off my thumb, I throw the rest of the wrapping and bag away, tucking my doughnut in its bag into my handbag. Then, holding the burger gently between my teeth, I pull one of my gloves out of my pocket and slip it onto my right hand.

As I pick my coffee back up, my glove protecting my fingers from the heat, I notice Adam is watching me with a look of wry amusement on his face.

"Why didn't you just ask for no pickles?"

"Oh, I never think of it till I have the burger in my hand."

Still smiling, he takes a big bite of his burger, somehow not needing to go through the same palaver I did. My burger is rapidly cooling down, now it's exposed to the night air, so I take a large bite too. There's something so wrong and yet so right about fast food. I can't remember the last time I had a McDonald's and it feels a little illicit, like I should be too mature for this sort of thing. McDonald's always reminds me of birthdays as a tween, when gathering there with friends for a meal before the cinema was the height of celebration sophistication, especially if the grown-ups sat apart from you or, even better, just loitered outside.

By unspoken consent, we turn and start walking in the rough direction of the Thames. Even though I don't know exactly where we are, I have enough of a grasp of London geography to be able to find my way to the river. Whereas Adam just seems to have a little A-Z in his head.

"So, why were you giving a teenager evil looks?"

"She was blatantly older than a teenager and I wasn't giving her evil looks, just maybe, you know, staring at her a bit. She caught me doing it and understandably it must have pissed her off."

"I guess she wouldn't have seen you as the kindred spirit you saw in her."

"Exactly. In my head, I still think I look like that." Here I go sharing my innermost thoughts again, it's like Adam's presence is some sort of truth drug, like he's my inhibition kryptonite.

"Really? Huh, it was weird seeing that girl in there, it reminded me just how different you look now. But then I see you faffing with your food and you somehow still look exactly the same, you know?"

"Not really." I can't decide whether he's contradicted himself or the gins are still having an effect. I take a big slurp of my coffee, just in case it is the gin. It's still scalding hot, and I feel the warmth flowing down my throat and into my chest. The heat and the bitter kick of caffeine make my eyes water and catch the back of my throat. I take in a deep breath of cold air to balance things out, resisting the urge to fan my scorched tongue.

"I guess that didn't make much sense, did it? I don't know, it's just with the glossy hair and smart clothes and all that, technically yeah, you look completely different and yet the minute I saw you through the crowds, over a hundred metres away, I knew instantly that it was you." He eats the last mouthful of his burger and scrunches up the wrapper, shoving it in his pocket. I'm inordinately pleased to see he still doesn't litter. I hate littering with a fiery passion.

I don't really know how to respond, so I decide to tuck into my doughnut instead.

"Mmm... this is so good," I mumble through my mouthful.

"Nice to see your sweet tooth hasn't diminished."

"No, but unfortunately my ability to eat gallons of chocolate and stay stick thin has, so I have to pace myself these days."

"Any other big changes?"

"Um, I wear fewer piercings now, my holes have pretty much closed up." Using the back of my doughnut-hand, I push my hair away from my ear, exposing my earlobe and the one set of chunky silver studs. "See."

"Very respectable," he smiles. "Hold on." He pauses on the pavement and stops me by taking my arm.

"What?"

"You've got a smudge of chocolate on your cheek now."

Tenderly he swipes the pad of his thumb across my cheekbone, his fingers resting on the sensitive skin at the top of my neck. It's such a small gesture, but it causes a huge reaction in me. Every millimetre of my skin prickles; I'm aware of my own heartbeat and a fizzing sensation in my chest. As he withdraws his hand, casually licking the chocolate off his thumb, my whole body suffuses with heat.

Fortunately, he seems totally oblivious to my body's traitorous reaction to him and continues walking, taking a casual sip of his coffee. I fall into step beside him, once more attempting a couple of subtle deep breaths.

What I really want to do is whip off my coat and cardigan and stand in the street until the cold air numbs some sense into me. Or, more accurately, into the parts of my brain and body that are refusing to cooperate with the 'don't get sucked in' plan that the logical part of me came up with at the start of the evening.

I make do with taking a sip of my coffee which luckily has already cooled considerably. The air must be even colder than I realised. This coat may be the ugliest thing I've ever owned but it is doing a good job of keeping me warm.

We're passing a park now, the bare trees casting strange shadows on the road like giant, gnarled hands. I carry on sipping my coffee and, feeling fortified by the caffeine, I attempt to continue the conversation.

"So, other than the facial hair, has anything changed about you? You're obviously not a vegetarian or teetotal or anything."

"Not really, oh, except I have a tattoo."

"You do not."

"I do, I swear."

"You got a tattoo?" I screech incredulously.

"Don't sound so surprised! I'm not that boring, am I?"

"No, you've never been boring, but a tattoo? I can't imagine it. Where is it?"

"On my back."

"No," I shake my head. "You're winding me up."

"Look."

He stops and places his coffee down. Unzipping his coat, he hands it to me before turning and pulling his shirt and jumper up. For a second, I think he's going to take them off, but he just bunches the material up around his neck.

I gulp at the sight of his smooth skin and broad shoulders. I've always had a weird thing for men's backs. I just find them sexy. Something I vividly remember Jenny and me bonding over after watching the second Pirates of the Caribbean film and getting a little tingle from a topless Orlando Bloom.

I attempt to resist for all of a second, before my hand reaches out and touches his skin, under the pretence of pushing his shirt a bit higher, even though I could already clearly see the tattoo. He is warm and smooth and suddenly I'm hit by the strongest memory of my hands stroking, then clutching at this same back, feeling the muscles moving under my fingers. I'm rocked by a wave of lust.

"What do you think?" he asks.

My fingers trace the black lines fanning out from his spine across his shoulder blades. I try to focus on the pattern and not on the feel of his skin beneath my fingertips. I go to speak, but a little croak comes out instead. Clearing my throat, I try again.

"It's nice."

"Nice?" he laughs pulling his top back down. My fingers feel bereft. "Oh dear, I'm pretty sure 'nice' from an artist means they don't like it."

"No, not at all, I think it's a fantastic pattern. Unique without being weird or over the top." I don't mention that I'd like to trace it with my tongue. Jesus, where are these thoughts coming from? Can I still blame the pink gin? "Where did you get it done?" I say instead.

"A little place in Camden Lock actually. It was a graduation present to myself," he continues while relieving me of his coat and zipping back into it before putting his gloves on. Phew, no more exposed skin.

"Was it a little bit of rebellion? Like 'I'm about to become a real grown-up with a sensible job and wearing a suit, but underneath I'm a tattooed hard man'?" I joke.

"Something like that, I guess," he laughs and picks up his coffee before we continue on.

# Chapter Fourteen

## Then

Rose knocked on the door, feeling nervous for the first time since her first visit to the house six months before. She was nervous but she was also excited. So excited.

The feeling had been mounting for a couple of weeks, ever since Adam's parents had announced that they were going away for a romantic weekend while Damien was staying in respite care.

Things between Adam and Rose were at boiling point. Ever since declaring their love for each other a month before, their relationship had taken on a new level of intensity. The only thing that they didn't share with each other now was their bodies. Plus, they were seventeen with raging hormones and they fancied each other like mad. They were both keen to move things on to the next level.

Sometimes when they were kissing, Rose felt like she might explode so desperate was she to ease the aching lust that pounded through her body. They'd progressed from long make out sessions, to under the clothes fumbling. Being able to intimately touch Adam and to be touched by him thrilled Rose to her core and was the last thing she thought about every night before sleep.

They'd both been very pleasantly surprised a few weeks previously when Adam had given Rose her first orgasm just by touching her through her jeans. But it wasn't enough, their feelings for each other were too strong and they needed a proper outlet.

However, they'd both agreed that they wanted it to be special and not to be sneaking around or rushing it if they found themselves alone. They'd both started saving their allowances to pay for a night in a hotel but when Karen had said that the house would be theirs for the weekend it was a lifeline.

Once again, Rose had been impressed and touched at how maturely Adam had approached the whole thing from respectfully discussing it with her to accompanying her to the GP so that she could start taking the pill.

And now the day was upon them. It had been one of those beautiful spring days with a pure blue sky and a gentle breeze. The touch of warmth from a bright sun very welcome after the particularly cold winter that they had endured. They eschewed the canteen at lunchtime and ate outside in the sunshine, the sexual tension zipping between them so strongly that Rose felt like the air around them was vibrating.

Even Jenny had noticed something was up and, usually not one for gossip and sharing personal information, Rose had excitedly revealed their plans to her while they touched up their make-up before class. Jenny had squealed and hugged her and for the first time in her life, Rose had felt like a normal girl.

Rose shivered slightly and knocked on the door again, a bit harder this time. It might have been a beautiful day but it was only April and the warmth was fading with the sun. Then she felt a different kind of shiver as she saw Adam's outline approaching the door through the frosted glass.

"Hi," he said, as the door swung open.

"Hi," breathed Rose, drinking in the sight of him as she stepped into the hall. Like her, he'd changed since college and was looking delectable in dark jeans and a soft grey T-shirt which clung to his broad shoulders. She'd seen him topless a handful of times and her mouth went dry at the thought of seeing a whole lot more later.

He was clearly thinking along the same lines as he reached past her to slam the door before pulling her to him and kissing her deeply. Rose was ready to rip his clothes off there and then, but Adam managed to keep a vestige of control and, breathing heavily, he broke their kiss and led her into the kitchen.

He'd gone to a lot of effort; he'd cooked a lasagne, knowing it was her favourite and had even whipped up some mint chocolate Angel Delight because he remembered her saying that she loved it as a child.

She tried her best to eat, but the butterflies in her stomach, and Adam looking so gorgeous in the soft light of the candles that he'd thoughtfully put on the table, had completely stripped her of her appetite, for food anyway.

Adam didn't seem to be doing much better as he pushed his dinner around his plate when they weren't staring at each other across the table.

"Screw it," he finally said, throwing down his fork. "Can we please just go upstairs?"

"Oh God, yes please," cried Rose, laughing.

With a broad grin, Adam jumped up from his seat and picked Rose up, throwing her over his shoulder and running to the stairs as she squealed and laughed in delight.

At the top of the stairs, he gently lowered her to the ground and the atmosphere changed dramatically as she slowly slid down his body.

"Are you sure you want to do this?" he asked gently.

"I've never been so sure of anything in my life," she murmured and taking his hand, she led him into his bedroom.

The night was a revelation. They explored each other's bodies learning how to give each other pleasure. Rose, who had always assumed that she'd be uncomfortable naked in front of someone, trusted Adam so completely that she had no inhibitions and didn't care where he touched or kissed her as long as he kept doing it.

When they finally joined together, Rose was so ready for him that all she felt was exquisite pleasure and a sense of total completeness.

Adam woke first the next morning feeling like he was king of the world. Rose was nestled into him, her small body curved so perfectly into his, her bare bum smooth against his groin which was also now waking up and quite rapidly too.

The night before had been amazing, beyond even his wildest dreams. He was so glad that they waited to do it right and even more glad that he'd waited for Rose.

She stirred and turned in his arms, wrapping her leg over his and nuzzling into his chest. He was surprised at how instantly turned on he was. After last night, he didn't expect to still be so responsive. But he was aware that this had been her first time too and they'd had a busy night, he didn't want to end up hurting her by trying it on again this morning.

"Good morning," she murmured.

"Good morning," he replied stroking her back in long slow strokes. He felt so lucky that he was able to touch her like this, hold her naked body against his like this. "How do you feel?"

"Mmm, good," was the sleepy response.

"I mean, are you OK? Are you sore or anything?"

"A little achy, I guess, but in a nice way."

"Maybe we should get up?"

"It seems like you already are," she replied coquettishly as her hand trailed down his abdomen to his erection. And soon they were lost in each other again.

That Sunday afternoon as Adam walked Rose home on weary, slightly shaky legs, he decided that it had been the best weekend of his life. Rose had been so complimentary about his prowess that he'd been forced to admit to the copy of *FHM* that he had stashed under his bed and the article, 'How to Pleasure Your Girlfriend' which he had studied with vigour.

She'd made him show it to her and she had read it out loud, only managing to get through half the article before it was discarded for the real thing.

They'd finally left the house on Saturday night and wandered into town to pick up a DVD and a takeaway and some chocolate to provide Rose with her sugar fix (they had already found a creative use for the uneaten Angel Delight around lunchtime.)

In the shop, Rose had gleefully pounced on a copy of Cosmopolitan magazine with a headline that screamed '10 tricks to drive him wild in the bedroom'. And, despite having never bought a girly magazine in her life, Rose insisted on buying it and then trying out all ten with Adam as her willing subject.

"Thank you for the best weekend ever," Adam said as they reached Rose's door and he pulled her into his arms.

"No, thank you for the best weekend ever," she replied, squeezing his bum.

"I love you," he said simply.

"I love you," she responded, gazing into his eyes.

Rose shut the front door behind her and leant against the wall listening to Adam's footsteps retreating with a wide smile on her face.

"Is that you, Rosie?" called her mum's voice from the lounge. Rose left her bag in the hall and wandered into the room. Dawn was watching TV while painting her toenails a lurid shade of pink.

"Did you have a nice weekend at your friend's?" Dawn asked, glancing up at Rose.

Rose felt herself flush. Would her mum be able to tell by looking at her? Rose felt so different, so alive, that surely, she must be giving off some sort of glow. But, if she was, her mum was oblivious and turned back to her nails.

For a moment, Rose considered telling her. She didn't think she'd be cross or anything, quite the opposite, Dawn would probably be amused that her little girl wasn't a virgin anymore. As long as she'd been careful.

Two weeks into Rose's relationship with Adam, her mum had sat her down and given her a lecture about how men can't be trusted, and that Rose needed to be sensible and get herself on the pill. It was the closest they'd ever come to a motherly chat. Dawn didn't seem bothered about the idea of Rose having sex as long as she didn't 'get herself pregnant'.

So, while she could tell her mum where she had been and what she'd been doing she instinctively knew that Dawn would make some caustic remark and cheapen it somehow. Or tell her dad at the worst possible time just to get a rise out of him. Her dad was a bit more old-school than her mum and probably wouldn't like the thought of his daughter having weekend-long love-ins with her boyfriend. Not that her dad ever had any clue what she was up to anyway.

It was still tempting to say something though. Uncharacteristically for Rose, she was actually desperate to talk about it all and confide in someone.

"Where's Dad?" she asked instead.

"Work, where'd you think?"

"On a Sunday?"

Dawn just shrugged, absorbed in her programme. Rose turned to go upstairs.

"There's pizza in the freezer if you're hungry," Dawn called after her. "I'm going out in a bit."

Up in her room, Rose lay down wearily on her bed. She felt thoroughly exhausted but in the best possible way and she couldn't help smiling as she remembered all the different ways that she'd tired herself out this weekend.

She picked up her phone to text Adam but saw one from Jenny.

> Hey girl, I hope your weekend was everything you thought it would be. I can't wait to hear all about it — I want details tomorrow! But, you know, not all the details cos Adam's my mate and ewww

Rose went to reply, inordinately pleased that Jenny had thought to text. She had never had a close female friend before, not really. She'd changed schools so much in her teens that she was always the new girl, the outsider, and while she had ultimately joined friendship groups, she was always on the periphery of the group and never really connected enough with anyone to get close to them. Groups of bullies creating hell for Rose also caused her to be very sceptical of people and she didn't trust easily.

However, Jenny was fun and so honest, almost to the point of rudeness, that it had become easy for Rose to trust her and feel comfortable. Although they'd met because of Adam, they were starting to develop their own friendship too which pleased Rose more than she would admit.

At the last second, instead of clicking on message, Rose clicked the call button. It rang twice before Jenny picked up with an excited "Hiya!" Before Rose could get a word out Jenny barrelled straight on. "So, how was it? Was it amazing? Did it hurt?"

And settling back on her pillows, Rose had her first-ever real girly gossip with a trusted friend.

# Chapter Fifteen

I hate to admit it but as we step out onto the riverbank the little Christmas tingle in my chest that I experienced in Covent Garden comes back. We're by a small mooring and large coloured lights are strung up along the jetty casting patches of coloured light onto the dark water of the Thames. London stretches out around us, the ever-lit buildings twinkling away through the mist rising off the river, giving the city an ethereal quality. To my right, I can just make out the London Eye, its coloured lights glowing and shimmering through the haze, like a giant Catherine Wheel. I'm a little disappointed that I'm the wrong side of the river to see Big Ben and the Houses of Parliament.

Instead of the usual cacophony of noise that I associate with London, I can just hear the rushing of the river and the gentle hum of the city in the background.

We automatically turn left away from the dark, imposing shadow of what I guess to be Embankment Station and follow the avenue of trees that line the river's edge. There's no one else around and it feels almost eerie in the swirling mist.

"It's like the witching hour," I can't help but whisper.

"What's that?" Adam whispers back.

"You know, like in the BFG when Sophie looks out of the window and the whole town is silent and still and she sees the BFG for the first time."

"Oh." Adam chuckles. "I read that when I was about eight. How do you remember it?"

"I illustrate children's books, it comes with the territory. Besides, it was always my favourite," I admit.

"Actually, I have a confession to make."

I stiffen for a second, but his jocular tone makes me realise that this isn't going anywhere serious. "Oh yeah?"

"Yeah, I knew you were an illustrator."

"You did, how?"

"I bought some of your books for my godson, the dinosaur series. He loves them, by the way. I recognised the style and saw your name as the illustrator and so I googled it to see if it was you. It took a bit of time, you don't have much of an internet presence, do you?"

"Are you surprised?"

"No, not really. I never expected you to pop up on Facebook or anything."

"My publisher says I'll have to get involved with social media engagement when my own series gets published though." I practically shudder and I can see Adam smiling despite the dark shadows cast by the trees, blocking the streetlights. I suppose it never really is dark in the city.

"So, you've got a godson then?"

"Yeah, he's awesome, his name's Noah. He's the son of friends of mine from work. I'll definitely start getting him your superhero series when it comes out."

He continues telling me about Noah as we walk, the occasional passing car breaking the feeling of solitude that surrounds us.

"Look, this is the other side of Somerset House," Adam says, changing the subject suddenly.

"Wow, it's huge," is my imaginative response, but in my defence, it does look massive.

"Yeah, it's like a reverse Tardis, it seems much bigger from the outside. It's 'cos the internal square you saw is just part of the larger building."

"It's beautiful though," I respond, gazing up at the arched and pillared grey stone rising up beside us as we walk. "I love the idea that it's been here for centuries, barely changing, as the world advances around it. I know it's a kind of obvious thing to say but I do love the sense of history you get in London."

"Me too. You know, I've always thought if I could travel back in time I wouldn't go to the dinosaurs or ancient Rome or anything, I would just visit the places I know but, like, one hundred and fifty years ago, before cars and electric lights."

"I've always thought that too," I exclaim. "I think it every time I walk around Clifton where I live in Bristol; how lovely it would be to see it without the modern shops or cars or hordes of people."

"Yes and walking up to The Pump Room in Cheltenham past the dressed-up people out for their daily constitutional, when all the grand houses were houses and not converted into flats."

"Exactly. Did you ever read *Tom's Midnight Garden* as a kid?" I continue excitedly.

"I don't think so."

"It was another favourite of mine. This boy, Tom, goes to stay with his aunt or something in a converted flat. But at night, something happens and he can go back in time to when the building was a posh house. He plays in the gardens, which are a housing estate in the present, and skates on the river. It captured my imagination so much as a kid and I always think of it when I'm in an old building."

"I ought to read it," he replies with a smile.

"Yes, you should. From what I can remember, it's written in quite a mature way."

"A bit like *The Secret Garden*."

"Yes, exactly."

We smile at each other, that connection zinging between us again. I feel myself blush under his gaze and turn my face back to the river.

"Sorry to lower the tone," Adam says, "but I'm really desperate for a pee."

I giggle, surprised. That was not what I expected him to say. There I was thinking we were having a moment and he was just desperate to piss.

"You should have had a tactical pee when we left the bar, like I did," I remonstrate proudly.

"Ha, I'd forgotten all about your tactical peeing. Every time we went to the cinema or sat down to watch a film, you'd have to go to the loo."

"It's common sense when you think about it. We always tell children to go to the loo before leaving the house or sitting down to eat or whatever. Why shouldn't adults empty the tank in advance?"

"OK, all this talk isn't helping my situation. Are you all right here for a minute if I nip over to one of those trees across the road?"

"Yeah, I'll just stay here. Just make sure you don't get arrested for indecency or something."

"I think I'll be safe," he grins, gesturing at the deserted streets.

"Men are so lucky, being able to just go wherever they want," I mutter to Adam's back. He's just about to cross the road when I call out to him. "Hey, Adam."

"Yes?" He replies impatiently, turning back to me, practically jiggling. At any second I expect him to hold his crotch and cross his legs like my little cousin used to.

"Nothing," I reply triumphantly.

"Not funny." But I hear him chuckling as he dashes across the street.

Tucking my handbag securely under my arm, I rest my elbows and lean on the rough stone wall. The dark water swirls hypnotically beneath me, the lights of London a distorted reflection on the surface. The cold air rising from the river stings my cheeks and nose, but it's invigorating, so I snuffle my chin further into my scarf and continue to stare out across the city. I think of our conversation and try to imagine how this all would have looked one hundred years ago. What would be the same? What would have stood in the places where the modern tower blocks now glint and glimmer? It would have been much darker too, I expect I'd have even been able to see the stars.

I lift my head to the night and as expected, I can only make out an occasional pinprick in the strange glowing, navy sky that shrouds the city, the moon having disappeared hours ago.

A sharp buzz and ping from my handbag make me jump. Who would be texting me at this hour? Possibly Stu with some more abuse or perhaps a drunken apology? I fish around in my bag and locating my phone, pull it out. It takes me a second before I register that it isn't my phone that I've grabbed and unintentionally opened.

The text on the screen is from Jenny

> Hey, I'm up on a night feed (joy) and thought I'd check in. I still don't get why you cancelled on Mark coming to get you? I hope you're OK and it's not too late, I'm up now, so once I put Issy back down, I can jump in the car, just say, OK? Loves xxx

I'm still holding the phone dumbly in my hand when Adam appears beside me at the wall.

"That feels so much better. And, as you can see, I wasn't arrested. You OK?"

"Yeah, sorry, I forgot I had your phone in my bag and picked it up," I mutter handing the phone over. "You really should lock the screen, you know."

I watch his face as he scans the message and slides the phone into his pocket. He looks up and our eyes meet, causing me to turn away slightly.

"Is that Jenny Hyde?" I ask, in an attempt at casual, but even to my own ears, my voice sounds too strained and high-pitched.

"Yes," he responds flatly.

"How is she?" Still high and squeaky, damn it.

"Well, she's Jenny Sampson now, but otherwise still the same, still a bit bonkers. She's just had a baby actually, a little girl, Issy."

"I saw, I mean, I didn't mean to, but I saw the message." Gabbling now too, great. We lapse into silence, side by side staring at the water swishing and tumbling past us. Seeing Jenny's name has thrown me a bit. After everything that happened, she's the one I feel guilty about. She didn't deserve the way that I treated her in the end. I never meant for it to happen the way it did and I'm sure she's completely over it by now, but the guilt still niggles sometimes, when something reminds me of her or I see a flash of a dark afro in the street and wonder.

"She still talks about you, you know?"

"Really?" Seriously, can this man read my mind? "So, you're still close then?"

"Yeah, she's probably my best mate, all things considered. She's always been there for me. Mark, her husband, is great too, we've become proper friends which is nice."

Even without looking at him, I know that while he's saying all this, he's watching me, studying for a reaction.

"Why did you stop him coming to get you?" I blurt out, surprising myself as much as Adam.

He doesn't answer and I risk turning my head to look at him. He's just watching me with that serious expression again.

"Does Jenny know you've met me?" I continue.

"No," he finally responds. "I wasn't sure how she'd react and figured that it would be best as a face-to-face thing."

"Fair enough," I reply blankly and turn to start walking again.

Adam grabs my arm, clutching the thick padding of my coat.

"I told Mark not to come when I went to the loo in that first pub. I wanted to spend some time with you again. I hoped..." He goes to run his fingers through his hair, something that I remember he does when he's agitated, but encounters his bobble hat and pulls it off, kneading it in his hands instead. "I hoped," he continues, "that maybe we could talk about what happened, you know, with us. Get some closure or something. I know it was a long time ago, but it's haunted me. I haven't pushed you, 'cos I didn't want to make you uncomfortable, but we're here now, so do you think we could?"

"No, I'm sorry, I can't. Not now." Thrusting my hands into my pockets I turn and start walking along the path again. I'm aware of him falling into step beside me but keep my eyes fixed on the buildings ahead.

# Chapter Sixteen

## Then

Rose paced around her room feeling like a caged animal. She'd only spoken to him a few hours before but was desperate to hear his voice again. She picked up her phone from her bedside table, her thumb immediately travelling to favourites and Adam's number, there at number one. Just as she was about to press the call button, she had second thoughts, quickly typing out a text instead.

> Hey, what are you up to? Xxxx

She flopped down onto her bed, the phone clutched to chest with one hand while she turned up her music, using the remote with the other. As the song blasted out of the CD player, she shut her eyes, feeling a hot tear escape and trickle down her cheek. A vibration on her chest alerted her to a reply.

> U OK? I'm Just about to watch a film with my flatmates. I'll ring you after. Love you xxx

Refusing to give in to the tears that she could feel burning behind her eyelids, the hot, pinching sensation in her nose; she got up and went downstairs in search of food.

As expected, her mum was slouched on the sofa watching TV when she walked through the lounge to the kitchen. From a quick glance, Rose could see that she was already on her second bottle of wine.

Looking around the dismal little kitchen, the dishes piled in the sink, the remains of a loaf of bread abandoned on the counter next to an open jar of peanut butter with a knife sticking out of it, the broken cupboard door that Dad never got round to fixing, Rose was overwhelmed by a feeling of intense claustrophobia. Suddenly she couldn't catch her breath as a wave of despair, rage and she didn't know what else, crashed through her. She wanted to scream. She wanted to pull all the plates out of the broken cupboard and throw them to the floor. She wanted to rip the skin off her arms with her hands. Feeling like she might explode, she sank to her knees grabbing handfuls of her hair and tugging it until the physical pain in her scalp focused her emotions and quietened the noise.

"I don't want to be here," she sighed piteously to herself.

Then, in a moment of clarity, she knew the only thing that would make her feel better, she knew where she could go to feel normal again. Pushing herself to her feet, she ventured back into the lounge.

Her mum glanced up, taking a second to focus.

"Y'all right love?" she slurred.

"Yeah. Mum, can I still have the car for the weekend?"

"Oh, err, I don't know..." Her mum's brow furrowed as she tried to focus on her thoughts.

"You said I could, remember?" Rose only felt a slight pang of guilt taking advantage of her mum's state and lying to her, but it was not like she needed the car, she wasn't going anywhere. Anyway, this was kind of an emergency.

"Oh, um, course. Going to see him, are you?"

"Yeah," Rose answered, sidling to the door, keen to get going.

"You're a fool," Dawn said then, her voice changing, sounding hard and mean. "They're all the same, men. You can't trust them. You need to put yourself first."

Wishing she could put her fingers in her ears and shout 'lalalala', Rose just scurried from the room. Taking the stairs two at a time, she rushed into her bedroom, but not before she heard her mum call, "He'll destroy you. They all do."

She started throwing stuff into her holdall, her earlier despair gone and, in its place, a giddy elation. Two hours and she'd be with him. Hopefully, he'd meant that he was watching a film in the flat but even if they'd gone to the cinema, he should be back around the same time that she arrived.

She rushed down the stairs, grabbing her coat and the car keys from the hall before slamming the door behind her. She paused momentarily, wondering if she should leave a note for her mum in case she didn't remember in the morning, but decided to text her when she arrived instead.

Once in the car and easing into the Friday evening traffic, she did feel a little nervous. She'd only passed her driving test a few weeks before and hadn't gone on a long journey by herself yet. She'd only ever got the train to visit Adam, other than the first weekend when she went with his parents to help him move in. But she was confident that, once in Southampton, she could find the way to his halls.

Nearly three hours later and feeling very stressed, Rose pulled into the visitor parking at Adam's halls of residence. Getting to Southampton had been fairly straightforward but she'd got lost driving through the suburbs around the university buildings, becoming thoroughly confused and frustrated and wishing her mum would just buy a Satnav despite the cost.

Excitement and relief coursing through her, she practically ran to his building, her holdall banging against her shins. To her surprise and in direct contravention of the giant sign posted next to it, the front door of Adam's hall building was propped wide open.

Climbing the stairs, she realised why, as the sounds of a lively party drifted down to meet her, the music pumping louder with each step she took. As she neared the third floor, people had started to congregate around the staircase as both apartments had their front doors open, spilling partygoers out into the hallway. Stepping gingerly past a couple kissing messily on the staircase, she made her way up to the fourth floor and Adam's flat. To her utter dismay, they were in on the party too, the front door flung open and hallway teeming with people. She squeezed her way past a group of girls shrieking with laughter and spilling drops of rosé from their plastic wine glasses, and into the sanctity of Adam's room, doubly grateful that he was in room one and hadn't thought to lock his door.

In the relative peace of Adam's room, Rose leant back against his door and took a moment to collect her thoughts. So, he hadn't told her about the party, but maybe it was an impromptu thing or maybe he had gone to the cinema to get away from it all? Unlikely though, as Adam was always more of a partygoer than she was. She considered ringing him but realised that could be futile in the noise. Her only options were to wait here for him or go and find him. As much as she dreaded going into a party where she knew no one, her desire to see Adam was so acute that, after stashing her bag under his desk for safety, it propelled her out of the door and into the throng.

Rose let the door slam behind her and resisted the temptation to lock it. It had been a futile and horrendous twenty minutes trying to look for Adam in the four apartments having the party. She didn't see him anywhere and someone spilt cider all down her top.

She'd occasionally spotted one of his housemates, but having only visited Adam twice, during which times they mainly kept themselves to themselves, revelling in the time together, she didn't feel confident going up to them. Plus, all the ones she saw were hammered anyway and she wasn't in the mood to attempt conversation with a tediously drunk person.

Pulling off her top, she rummaged in Adam's wardrobe for her favourite hoody of his, resisting the temptation to lovingly run her hand over all the familiar Adam clothes. The hoody smelt of him and she pulled it on, nuzzling her face into the neckline, breathing him in. Instantly, she felt better. Flopping down on the bed, she tried ringing him but it went straight to voicemail. So, plan B, she'd hunker down here until he turned up, which he was bound to do at some point.

The weak, grey, light of dawn spilling in from Adam's window woke Rose and she sat up in bed, rubbing her eyes. She immediately reached for her phone, having eventually plugged it in to charge when it beeped at her in the early hours. Still nothing from Adam, despite the stack of missed calls he must now have from her. And why hadn't he come home? Where was he?

Rose had a raging thirst and her head was pounding from lack of sleep. She had stayed up until about two a.m.; drunk people kept stumbling into the room only to retreat again when they saw her. Each time her heart leapt, thinking it was Adam. And each time it wasn't, the disappointment got more bitter.

And now, as well as being worried about him, there was a gnawing fear in her heart that she was trying to ignore. If he wasn't sleeping here, maybe he was sleeping somewhere else?

Dragging herself out of the bed, still in last night's clothes, she staggered out into the hallway, heading for the communal lounge and kitchen at the end of the corridor. Someone was asleep against the wall opposite, snoring away. She tiptoed down the hall but as she got to the open kitchen door, she heard voices over the soft music that was playing inside. A hardcore selection of partygoers was obviously still going strong. She hovered outside, listening carefully in case one of the voices was Adam's.

Suddenly a door opened further down the hall and she instinctively dropped to the floor, pulling up her hood and turning her back to appear asleep. She did not want to deal with any of his flatmates right now.

She heard whoever it was enter the room and a brief conversation ensued with some laughing although now, with her hood up, she couldn't make out what was being said. Then footsteps came back out again, followed swiftly by another set.

"Hey, wait up," whispered a girl's voice. "So, did you do it?" she continued.

"Yes," whispered a second female voice excitedly.

"Oh my God!" squealed the first.

"He's still in my room."

"How was it?"

"So amazing, like honestly, really good."

"Oh wow, I'm so happy for you guys. But don't you feel a bit bad?"

"About her? No, it's not my problem. Adam is with me now and she'll just have to accept it."

And just like that, as she lay on the cold, itchy floor, Rose's world collapsed.

# Chapter Seventeen

We continue to walk in silence, our booted feet clomping on the frozen pavement and breath smoking into the chill air.

Great! Is this how it's going to be for the rest of the night? Uncomfortable silence. Just when I thought we'd got to a good place. I get that he's frustrated, and I get that he wants to talk about it all, clear his conscience or whatever, but I'm just not ready. I'm still working away frantically in my brain with the gaffer tape and I'm not about to rip it all off now.

Our rhythmic feet take us past more floodlit regal buildings and under a couple of dark bridges which would be very scary if I were alone. We pass the occasional group of people; other displaced souls like ourselves, wandering the city until dawn. It feels a bit like a special club. We all nod at each other in a knowing way and in breach of how Londoners behave — as if no one else exists.

I'm starting to feel thoroughly uncomfortable. I'm usually fine with long silences but this particular one feels too loaded. I start wracking my brains for opening gambits but come up blank.

"Once we round the corner up here, you'll be able to see The Globe on the other side."

Thank you, Adam.

"Oh, cool, that must mean we're close to St Paul's, right?"

"Yeah, it's just along here, you should be able to see the top soon."

"I love St Paul's. Would you be up for diverting from the river and wandering up to it? It would be nice to see it all lit up but without the crowds and buses and stuff."

"Of course, tonight is all about going with the flow, right?"

There's another brief lull in the conversation but it feels less strained this time. Maybe I'm just imagining all these feelings though? Transmitting what I feel onto him?

"So, come on, be honest," Adam says suddenly but with a teasing hint to his voice, "there must be something you still like about Christmas?"

"Hmm..." I stroke my chin for dramatic effect, causing Adam to smile. "Well, I have to admit, I am a bit of a sucker for fairy lights. Not just at Christmas though, I like them all year round, they're just pretty. And... OK, well, I love The Salvation Army."

"The Salvation Army?"

"Yep. I just admire them so much. Every year, whatever the weather, they dress up in their special suits and play beautiful carols to busy shoppers. Proper carols too, none of the tacky December radio fodder. They give up their time, their talent, all for a good cause because they believe in something and want to help others. That's the real meaning of Christmas, if you ask me. They are the embodiment of true Christmas spirit."

"Wow. I did not expect that answer."

"Well, it's the truth," I shrug. "Every December I go into town on a Saturday and find them and I stand and listen to the whole set, drinking a hot chocolate, and giving them a good donation at the end. It's my only real Christmas tradition, I suppose. It's the only time I ever feel Christmassy."

"I wish you'd said earlier, we could have tried to find you some as part of your de-Scrooging," Adam jokes.

I narrow my eyes at him and continue, "I worked for them one year actually."

"But you can't play an instrument. Or can you now?"

"Not for the band!" I roll my eyes. "In one of their food kitchens. You know providing meals for the homeless and people in need."

"Really?"

"Well, throughout my twenties, I'd given up on Christmas with either of my parents and I kept trying other ways to pass the time. I went abroad a few times or spent it with friends and one year I thought I'd be a bit selfless, you know?"

"Just the one year?"

"Yeah," I admit meekly. "It didn't work out how I expected."

"Let me guess, you found it too hard seeing all those people in need?"

"Yes, exactly." I stop and stare at him. He still gets me. "I kept feeling emotional, nearly bursting into tears and got so flustered, I cocked things up and then I felt worse. I was upset for days afterwards. So, selfishly, I never did it again. Does that make me an awful person?" I hide my face with my hands as we continue walking.

"God, no! It's great that you wanted to do it in the first place. Work like that takes a certain sensibility. You have to be kind, obviously, and very devoted, but you also need to be pragmatic and stuff. We experienced it with Damien and carers. Sometimes the ones who cared too much couldn't detach themselves from the reality of the situation and found it too upsetting. I think it's linked to you being so creative."

"What do you mean?"

"I think creative people tend to empathise more, it's because of your strong imaginations. Miss Pheasant would probably have said you see too deeply into the human psyche or something. I mean, look at how you love to people watch and make up stories about them, well, you used to anyway. So, to you, those men and women who came in for their dinners weren't just random homeless people. They were someone's son, someone's grandpa, a girl who was abused, you see it all and you can't detach from it."

I actually feel a bit tearful, what is wrong with me tonight? Maybe it's hormones or something? But he's right, he's summed it up perfectly. We haven't seen each other in over a decade and yet he still knows me better than anyone else in my life. And the realisation of that is just incredibly sad. I swallow hard and snuggle my chin further into my scarf.

"I've always thought you'd make a good actress actually," he continues in a lighter tone.

I harrumph into my scarf.

"Not the performing in front of people side of things, obviously, but your ability to read people and emotions would make you great at getting into character."

"Yeah, maybe," I mumble, "but I don't fancy testing that theory any time soon."

"I guess we'll just have to assume I'm right then," he smiles.

"You may have a point about the over-empathising, but that's all I'll concede."

"Fair enough."

"And before you say it, yes, I know, it does make me a hedgehog."

"I wouldn't have dared after the last time," he says in mock horror. "You'd probably slap me or something."

"Good, just so we're clear!" I nudge him playfully. "Oh look, there's The Globe."

We continue to walk but our pace naturally slows as we look across the river at the recreation of Shakespeare's theatre, glowing under purple lights and looking thoroughly out of place, surrounded as it is by steel, concrete and glass.

"We could try to sneak in, if you like. You could have a go on the stage, see if it suits you?" Adam suggests deadpan.

"I would assume you're joking but after how smoothly you conned our way into that party, I'm not so sure. Maybe you're not even an architect like you claimed, maybe you're actually just a grifter these days?"

"Nah, you can admit it. I was honest with you, you've googled me too, haven't you? You know I'm a bona fide architect."

Damn, he's got me there. And I hate lying, so I'll just have to come clean.

"OK, maybe I did once or twice."

"Ha, I knew it."

"Don't get all smug, it's not weird, everyone googles their exes at some point. Or stalks them on Facebook, like some of my friends seem to."

I can feel it again, that crackle in the air. We're getting into dangerous territory, talking about our relationship. I know it's childish and I know it makes no sense, but I just don't want to hear it from his lips; I don't want to know about the girl he chose over me. I just don't. So, as usual, I blurt out the first thing that I can think of to divert the conversation.

"Speaking of exes, I told you all about stupid Stu, but you never gave up any information about your ex. You said you were together for quite a long time. What happened?"

I'm not sure why I asked that aside from curiosity winning over common sense, I should've asked him about his job or something less contentious.

"Oh, it's complicated. A bit like what you said about you and Stu. I'm not really sure why Cathy and I ever got together in the first place, we weren't massively suited. But we got on OK, and she was pretty and easy going and so we just carried on. It wasn't a bad relationship, but it wasn't great either; we never really got close. We both lived quite separate lives.

"When Damien died, I told myself that she was giving me space. I thought she was being understanding, letting me spend as much time with my family as I needed and sort of staying away. But actually, I think she just didn't care enough to be there for me. I could have done with someone to lean on though, you know? I needed a shoulder. At least I had Jenny and Mark, they were amazing. But once I clawed my way out of the grief, I realised that Cathy and I had nothing real, nothing substantial and what was the point? Turned out I was right because when I brought it up with her, she told me she was already sleeping with someone else. I found out later that while I was dealing with the fall-out from losing Damien, she was shagging some bloke from her gym then too."

"What a bitch!" I exclaim.

"Yeah, but you know what? It made me realise that I didn't care as much about her as I should have. I mean, I was gutted, and my pride was hurt but I wasn't devasted, not like when... well, not as devasted as I should have been after five years. I felt like a bit of an idiot, if I'm honest."

I don't know what to say so I just take my hand out of my pocket and give his arm a comforting squeeze, not that I'm sure he can feel it through all the puff.

We reach the foot of the Millennium Bridge and turn left towards St Paul's. I gasp a little when it comes into view, its majestic domed tower, glorious against the dark night, framed by the buildings on either side of the road leading towards it. It's at times like this that I wish I had taken up photography as I'd always secretly wanted to do. But then a photograph wouldn't capture the stillness of the frozen air or the sense of history emanating from its walls.

We walk in almost reverent silence towards St Paul's, the building growing with each step we take as more of it comes into view, each feature highlighted by the golden uplights.

"I've never seen it not surrounded by people," Adam whispers. He feels it too.

Adam and I take our time walking around, enjoying the peace. It feels like we're out of time, like the world has paused and we're the only ones awake. It feels a little like magic, like this place is just here for us. It's so beautiful.

Once we've walked all around, we agree to rest for a bit on a wall that gives us a lovely view of the building through the twisted branches of a dormant tree.

"There's something so magical about buildings lit up at night, isn't there?" Adam murmurs.

I nod my head in agreement. I'm so glad we're here, that I'm seeing London in a way that so few people ever get to. And yet, I haven't been able to relax. Something about Adam's story, about Cathy and his whole situation. Try as I might, I can't stop thinking about it.

I've always been focused on what Adam did to me, cheating on me like that. I loved him so much that I couldn't see beyond my own pain, my betrayal. And I've carried that around with me for so many years. Given Adam the mantle of bastard in my mind and refused to let myself think of him, well, attempted not to, anyway.

But, just like how he knows me, I know him too. He's not a bastard. He's a genuine, nice, straightforward person. He's not evil; he wouldn't have set out to hurt me. I truly believe that he did love me once. He gave me so much in our two years together, so much happiness, so much confidence in myself. I don't think I'd ever have pursued art in the way I did if it hadn't had been for his belief in me at a critical stage of my life.

He was just eighteen. Just a kid really and he went away to university and he met someone else. It's not exactly uncommon. It happens in every country: young lovers, determined to stay together but the distance, the individual growth while miles apart, put too big a strain on the relationship.

OK, yes, he should have dumped me before sleeping with someone else. But, actually, thinking about it, it was just after my dad moved out. Maybe he'd been planning to but hadn't wanted to pile on to my problems? Maybe he planned to wait a few weeks? He was always thoughtful like that. But then, he was an eighteen-year-old at a college party and a girl he liked wanted to go for it. He'd have to have been some sort of monk to turn that down when he probably thought I'd never find out anyway.

I can't really blame him for what happened after. For how things turned out. And yet, I have been blaming him... for years. I'd put so much blame on a young man's head. It's not been fair of me. Actually, in a lot of this, I haven't been fair, not to Jenny, not to his mum. All these years they must have assumed that I'm the mega-bitch in all this. And I suppose I am in a way. I wasn't even fair to him. I should have let him do it properly; end the relationship gently, as I'm sure he intended to.

"Shall we move on? This stone is numbing my bum," Adam says suddenly, breaking the silence that had enveloped us.

"Yeah, sure, back to the river?"

Our footsteps echo as we continue back down to the Millennium Bridge where we turn left and carry on along our path, the pavements glittering with frost and the ethereal mist swirling about us.

Adam has started talking about the redevelopment of some of the warehouse buildings along the river. Something I'd usually be fascinated by, but I can't tune in properly. I keep thinking about how things could have gone differently.

I can see it; a young fresh-faced Adam, sitting me down in my room, telling me gently how I'll always be special to him but that since being in Uni, he needs to stretch his wings. I'd have been devastated, sure, but without the horrible knowledge of betrayal sickening my gut.

He'd probably have asked his mum to keep an eye on me and Karen would have insisted we meet for coffee a few times. Maybe Adam and I would have become friends. Maybe not, maybe that's a step too far. But, still, it's a much nicer series of events than the reality.

"Are you OK?" Adam asks gently, breaking into my musings.

"I'm fine."

"Are you sure? You've gone very quiet. Are you getting too tired? Do you want to try to find somewhere else to go?"

The path has stopped, and we've had to turn away from the river's edge to follow a warren of streets until we can join the path again. Here, under the stark streetlights and tall, imposing buildings, it feels less magical and more creepy. I'm very glad Adam is by my side.

He's looking at me with such genuine concern that it causes my chest to ache a little bit. He's not a heartless bastard, he never was. And then, with that firm knowledge, I feel lighter. A heavy cloak of hate has been lifted from my shoulders. I feel free. Without thinking, I stop and hug him, wrapping my arms around his back and burying my chin on his shoulder.

For a second, I feel his surprised resistance and then his arms are around me and he's hugging me back. I feel a bit like I'm wrapped up in a giant duvet, which I suppose I basically am.

After a few seconds, with much rustling of puffa, I pull away with a smile and continue our brisk walk, Adam falling into step beside me.

"What was that for?"

"I just... I guess I had an epiphany, I suppose."

"Sounds interesting. Care to share?"

And although my heart is beating a bit faster and that feeling of dread is starting to sweep over me, I decide I do.

I'm fed up with running away when things get hard. I stop and turn to Adam.

"I know I said earlier that I didn't want to talk about our past, but you have to understand that I've been carrying this hurt around for a long time. And it made me bitter and it made me hate you. But I realise now that that's not healthy. I know what you did, but you were only eighteen and I'm an adult now, and I should know better. I'm supposed to be empathetic and all that, but I wasn't applying that empathy to our situation. I've hated you for all these years and I just want to say, I'm sorry for that. And I'm sorry for being so difficult at the start of tonight when you were just being nice. I was just holding on too tightly to a grudge, but you've been so great all evening and a clean slate, like a proper one, would be nice."

Phew! I'm rambling now. I'll quit while I'm ahead. I said what I needed to. I look up from where I'd been staring at the floor during my outburst. I don't know what expression I expected to see on Adam's face, surprise maybe? Pleasure that I was relieving him of his emotional burden. But the expression I do see chills me.

He is staring at me, a bit like how he did in the bar, but now with a fierce glint to his eyes. Through the shadows cast over his face, I can see the tense line of his jaw, the small beat of a pulse in his neck. His shoulders are rigid and square. Honestly, he looks furious.

"What do you mean, you hated me? You had a grudge?" he growls through clenched teeth.

"I know that you cheated on me, OK?" I mutter, looking away again. "I know you met someone else."

"I did what?" he practically roars, causing me to flinch as his voice reverberates around the empty streets. He is breathing heavily, the rise and fall of his chest clear despite the thick coat, his breath like smoke, fury coming from him in waves. I stagger back until I can feel solid brick at my shoulders and press myself to the building.

Adam towers over me. With the streetlight behind him, he's just a silhouette until he takes a step closer. His face is inches from mine. I instinctively look down. What the hell is happening? I want to run, run and hide, but I feel trapped.

He roughly takes my chin, lifting my face up so I'm forced to look at him.

"I never cheated on you," he says hoarsely. "Never."

# Chapter Eighteen

## Then

Adam paid the taxi driver and with Dave's help pulled Tommy out of the back, half carrying, half dragging him in through the front doors, grateful that Tommy was quite slight, although that may have been part of the problem. Once inside, they headed straight for the reception desk where a middle-aged woman glared at them through the hatch.

"Hello, erm, our friend's had too much to drink. We think he may need a doctor."

"Name?"

"Erm, mine or his?"

"His."

"Oh, sorry, Thomas Reynolds."

"Date of birth?"

"Oh, I don't know. Dave?" Dave, struggling to keep Tommy upright while Adam was talking, just shook his head. "He's eighteen," Adam offered and was rewarded with a particularly vicious glare.

"Take a seat there and someone will be with you."

They shuffled over to the nearest seat where they dropped Tommy who murmured something incoherent before slumping over and almost falling off till Adam grabbed hold of his jumper and shifted him up again. Luckily just then, his name was called and a friendly-looking nurse appeared with a wheelchair.

"Just one of you to come in with him, please?" she said calmly but in a tone that brooked no argument.

"I'll stay with him," Adam offered.

"Are you sure?" asked Dave half-heartedly, already visibly backing away towards the door.

"Yeah, he's my flatmate."

"OK, keep us posted, yeah? Good luck, mate." And then Dave turned and almost ran out of the hospital, no doubt straight back to the party and the crate of beer he had stashed under his bed in the room below Adam's.

Adam sheepishly followed the nurse as she pushed Tommy briskly through a swinging door and into a triage room. This was so not how he wanted to spend his Friday night. He hadn't even wanted them to throw the damn party in the first place, but once they heard the third floor were having one, his flatmates took a vote and he lost.

He took his phone out to text Rose.

"No phones in here, please," snapped the nurse so he hurriedly put it away again. "Now, can you tell me how much your friend has had to drink?"

Adam trudged wearily through the gates wondering if he should have just shelled out on another taxi after all, rather than waiting for the first bus of the morning, but it just seemed an unnecessary expenditure. If he hadn't been so exhausted, he may have noticed Rose's car in the car park, he may have even seen her slumped over the steering wheel, howling in anguish, but he didn't. He just carried on up to his room, passing the detritus of the night before.

The first thing he noticed when he opened his bedroom door was the dishevelled duvet. He should have thought to lock his room, but he'd been so worried about Tommy when they couldn't get him to wake up, that he wasn't thinking of anything else but getting his flatmate to hospital. And now, for his trouble, someone had probably had sex in his bed. Gross. Too tired to change the sheets now, he remade the bed, flipped the pillow over and lay down on top of the duvet, plugging his phone into the charger.

He felt awful about Rose, she'd be wondering why he hadn't called her and had probably tried to get in touch with him. But, when he finally got a chance to use his phone, while Tommy was having his stomach pumped, the battery had died.

He was going to have a lot of explaining to do. He should have just told her about the party in the first place, but she'd had such an awful week with everything going on at home that he didn't want her to think that he was having a great time without her. He wasn't, he missed her every day. When she rang him on Wednesday night in tears to say her dad had moved out, his first instinct was to book a train ticket to be with her. But they'd both agreed to every other weekend and his dad had already lectured him about the importance of getting involved with Uni life.

His phone pinged into life to show a bunch of missed calls from Rose. It was only seven a.m. and was too early to ring her now. Adam decided to have a little sleep and ring her when he woke up, he was sure she'd understand once he'd explained.


A knock on his door woke him up a few hours later.

"Come in," Adam croaked.

It was Adam from across the hall. Having two Adams on the same floor had become confusing, their flatmates usually referring to them by their surnames too, then eventually just their initials. This Adam was usually known as A.F.

"Hey man, sorry to bother you, we just heard about Tommy, is he OK?" A.F. asked, his face full of concern.

"Yeah, he will be, he had his stomach pumped so was in overnight. I got hold of his mum and they were coming to get him this morning."

"Woah, he's going to be in some shit."

"Kind of his own fault though, for downing all that tequila."

"Yeah, I guess. Shame you missed the party though, it was epic. Me and Kayla got together."

"No way! Good for you."

"Yeah, I'm pretty psyched about her. It might cause problems with Suze though, cos I guess she liked me or something, but hopefully she'll get over it. Anyway, I'll let you sleep. Thanks for looking after Tommy like that, man, we all owe you one. Laters."

As the door closed behind A.F., Adam rolled over and picked up his phone ready to call Rose, but she'd already messaged him. Just one sentence.

> This isn't working for me anymore. We're over.
> Please don't contact me.

Adam hammered on the door, rain pelting down the neck of his thin jacket. He'd tried to ring Rose all day, getting more and more frantic when she didn't answer and eventually getting on the train back to Cheltenham. He'd run to her house straight from the station. The hall light eventually came on and the door opened to reveal Rose's mum, Dawn, looking a little dishevelled with the imprint of the couch cushion on her cheek.

"What do you want?" She seemed genuinely confused to see him standing there, but then Rose said she'd been hitting the booze hard this week. He pushed past her into the hall, his usual respectful manners flying out the window, water dripping off him like he was a wet dog.

"Rose?" he called.

"She's not here," Dawn said sourly. "I thought you'd know that."

"I need to see her; where is she?"

"She's gone with her dad."

"What do you mean? Gone where?"

"To live with him, in Cirencester."

"But she can't have, what about her course?"

"She's going to commute or something." Dawn shrugged sorrowfully.

Without asking permission, Adam darted up the stairs and burst into Rose's room. It was like being punched. The room was bare, no duvet on the bed, her CDs and books gone. The only sign of Rose was the picture of the two of them in a frame on her bedside. It was her favourite picture. She'd left it behind.

# Chapter Nineteen

Time is a funny thing, the way it plays tricks on you. How ten years can suddenly feel like one, or how one moment can seemingly stretch for minutes. I'm sure it's only been a second since Adam spoke, but it feels like we've been staring at each other for ages. The only sound our laboured breath. My mind is in a whirl. Why would he bother lying about it now, what's the point? And with such vehemence too. Maybe he should be the one at The Globe? Has he just forgotten the order of the events? Was I that insignificant?

He's glaring at me, obviously expecting me to say something but I can't marshal my thoughts. A car comes around the corner, the bright glare of the headlights burns my eyes and causes me to flinch further back against the wall, shielding my face with my hand. I hear the engine slow down.

"Are you all right there, luv?" calls a gruff voice.

Adam steps back from me and moves off to the side, looking shaken. Now that he's moved, I can see the owner of the vehicle: a big, burly cabbie in a flat cap stepping out of his taxi and looking menacingly at Adam.

"I'm OK, thanks," I stammer.

"Are you sure? Looked like this chap was botherin' you."

I suppose it would have looked like that; the way I was cowering against the wall, Adam looming over me. Of course, he was actually bothering me but not in the way that the cabbie imagined, and not in a way that I could ever explain.

"No, he's fine," I reply, trying to paste a smile onto my face. Clearly, I would in fact make a crap actress as the man remained with one foot on the pavement, looking unconvinced and throwing another glare at Adam for good measure.

"I've just finished my shift, but I can give you a ride home if you're local?"

"Oh, that's very kind of you, but home is in Bristol, so I don't think I could cover that fare." I manage a more genuine smile this time.

"Ah, you're some of those lot supposed to be on the trains, are ya?"

"Yes, we are," I reply, going to stand next to Adam to show that I'm really not scared of him or anything. I consider linking my arm through his but think that might be a step too far.

"A lot of the churches have opened up to take people in through the night. I've a list if you want to find one, or it's all over Facebook," continues the cabbie with slightly less concern in his voice.

"Oh, thanks." Then I turn to Adam and ask quietly, "What do you think?"

He looks at me with that serious, intent expression again. It's actually quite sexy. Oh my God, what is wrong with me? Why am I thinking like that right now?

"Up to you," he shrugs but I can still feel his tension; he's practically vibrating. "But I think we've got things to finish here, don't you?"

I turn back to the kind cabbie, who does seem to have relaxed a little and is now leaning casually on his door.

"We're happy walking around for a bit more, thanks, but it's really good to know about the churches in case we get fed up."

"All right, if you're sure." He glares at Adam one final time before slipping back into his seat.

"Thank you for stopping though, it was really good of you."

He readjusts his cap and with a salute-like wave drives off, leaving us to the silence once more.

"I think we need to talk, don't we?" Adam says grimly.

"Not here though." I shiver. "It's too, I don't know..." I look around at the tall, dark buildings, the black glass of their empty windows feeling like a thousand eyes. "... claustrophobic."

Adam marches ahead, confidently leading the way, as I struggle to keep up through the silent maze of streets and alleys until we descend a twisting concrete staircase aside a bridge and are once again on a path by the river. He waits until we are out from under the shadow of the bridge and in front of a small patch of shrubs and grass at the base of a block of flats before he stops and leans heavily on the wall, looking out over the Thames.

I fall into place beside him, taking a moment to catch my breath, the cold almost burning my lungs with each mouthful of frozen air. Across the river, The Shard is in front of us, phallically rising from its nest of skyscrapers, glinting and sparkling darkly. I've never liked The Shard. Of course, I'm impressed at the concept and the workmanship, but all that glass and steel just feel too cold, too hard and aloof. Even the name, apt as it is, makes me think of something broken and jagged and wrong.

I lean further over the wall, to look past Adam who is staring moodily into the inky water. And then I can see Tower Bridge and instantly feel a little better; the beautifully lit, blue-painted steel and iconic towers a symbol of the things that I love about London. For some reason, the iconic image, strong against the night sky gives me a little surge of bravery. I can do this; it's just a difficult conversation, for fuck's sake. I'm not the person I was anymore, I can do this now.

"I was there," I say, my voice cracking. I clear my throat and continue. "The night of the party, at your halls. I was feeling awful and just wanted to see you, so I borrowed Mum's car. I waited in your room all night, but you never came back."

He's turned to look at me, but backlit by the lights of Tower Bridge his face is a blank mask and I can't make out his expression. He's not making a move to say anything, so I carry on.

"It was about five or six in the morning when I went to get a drink and I heard these girls talking. One of them told the other that you were in her room, that you'd slept together. So, I ran. I couldn't face seeing you, hearing about her. Having to sit there while you tried to let me down gently. So, I cut myself off from you, and I feel bad that I lost Jenny, and I feel bad that I never saw Damien again or your parents, but I was young and so, so hurt."

I can feel myself trembling but I'm not crying, which I'm proud of. And I'm ready to listen, to hear his side, hear her name, finally put it behind me.

"But that wasn't me," he says hoarsely. "I wasn't there."

I thought it felt like a punch in the gut when I first saw Adam standing there at the train station. It's nothing compared to what I'm feeling at this moment. This is a karate kick to the solar plexus. A sweeping sense of dread is spreading from my chest. I can't breathe.

"What do you mean?" I manage to gasp.

"That wasn't me. I was at a hospital all night while my flatmate was getting his stomach pumped. You heard wrong."

"But... but she said 'Adam'. She did, she said she was with Adam." I can hear the panic in my own voice, it sounds shrill and strange, echoing across the river.

"Adam Foster. She would have been talking about Adam Foster," he responds flatly. He turns and leans back on the wall, putting his head in his hands.

Time has slowed down again. I'm aware of every little sound: Adam's breathing, the rush of the river, the faint, distant noise of traffic, my own pounding heartbeat, the blood rushing in my ears. I almost feel like I'm not even here, like I'm disassociated from my own body. It's all rushing through my head like a sped-up montage. Being in Mum's kitchen, feeling so wretched, driving to Adam's, the awful party, feeling so alone and scared. And the searing, wrenching heartbreak.

It's such a common expression, broken-hearted. And really, it's stupid, of course, your heart doesn't actually break. But, honestly, that's how it felt, like something in my chest was ripping in two. The pain of it had destroyed me, eaten me up from the inside. Most people when they talk of heartbreak, they're being glib, they don't really know. Like when someone calls a headache a migraine, or a cold the flu. Until you've been there, until you've really had your heart broken, metaphorically, of course, you don't actually know.

And it was all a misunderstanding. He hadn't cheated. I went through all of that, all of it for nothing. All these years, all the bitterness I had, it was my own doing. My own lack of faith in him, in us. I feel dizzy.

Suddenly, through the swirling, roller-coaster of thoughts, I'm aware of a tight cramping in my stomach and gripping the wall tightly, I lean over and throw up into the Thames. When I'm done heaving, I sink onto the wall, resting my cheek on the rough, freezing stone while my body quakes.

I'm aware of Adam behind me, gently rubbing my back though I can barely feel it through all the padding.

"If only you hadn't run away, if only you'd let me talk to you, I could have explained. You should have trusted me."

He says this without harshness or any hint of recrimination, just sadness. But it's an unnecessary statement, I realise all that. I'm suddenly, vomit-inducingly aware that everything I lost was my own doing. All of it.

I squeeze my eyes shut, as hot, silent tears start to stream down my face and onto the stone.

"Hey, it's OK," Adam murmurs gently. "It was a long time ago. I understand why you did it; anyone would have thought the same in your position. And you were already vulnerable back then. I know you hate me saying it but emotionally you were always so fragile, I always got that. That's why I could never have done it, what you thought I did. But that's not the point, the point is that I get why you ran, I understand how that would have been your instinct, to shut yourself away from me. I understand."

He strokes my hair away from my face. "Come on," he says gently. "That wall must be freezing."

It probably is, but I don't really notice it. Nevertheless, I allow him to guide me back onto my feet. He tenderly wipes my cheek with his gloved hand. It feels warm and soft and a small part of my wants to nuzzle into his palm like a cat. But I can't. I can't do anything except stand there numbly while the thoughts crowd in, rushing in darkly, like the dank water of the Thames behind us.

"It's OK," he says again and folds me into his embrace.

But it's not. It's not OK. I can't breathe. The door in my brain, the one I've barricaded for so long, is wide open and the fire is raging. I can feel the panic rising, the pain in my chest, the itching of my flesh. Suddenly his arms aren't comforting, they are steel bands around me, and I'm trapped. I'm drowning. I push him away and start running, blindly. I don't know if he's behind me; I don't know where I'm going, but I can't stop. I need to run. I need to breathe.

My feet pound on the icy cement, the cold air burning my lungs. I clutch at my handbag like it's a life jacket. I want to claw at my skin, rip at my hair, but I run.

The lights of Tower Bridge are getting brighter as the towers rise up before me, but all I'm aware of is the blackness swirling around me, trying to smother me. The path opens up into a big square. I round the corner and then I'm sliding and falling to the floor with a muffled thud, knocking the breath from my body.

It's acted like the slap in the face that I needed. I know what this is, this is a panic attack. I can be in control again.

Pushing myself up from my prone position and careful to avoid the patch of ice that led to my fall, I shuffle back against a tree, not even caring if a dog has relieved itself there recently. Still trying to quell the panic, my eyes search frantically for something to focus on.

I can still see one of the towers of Tower Bridge and so I start to count the windows as I breathe deeply in through my nose and out through my mouth. Forty-two that I can see. Good. I can feel it working. The Tower of London is in front of me and I start to count the windows that I can see there too. Concentrate on this little task, just like I was taught, and the darkness will fade. Please let it fade.

# Chapter Twenty

I'm not sure how long I sit counting but after a while I feel the panic recede and my heartbeat calm down. I'm not shaking anymore either. Then I see him, hovering just to my right, a few metres away, leaning against the brown stone wall of an old building, watching me intently.

I lift my arm in acknowledgement and turn my gaze back to the soft glow of the Tower of London. Not one of my favourite buildings, but pretty when all lit up, nonetheless. And far too lovely given some of the atrocious things that occurred there.

I did the tour once, years ago, and I can't remember much about it except it confirmed that I hate medieval history. It's all so dark and cruel. People just must have had less humanity back then.

Thinking of how people would have suffered in those rooms and chambers should make me feel better, put my problems into perspective, but it doesn't. It just piles on to the sadness I feel.

Adam is approaching me warily, a bit like one would a rabid dog. The picture of it: me as a snarling, drooling beast, frothing at the mouth causes a glimmer of a smile to touch the corners of my mouth.

I turn my face to him. He looks pale and tired but above all, worried. Understandable, I suppose.

"Are you OK?" he asks gently, still a few feet away. "I saw you fall, but I thought, well, I guessed you needed space, so I didn't..." He trails off, then asks, "Are you hurt?"

"No. This ugly coat is useful on so many levels, it's puffiness took the brunt of the impact."

"Good."

Silence reigns. A couple of women, wrapped up like us, walk past. I see them looking at us discreetly, probably wondering why I'm sitting on the ground when there are lots of perfectly good benches dotted about. It's a good question.

I stagger to my feet using the tree trunk to pull myself up. I can tell Adam is itching to offer a helping hand but is staying back. Poor bloke, I've done it again, run away from him.

"Sorry," I say simply, tears once again springing from my eyes. "I'm sorry I ran; I was having a panic attack."

"You've had them before?" he asks simply.

"Yes, I used to get them quite a lot. I haven't had one for years though. I didn't even recognise what was happening at first."

"But you feel better now?"

"Yes, I have some exercises to do. You focus on something else, counting things works for me, and deep breathing and stuff."

I'm suddenly aware of the sour taste in my mouth and I ferret in my bag for the box of mint Tic-Tacs that I usually have floating around in there and some water. I take a long swig from my bottle and pop some Tic-Tacs in my mouth, offering the packet to Adam. He shakes his head but seems a little relieved that I'm doing normal things. His face has lost some of the taut worry of a few minutes ago.

I look at him, the lamplight casting angular shadows across his handsome face but his eyes full of kindness. God, I love him.

Oh crap, do I? Do I really? Still, after all these years? Or is it just all this emotion clouding my mind? All the memories. All the what ifs? I can't think about that right now though, one thing at a time.

"There's something I need to tell you," I say simply.

# Chapter Twenty-One

## Then

Rose pulled into the garage forecourt and yanked the handbrake on rather too forcefully. She sat for a moment summoning the energy to step out of the car. At least she didn't have to visit her mum again now until Christmas Day. A day she was already dreading.

Rose felt awful, truly awful; in fact, there needed to be a new word to describe how she felt, there was nothing currently in the dictionary that had it covered.

It had been five weeks since that night, nearly six weeks since she last saw Adam, held him, smelt him, was loved by him. She barely slept or ate, she just about managed to get into Uni but she doubted that she'd pass her first semester at this rate. She found it hard to care, though.

Her sense of loss and betrayal was so acute that she spent every waking hour feeling like there was a knife embedded in her sternum.

How she'd driven home that morning without crashing was a mystery to her; she could barely remember the journey. While her mum lay snoring across the hall, Rose had packed up all her belongings in whatever bags she could get her hands on, eventually resorting to black bin bags. Tears had streamed down her face as she worked frantically, only stopping occasionally when uncontrollable sobs wracked her body.

The only concise thought she'd had in her head was that she had to get away.

When her dad had moved out, he had offered for her to go with him, extolling the virtues of the flat he'd rented with a spare room just for her. At the time, she'd opted to stay where she was as it was easier to get to Uni, but also, mainly, because it was near to Adam's house. Now the last place on earth that she wanted to be near.

Once all her stuff was packed, she'd phoned her dad and he'd taken an extended lunch break to come and drive her over to his place. A rare honour indeed. Although he was probably just pleased to feel he had one over on her mum. She'd spent the rest of the weekend curled up in bed, only venturing from her room to smash her phone under a brick in the back yard and deposit the remains in the bin.

With a deep sigh, Rose forced herself to step out of the car. It was running on fumes and if she didn't put some petrol in, there was a chance that she wouldn't make it back to Cirencester. Too worried about bumping into anyone that she knew, she'd waited until she was well clear of Cheltenham, before finding a garage.

Persuading her dad to buy her a cheap car had been surprisingly easy. He was probably feeling a bit guilty about refusing to fund her application to university to study art which he considered a 'silly waste of time'. She'd stuck to her guns about going but lack of funds meant that she was forced to stay local and live at home, limiting her choices to The School of Arts in Cheltenham. Luckily, it was a good institution and she had been enjoying the course, back when she could enjoy anything.

Her world had become so small. She drove to her lectures and classes, drove to her mum's once a week and otherwise sat at home, more often than not on her own as her dad was usually working. He was going to be home tonight, though and had asked if they could have tea together, so she'd better get a move on.

Rose twisted off the fuel cap and lifted the nozzle from the pump, barely registering her actions, as was the case with everything she did these days. As she squeezed the fuel into the car, the smell of petrol wafted up, causing her to gag.

But not just gag, her stomach cramped and she could feel the bile rising. She was going to be sick! Abandoning the pump in the car, she ran to the bushes surrounding the forecourt and got there just in time to heave into the shrubbery.

As usual, she hadn't eaten much so the vomit was mainly bile which burnt her nose and throat and caused her eyes to water. When she was confident that she was done, she sat down shakily on the kerb, her head in her hands, taking some long, deep breaths.

"Are you OK, lovely?" asked a soft lilting Welsh voice.

Rose looked up to see a young woman with her blonde hair in a messy bun and what looked like a chocolate stain on her pale blue hoody, smiling kindly at her.

"Would you like a wet wipe?" she asked, offering her a packet to pull one from. Rose took one gratefully and wiped her mouth.

"Heavy night last night, was it?" the woman continued.

"No," croaked Rose, balling up the used wipe in her hand. "Must've been something I ate."

"Oh, love you, petrol stations are the worst when you're poorly. When I was pregnant with my Charlie," she nodded over to the car behind her where a chubby blonde toddler was waving his arms impatiently, "I couldn't stomach the smell of petrol at all, made me throw up every time it did. My husband always had to get the petrol for me. Are you going to be all right getting home?"

"Yes, thank you for being so kind," Rose murmured, her mind working overtime.

All she'd eaten that day was some toast, a bag of crisps and an apple. Nothing that could make you sick. Her parents were both fine and she interacted so little with anyone else that she couldn't possibly have caught something.

Panicking now, she started thinking back over the last few weeks - had she had a period while living at her dad's? No, she hadn't. She'd been feeling so wretched that she didn't even notice. She couldn't be, though, could she? She was on the pill — well, she had been until she left, there didn't seem any point once Adam was gone. She had heard stories about it not always being 100% effective though. What if she was in that unlucky 1%?

She drove the rest of the way to Cirencester on autopilot, stopping at the large Waitrose on the edge of town, grateful to find it still open. She purchased a double pregnancy test just to be on the safe side and squirrelled it away in her bag, guessing correctly that her dad would insist they ate straight away.

She barely touched her food, just pushed it around her plate and she struggled to follow anything her dad was saying. This wasn't such unusual behaviour for her at the moment, though, so her dad didn't notice anything amiss.

Having always assumed that her dad barely registered her presence at all, Rose was unaware that Keith had actually become very concerned about his little girl. She was so skinny, listless and miserable. He knew something had gone on with the boyfriend, but she was only young and she should've snapped out of it faster as far as he was concerned. He was at a loss to know how to deal with the situation and he didn't like it.

After what felt like aeons, Rose had been able to excuse herself and, on the pretence of running a bath, she locked herself in the bathroom. She'd been holding in a wee all through dinner and so it was no challenge to go on both sticks from the box – just to be on the safe side – while the bath filled.

When the required three minutes (which had felt more like fifteen) was up, she turned off the bath taps and almost crept to the loo where she'd left the tests facing up on the cistern. At the sight of the very clear double pink lines in each window, she lost the little dinner she'd eaten into the toilet bowl.

Over the next few days Rose went through every imaginable emotion several times over and by Christmas Day, felt entirely wrung out. At least she was able to attribute the puffy face and bloodshot eyes to her break-up. The vomiting, which was starting to become a little more frequent, was harder to hide.

For the first time in her life, Rose was grateful that her parents didn't show a massive amount of interest in her, so they hadn't worked anything out. She couldn't help but wonder what Karen's reaction would be. Shocked at first, no doubt, but then so loving and supportive.

It hadn't even occurred to Rose not to have the baby, although at times she had considered adoption. But she knew herself too well. She really was a hedgehog. Her often-spiky exterior hid a heart that was so capable of love. She knew that once she held that child in her arms, hell, once she felt that first kick, she'd never be able to give the baby up.

No, the decision she'd really wrestled with was whether or not to tell Adam. He might be a cheat and a liar, but she knew that when it came to something like this, he'd do what he considered to be the right thing and stand by her. She couldn't stand that. Having him there at the scans, at the birth, being all supportive but with his new girlfriend hanging around in the wings.

Or maybe the girlfriend would change her mind about him once he came with a kid and leave him. Then what? Maybe he'd turn back to Rose as a consolation prize? Or just because they had a baby together? She loved him with all her heart and she didn't want him ending up with her out of a misplaced sense of duty.

She'd wait until she had the baby and then she would let him know. She couldn't live with herself if she deprived that whole family of knowing their kin. She also wanted her baby to share in the love they had for each other and to be part of it, even if she wasn't. Rose was sure that once the baby was here, she'd be able to be more emotionally detached from Adam and the whole family. She hoped so, anyway.

"Mum, come on, it's Christmas Day." Rose shook her Mum not too gently. "We're going to be late for dinner if you don't get up soon."

Dawn shuffled up in bed and rubbed her eyes. "What time is it?" she groaned.

"Half eleven," replied Rose, handing her a mug. "Look, I've made you a coffee. Jump in the shower and I'll wait for you downstairs."

Satisfied that her mum wasn't going to go back to sleep, Rose sat despondently in the sitting room flicking through TV channels until she found one showing It's a Wonderful Life, of course.

This Christmas was supposed to be so great. Last year her mum had decided she couldn't be bothered with the mess of cooking Christmas dinner so had booked to go to their local. It wasn't strictly the closest to the house, but it was the one where her mum had become a regular. She had this new group of mates, The Coven, Keith called it. All of them a bit too reliant on drink and all of them either single or with partners of the same mindset.

They were what Rose thought of as 'pub friends'. Her mum thought they were all great and a good laugh and they all spent enough time together, but they weren't real friends. They weren't the ones driving Dawn to the hospital when she twisted her ankle on the stairs at two in the morning. They didn't text her every day to make sure she was OK. They wouldn't visit Dawn if she was sick and bring her shopping.

In fact, Rose was fairly confident that if, one day, Dawn stopped going to the pub, she wouldn't be missed, not really, none of them would. There would always be someone else to have a drink with, so they didn't have to be the one drinking alone and admit it was about the alcohol, not the socialising.

Last Christmas, Dawn hadn't long discovered these new 'friends' and so the pub idea seemed decent. As soon as they'd finished eating, The Coven descended and Dawn chose to stay at the pub rather than go home with Rose and Keith.

Christmas used to be the one time that Rose felt like they were a proper family, like other people, but she hadn't factored how much her parents' relationship had already deteriorated. Once they'd got home, her dad popped the telly on and was asleep within minutes. Sitting twiddling her thumbs, Rose had rung Adam who had invited her round to his house straight away instead of waiting until the evening as they'd originally planned.

She spent a wonderful afternoon in their cosy home, dancing to Christmas music and playing board games while snacking on chocolate snowmen and gingerbread. In the evening, after a cursory text to her parents, and after Adam's grandparents had left, they'd snuggled down in the lounge with the fire roaring, drinking Bailey's hot chocolate and watching a film.

This year she'd negated making plans with her parents at all and had been so excited about spending the whole of Christmas with Adam and his family. She'd even been excited about going to Midnight Mass with them on Christmas Eve, something her agnostic family had never done.

She'd felt so much a part of their family and always so welcome. A week and a half after Adam had left for university, her parents were having a particularly vicious row and Rose, unable to bear listening to them anymore, had left the house in tears.

Her instincts took her to Adam's house, the one place she felt comfortable, and Karen had welcomed her with open arms. They'd sat in the kitchen having a chat over a cup of tea, then they'd done each other's nails and watched trash TV while Dan and Damien had some 'guy time' as Dan called it, to much mocking from his son.

When it got to ten o'clock, Dan had popped his head around the door to say goodnight.

"Are you staying over, Rose?" he'd asked simply.

"Can I?" she'd responded hesitantly.

"Of course you can," Karen said, so matter of fact that it made Rose want to weep with gratitude. "You know you're always welcome, even with Ad not here. Just text your mum, yeah?"

That night, Rose had snuggled up in Adam's bed, that still smelt of him, in his familiar room. Once they'd turned eighteen, Adam's parents had decided she was allowed to sleep in his bed when she stayed over, something that had become so frequent she now had her own drawer in his room. That night, tucking a pillow in behind her so she could pretend it was him, she slept more soundly than she had since he left.

The next morning, over fresh orange juice and toast, the weak autumn sunlight giving the kitchen a soft yellow glow, Karen had given Rose her own key to use whenever she liked. The key was still on her keyring. She hadn't had the heart to throw it away.

But now, instead of the glorious Christmas she'd been looking forward to, her dad was working, and she was joining her mum and her cronies for dinner in the pub. Rose planned to leave them to it the moment she finished her Christmas pudding.

Knowing about the baby growing inside her had given Rose the impetus she needed to start looking after herself again and she was forcing herself to eat proper meals with as much fruit and veg as possible. The food tasted like dirt in her mouth, but she pictured her little baby and forced each meal down.

She looked at her watch: they were going to be late if her mum was much longer but Rose didn't have the energy or inclination to go and chivvy her along. But then she heard Dawn clattering down the stairs.

She scurried into the room with a trying-too-hard bright smile on her face as she started scouting around through the clutter for something.

"Help me find my purse, will you, Rosie?"

With a sigh, Rose dragged herself up from the sofa and starting hunting through piles of magazines, discarded clothing and other detritus that lay scattered about the place. Never particularly houseproud, Dawn's ways had become even more slovenly now that Rose and her dad weren't there to tidy up after her.

"Found it," Dawn declared triumphantly and in the nick of time, as all the bending over was making Rose feel decidedly queasy.

Shuffling behind Dawn into the hallway, Rose watched as her mum checked her reflection in the mirror and put on some jewellery, previously discarded on the sideboard.

Dawn still had nice bone structure and if you could see past either the permanent glaze or the morning-after bloodshot, her eyes were still a vibrant blue. Rose had always wished she'd inherited her Mum's fair hair instead of the dull brown of her dad's.

She could see why her dad fell for Dawn all those years ago, enough to leave his first wife anyway. However, the drinking was starting to take its toll on her looks. This morning, her make-up was caked on a bit too thickly, obviously trying to disguise the dark circles and pale skin of her Christmas Eve hangover.

Instead of the glamorous appearance she was obviously going for, the thick foundation clung to the slight lines of her face, and the garish lipstick highlighted the feathering around her mouth from years of smoking. Both of which combined to make her look older than she actually was.

Not for the first time, Rose felt a deep sense of sorrow for her mum. For the potential she had and was wasting.

Suddenly aware of being under scrutiny, Dawn turned and for once, looked properly at her daughter.

"Are you OK, Rosie? You look awfully pale?"

"I've had a bit of a bug," Rose mumbled, desperate to suddenly tell her mum everything, to be pulled into a warm, loving embrace. But no sooner had she had the thought than she dismissed it. They'd never had that sort of relationship, and besides Dawn had already turned her back and was slipping into her coat. Her brief show of motherly concern was done for the day.

They trudged wearily to the pub, everything in Rose screaming at her to turn and run in the opposite direction, towards Adam's house. There she'd be coddled and looked after. She'd get to see him, breathe him in, hear his voice again. For a few minutes, it would be pure heaven.

But her feet kept on walking forwards. There was no going back.

It was the early hours of Boxing Day morning, back at her dad's flat when Rose was dragged out of sleep by a cramping, twisting pain deep inside her stomach. Switching on the bedside light, the glare causing her eyes to water, she pushed back her duvet.

A dark crimson stain was spreading across the crotch of her cotton pyjamas. She watched it for a moment, as it moved fibre by fibre, saturating the material, ruining it forever, her brain not quite able to register what she was seeing.

As she was gripped by another wave of pain, she let out a long, guttural cry of anguish.

Then her dad was there, stroking her hair and murmuring soothing platitudes.

"I'm pregnant," she whispered hoarsely.

She felt herself being wrapped in a blanket and lifted by strong arms, as her dad carried her princess-like down the stairs. Finding herself held, in safe, solid arms was too much for Rose, she couldn't stay strong anymore; she clung to her father and howled.

# Chapter Twenty-Two

We walk over to a row of benches set between trees, their backs to the castle. Once again, we're facing out onto the river. All is silent and still except for the occasional whooshing of a vehicle passing over Tower Bridge.

Adam sits down first, turning slightly towards me, his arm resting casually along the back of the bench. I perch on the opposite end. Despite feeling calmer, I'm still hyper-aware of every sound, smell and sensation. Adam's scent, the crisp tang of the night air, the muted old-fashioned streetlights buzzing and glaring at me, the twinkling of the fairy lights strung into the trees, the endless rushing of the water.

At first glance, Adam would seem oh so relaxed, but I can see the tension in his jaw, in the set of his shoulders. Am I right to be doing this? Will I just be passing on my burden to him? Haven't I put him through enough?

He smiles at me encouragingly. I wonder what he's thinking right now. Maybe he's regretting approaching me in the train station a few hours ago. Was it just a few hours? It feels like weeks.

But it is better this way. I take a deep breath and for once, look right at him as I speak.

"A few weeks after I moved to my dad's, I found out I was pregnant."

"Am I a father?" he gasps, the colour draining from his face, his eyes glinting like steel.

"No. I lost the baby," I say hurriedly. "It was Boxing Day morning. My dad drove me to the hospital, he even put his siren on, but there was nothing they could do." I look down at my clenched hands. A tear plops onto the wool of my glove, resting for a moment, a perfect dewdrop, before dissolving slowly into the fabric.

"Oh my God."

We sit in silence for a moment while he digests what I've just told him. I watch him staring statue-like out to the water, the slight flickering of his irises the only indication of the frenetic thought process that must be going on.

"I'm so sorry you had to go through that," he eventually says, turning to look at me. "It must have been so hard, especially on your own."

"It was the worst time of my life. I already loved her, you know."

"Her?"

"I always felt she was a girl."

He just nods.

"But my dad actually stepped up," I continue. "He didn't magically become a perfect parent overnight or anything, but he took me to the GP, and I got some help, antidepressants and eventually counselling. Dad still worked a lot, but he took me to every session and made sure he was around afterwards so that I wouldn't be alone."

"That explains something actually." I look at him curiously but don't interrupt. "I saw your dad just after that New Year and he was, well, weird, to put it mildly."

"What do you mean you saw him?"

"Look, I missed you so much and was desperate. I had no idea what had happened, where you'd gone. I was frantic."

I clench my fingers together, the guilt over my actions flowing through me.

"I'd tried your mum a few times," he continues, "but all she would say was that you were with your dad and she wouldn't say where that was. So, before I had to go back to Uni, I thought I'd track your dad down. I knew where he worked so I started hanging out in my car near the station, the plan being to follow him home."

"You stalked a policeman?" I ask incredulously.

"Yeah, pretty much. But I hadn't factored on your dad being good at his job. Of course, he clocked me in my battered red Corsa and eventually came out and had a word. It was so strange because he managed to be nice but threatening at the same time. It was like he felt sorry for me and hated me all at once. He told me not to worry about you, that you were fine, but he was emphatic about me never trying to contact you again. It was quite unnerving. But I got the message loud and clear. It did leave me with more questions, though; when he talked about you, he seemed so... I don't know, worried, sad, something I couldn't put my finger on. For a while, I was convinced you had cancer or something and that was why you left me, so as not to put me through all that, but then I realised your mum wouldn't have been so chilled. Now of course, it all makes sense."

We sit in silence for a moment. Dad never told me he'd seen Adam but then I was in such a bad place and Dad was so worried about me that I'm not surprised. I can't help but feel a little pissed off, though. If I'd known the lengths to which Adam was going, to try to contact me, perhaps it would have changed things. Perhaps I would have got in touch with him to hear his side. Perhaps it all could have been different.

Thinking like that does no good though. I can't live my life in 'what-ifs'. What happened, happened, and that's all there is to it. It doesn't stop a terrible lump from forming in my throat, though.

"So, the counselling you had, did it help?" Adam asks gently.

"Yes, a bit. I had a lot of guilt, I felt it was my fault because I hadn't been looking after myself. I was so heartbroken at the time that I wasn't eating or sleeping properly. She assured me that I wasn't to blame, that it's just one of those things. One in four pregnancies, apparently."

"So, you didn't... I mean..." Adam shifts uncomfortably. "You did want to keep the baby then? Despite all that happened, what you thought I did."

"Yes, once I got over the initial shock, I did. I mean she was part of you, of us, you know? Even though I hated you. At the time," I add quickly. He just smiles briefly. "I knew I would love the baby with my whole heart. I guess it was just never meant to be."

"I wish I'd known. I wish you'd told me," he mutters. "We could have gone through it all together, I could've been there for you. I'm not having a go, I just..." He trails off looking despondent.

"I know. I can't believe I fucked up so badly."

Tears start coursing down my cheeks again and I wipe them away quickly with the back of my hand. I'm like a leaky tap all of a sudden, I can't seem to stop.

I can tell Adam is watching me and I try to gather myself but then he wraps his arms around me and I nestle into his chest, tucking my feet up onto the bench. With my face buried in the puffy material of his ugly coat, I let the tears fall.

The cold in my legs pull me out of sleep and I blink blurrily, my eyes feeling swollen and sore. With each blink. my surroundings come into focus, what I first thought were stars show themselves to be fairy lights entwined around bare trees. One half of my body and my lower legs are freezing, my hip is stiff and cramping slightly where I've curled my legs up. The tip of my nose is stinging.

The rest of me is toasty warm though, where I'm snuggled up to Adam. I can feel the slight weight of his head resting on mine, his arm relaxed around my shoulder. I can hear his slow, rhythmic breathing, almost heading towards a snore, and I can just about feel the rise and fall of his chest against my cheek.

I don't want to move, I want to savour this moment, this feeling of being safe. But my body is protesting and I really need to shift soon to get the blood flowing around my legs again and some heat through my body.

Without moving my upper body too much, I swing my legs around so my feet are on the ground. My hip instantly feels better but bloody hell, it's cold! My wriggling hasn't woken Adam, although it's brought my face closer to his neck. If I strain my eyes upwards, I can see the line of his jaw and the short dark hairs that make up his stubbly beard.

It then hits me. I'm sleeping with Adam again and I can't help but smile a little. Just twenty-four hours ago I would have bet my house on that never happening again.

I used to love sleeping with Adam. And I do mean sleeping, not just the sex, although that was rather wonderful too. The best thing about turning eighteen was his parents allowing us to officially spend the night together in his bed. From then on, I stayed over pretty much every Friday and Saturday night and it was the best sleep I ever had.

We'd always fall asleep with my head on his chest, tucked just under his chin. His skin warm and soft beneath my cheek, his arms around me, our legs intertwined. He used to gently stroke my bare back with his fingertips. I used to warm my permanently cold feet up on his shins. I'd forgotten until this moment. Or had made myself forget anyway.

I always say I'm not a cuddly sleeper, that I need my space in bed. Aside from the brief obligatory post-coital cuddle or early morning fondle, I don't think I ever cuddled any of my other boyfriends to sleep. And, yet, now I think about it, Adam and I would spend the whole night wrapped in each other, some way or another. Even a ferocious heatwave, the summer after we turned eighteen, didn't stop us: we still held hands or linked our legs, refusing to let go of each other even in sleep.

Was it an age thing? Teenagers are renowned for being able to sleep anywhere. Now that we are older, would it be different, would I actually need my space? It seems my hip can't even cope with being in one position for a long period without cramping up. Could I really sleep wrapped up with someone? Or does it come down to who that person is?

I allow my mind to drift just for a moment. I allow myself to wonder what it would feel like now to wrap my naked body around his. How would his chest hair feel? He only had a light smattering when we were together. How would his manly, adult thighs feel tucked underneath mine? Pretty damn good, I imagine.

A slight frisson of lust ripples through me, heating my insides and causing my thighs to tighten in response. I force my mind away from that rabbit hole and attempt to gently pull my body away from the warmth of Adam.

He jolts awake instantly, his arm tightening instinctively around me. Our faces are inches apart and I watch his look of sleepy bewilderment morph into a gentle smile as he focuses on me.

Reluctantly I pull myself away from his embrace and pull my scarf up to try and warm my frozen nose.

"I guess we fell asleep," he says sheepishly and looking adorably befuddled.

"How long do you think we were asleep for?" I ask.

He pushes back his sleeve and squints at his watch. "Just over an hour, I'd say."

"I'm frigging freezing," I groan through my scarf as I jiggle my legs and wrap my arms around my body.

"Yeah, me too," Adam replies standing up and stamping his feet. His coat isn't as long as mine and he wasn't all tucked up like I was. His legs must be like blocks of ice. "Do you want to find a church to hunker down in like that taxi driver suggested?"

"I don't mind," I reply, being polite. But actually, I don't want to. I'm not ready for this night to be over, as crazy and dramatic as it has been. I feel like I want to see it through.

"You always used to say, 'I don't mind' to be polite, when actually you had an opinion but you just didn't want to say it."

"How do you remember this stuff?" I smile. "But yes OK, Mr-Know-it-All, I don't really fancy huddling in a church with a load of strangers, feeling like a refugee. But I didn't want to say so in case you're freezing and fed up of me and desperate to get inside."

"Never!" he exclaims. "This was my idea, remember? I'm happy to see it through if you are. Come on." He reaches out his hands and pulls me to my feet. "If we walk quickly, we'll soon warm up."

My head swims a little as I stand, the streetlamps blurring slightly as my eyes refocus. Tiredness has made me woozy and lightheaded, a bit like when you've had a few drinks, but it doesn't hit you till you start moving.

"Ugh, falling asleep was a mistake. I feel horrible now." The gritty feeling in my eyes reminds me that I probably look horrible too. I doubt crying myself to sleep has done my face any favours. I shouldn't have redone my eyeliner in that bar — ghoulish panda is not a good look. I rub the pads of my thumbs under my eyes in a blind attempt to improve things. For all I know I could be making it worse.

"I have something that will perk you up," Adam says brightly rummaging in his pocket. With a triumphant smile, he pulls out a white McDonald's bag. "Here you go," he says passing it to me.

Momentarily confused, I open the bag. It's his doughnut! I'd forgotten that he hadn't eaten it. I pull my gloves off with my teeth and shove them in my pocket, the skin of my fingers stinging sharply the second they're exposed to the night air. I wonder how cold it is now. I tear the doughnut in two, handing one half to Adam.

Despite being a few hours old now, the doughnut is still delicious, and I swear I can feel the sugar hitting my bloodstream as I allow the chocolate to melt on my tongue before chewing the soft dough. Although to be honest, pretty much anything dipped in chocolate would hit the spot right now.

Adam, in the meantime, in typical bloke style, has polished off his half in two bites while hopping from foot to foot in an attempt to warm up.

"Better?" he asks as I pop the last bite into my mouth and hurriedly put my gloves back on to my pink, stinging hands.

"Marginally," I reply, joining Adam in his jiggling by bouncing up and down on the soles of my feet, "but I still feel weird and woozy. I'd murder a coffee."

"I've had an idea about that."

"Oh yeah?"

"Well, you've already seen two of London's best Christmas trees, so we ought to make it a hat trick really and see the one on Trafalgar Square."

"But that's ages away," I moan.

"I think we'll be able to catch a night bus, and I'm sure over there, we'll be able to find a shop and purchase something caffeinated. Or we could..."

I put up my hand to stop him.

"You had me at night bus."

He grins and gets his phone out of his pocket. I resume my bouncing in an attempt to get some feeling back into my toes as he taps away on his screen.

"Yep, we can get a bus from Tower Underground that'll take us to Trafalgar. There's one in ten minutes."

"Right, come on then." I turn decisively and start walking back up through the square towards the city and the gleaming peak of the far-too-phallic gherkin which is winking at us over the skyline.

"You know we'd warm up faster if we ran," Adam says, falling into step beside me.

"Ugh, I don't have the energy for running," I grumble.

"Jog then?" is his cheeky response.

I attempt to give him a dirty look, but I know I don't pull it off.

"How about skipping?"

I give up pretending to be serious and allow a giggle to bubble out.

"As if you would really skip somewhere."

He stops dead and looks at me.

"You reckon?" he asks with an eyebrow raised. I was always jealous that he could do that; I have no control over my brows. I make do with staring challengingly at him. The same energy zips between us as it did when we first agreed on this night.

Adam grabs my hand, turns and starts skipping through the square. Large, over the top, comedy skips, pulling me behind him. Well, if you can't beat them...

Gripping tightly onto Adam's hand I start matching him skip for skip and, giggling like children, we skip our way up to the bus stop.

# Chapter Twenty-Three

I pull the plastic lid off my coffee cup so I can better breathe in the rich aroma and warm my face on the steam. Adam was right about finding a shop. There was a twenty-four-hour Co-op near Trafalgar Square that blessedly had a Costa coffee machine.

I still feel a bit woozy and strange but hopefully, the coffee will help. This whole night is starting to feel surreal, like a strange dream that I'll only remember glimmers of tomorrow. Our time down by the riverbank already feels like something I imagined; the swirling mist and glittering frost and sense of existing outside of time, like the city had paused around us. Here among the modern streetlights, mild traffic and decorated shop fronts, it's a different world.

Slurping our coffees, we head towards Trafalgar Square. I had been hoping to have it all to ourselves, like St Paul's, but instead, occasional cars and taxis are circling the surrounding roads and a few clumps of people are gathered on the square itself. One group who look like they could be students are assembled on the base of Nelson's Column. They're playing music and clearly ignoring central London's no public drinking rules as they frolic about. I can't help but worry about one of them falling off.

Ugh, a lot of things have changed tonight but clearly the fact I've turned into a middle-aged worry wart isn't one of them.

Ignoring the partying students, I'm drawn to the fountains, lit in bright blues and purples. They look magical, especially against the backdrop of the grand, columned façade of The National Gallery, glorious under golden lights.

We lean on the fountain walls, watching the water dance and tumble. Despite the tinny throbbing music coming from

Nelson's party gang, it's very peaceful. I can see various coins shimmering at the bottom of the pool and without thinking, reach for my purse in the depths of my handbag and find a couple of twenty pence pieces, which is lucky because I rarely have cash on me.

Wordlessly I pass one to Adam and I watch him as he holds it in his fist, closing his eyes briefly and then he tosses it into the pool where it lands with a satisfying plop.

"What are you going to wish for?" he asks, turning to me.

I look down at the coin still lying in my gloved palm. Good question. Not that I actually believe in wishes in fountains, it's just a silly tradition. But if it were real, if I had one wish, what would it be? I have a nice house, a good job, my health. They're the main things, aren't they? Well, except for love, that's the biggie, isn't it? People always wish for love. Is that something I really want again though, love? Is it worth all the pain that can come with the pleasure? I don't think that it is.

I realise that Adam is staring at me and I'm still holding on to the stupid coin. I fling it into the water and find myself wishing for 'happiness' as it cuts through the fountain stream and lands in the water.

"I can't tell you," I smile at Adam, "because then it wouldn't come true."

"So what do you think of the tree then?" Adam asks, turning to look at the giant pine towering above us in the centre of the square.

"This is the one the King gets as a gift each year from Norway, isn't it?"

"Yeah, I think so, although I always thought it was a gift to the people of Britain, rather than just the monarch. But do you like it?"

"It's certainly big, but we all know size isn't everything."

"Yeah, but women always say that and never actually mean it," grins Adam with the confidence of someone who, if memory serves, knows he never has to worry about the size of... things.

I appraise the tree some more. It's simply decorated with just vertical strings of fairy lights so if it weren't for the coloured fountains and impressive frontage of the national gallery surrounding it, it would be nothing special.

"It's OK," I finally concede. "Obviously, I like the fairy lights, but I think Somerset House was my favourite. It was just so full-on, you know. I mean if you're going to do Christmas, you might as well give it your all and really go for it."

"I couldn't agree more," laughs Adam. "Up for some more walking?"

Downing my coffee, I nod my head.

We stroll down to the river once more and walk out to the middle of Westminster Bridge so that I get to see Big Ben and the Houses of Parliament looking as impressive as I thought they would, glowing through the frosty mist. As we walk back, past Westminster Abbey and along St James Park towards Buckingham Palace, we start talking about the baby. Our child who could have been. We wonder what she would have looked like. I decide she'd have had my facial features but Adam's eyes and light hair. He says he can't picture anything but a mini version of me. We argue light-heartedly over what we would have called her.

We talk about how old she'd be now and what she'd be doing. I love that he never questions my sense that she was a girl, even though it's totally unfounded. I love that, this whole time, he has never suggested that she would have lived, were we still together. It's set in stone that we would have lost her anyway and that, as daft as it sounds, lifts my burden a little. But most of all, I just love that we talk about her.

I've never talked about her with anyone before. Dad never mentioned what happened that night after he bought me home from the hospital. He never asked any questions or talked about it in any way and I've never been an emotional sharer. For the first few years, he was particularly thoughtful and solicitous around Christmas, although that has lessened with time.

However, each year on Boxing Day, he gives me, or makes sure I receive, a bunch of flowers. It's never discussed but it's his way of acknowledging the anniversary and letting me know he cares. Each year, without fail, even though I know it's coming, I shed a little tear over that bunch of flowers.

He's the only one who knows what happened. Even my closest friends don't know. Partly because all the friends that I have, I made after that time and, as I say, I'm not a sharer. It's not that I'm ashamed of what happened, it just hasn't come up. I'm sure if a friend went through a loss like that, I would tell them I've been there and offer a shoulder to cry on. But to my knowledge no one has.

It means that she only lives on in my mind and that annual bunch of flowers. Being able to have the 'what-if' conversation, being able to talk about her and acknowledge what she could have been, is so liberating.

Emerging from the shadows cast by the skeletal trees that line St James Park, Buckingham Palace appears before us in all its splendour. Although the up lights placed in between the columns creates a kind of spooky, shadowy look which reminds me of a kid putting a torch under their chin to tell a ghost story.

As we get closer, I can see the Palace Christmas tree, another fine specimen, in the entranceway.

"Charlie is home," says Adam nodding at the flag flying proudly.

"It's weird to think he's in there now, fast asleep."

"Do you think he snores?" he asks.

"Do you think he lets the dogs sleep on the bed with him?"

"Do you think he wears PJs with little crowns all over them?"

"And a little crown-shaped nightcap," I giggle.

"Seriously though," Adam says, "I wonder how many people are asleep behind those windows right now? How many staff are there? How many bedrooms are empty?"

"I'm sure we could google it," I offer.

"Yeah, but that takes the fun out of wondering."

We've reached the gates and both stare up at the many blank windows reflecting the pink lights. I can't stop picturing the King now in his crown PJs, snoring away.

Actually, it's weird to think how many thousands of people are fast asleep, tucked up in their beds all around us while we're out here in the night. It's that surreal otherworld feeling again. I also wonder how many night owls or disrupted sleepers have glanced out of their windows tonight and seen us wandering the streets and wondered about us.

Like many people, I'm fascinated by stuff like that. I love passing by windows at night and seeing the snatches of life going on behind them, especially when you can see several homes at once. A couple sat at the table having dinner, a parent reading to their child, a group of mates huddled around the TV. A kaleidoscope of lives. I find these glimpses unfathomably comforting but I couldn't say why. It's linked to my enjoyment of people watching, I suspect.

I'm always intrigued by the concept of all our lives playing out alongside each other, like different strands of string, all intertwined but rarely touching. How split-second decisions can suddenly connect two people, or how you could pass the same person multiple times in your life but never be aware of each other. Tonight being the perfect example of the split-second timing that has caused our paths to cross again.

What if Adam hadn't looked in my direction at the train station? This whole night wouldn't have happened, all those questions would have forever remained unanswered.

"What are you thinking about? You look so serious," Adam asks.

"Quite deep philosophical stuff actually," I answer truthfully.

"Like what?"

"About how we co-exist with so many millions of people and yet actually meet so comparatively few. Whenever I am at tourist spots like this — not tonight obviously..." I gesture at the silent street. "I wonder how many photos I'm in, in other people's houses? Like, is there a family in Japan who have a holiday photo up in their lounge and I'm there in the background. If I looked at the photos that I took at that Coldplay gig in 2011, would I spot you among the crowd?"

"You need some sleep," Adam jokes kindly. "I know what you mean, though. I read a story ages ago, it had gone viral on Facebook, so I doubt you saw it, but it was this couple who had been married for a few years. They were looking through some of her old family photos and they found one from a childhood holiday where she was on the beach with her siblings and the family sat just to their side are his. They spent the whole day on this beach next to each other, maybe even played together and they would never have known their paths had crossed before if they hadn't found that photo."

I'm about to respond when Adam's phone pings shrilly.

"Sorry, I'd better reply to that, it's probably Jenny checking in. Or my mum can't sleep."

He pulls his phone out of his pocket and I turn to look at the colourfully lit fountain for something to do while trying to ignore the wave of guilt that is crashing over me.

"Yep, it's Jenny," he says with a smile as he taps out a response. "She's like a mother hen."

"How come she's up so early?" I ask, attempting nonchalance.

"The baby has her up feeding every few hours. I suspect she is enjoying texting someone who is actually awake and able to respond," he smiles. "She was making sure I hadn't frozen to death."

"What does she think you're doing?"

"I'm not sure; I've kept it vague."

"Good idea," I nod. "She must hate me."

"She doesn't hate you," he says gently. "She just, well, once I've explained what happened, she'll understand."

"I've always regretted losing touch with Jenny, you know. I never meant for it to happen. I smashed my phone that weekend in a fit of self-pity or something, but I figured that once I'd licked my wounds for a bit, I'd email her and explain and stay in touch. But then the baby happened and afterwards, I was such a mess. Once I started to feel better, got myself together, it just seemed easier to lock the door on that whole chapter of my life. Try and forget about all of you."

"And how did that work out?" Adam asks a touch sarcastically.

"Pretty well actually," I snap.

And it did. I locked them all away and refused to think about it. I'd moved house enough as a kid that cutting ties wasn't exactly new to me, I adapted and carried on and I've done OK. I may not be the perfect picture of mental health but who is?

We glare at each other for a moment. I'm daring Adam to say something else, make some assumption that my life without him, without all of them, was somehow less. He obviously has an opinion and is deciding whether or not to poke the bear by sharing it.

Suddenly his stomach lets out a huge rumble, breaking the tension and making me almost smile but I swallow it down.

"Hungry, are you?" I ask politely.

"A bit, I guess." He shrugs. "Oh look, a light has just come on downstairs." He points at the palace. He's right, some of the lights on the ground floor have come on, not that you can see anything, but the glass is brighter.

"I guess the butler must be up getting Charles' day started."

"Wow, so it's almost morning," I murmur, trying to quell my disappointment that this night is nearly over and real-life approaches.

"Well, yeah," says Adam. "I suppose some crazy people would be getting up at this hour, but it's not dawn for a while."

"But doesn't that mean that some early breakfast cafés might be opening up soon?"

"Yes," Adam cries, his eyes lighting up as he scrabbles for his phone.

I watch him, his brow creasing cutely as he concentrates on the screen followed by a look of triumph as he finds what he's looking for.

"There's a place about twenty minutes away that opens at six. You up for walking there?"

"If tea and food are involved, I'll walk anywhere," I smile, our previous sour moment forgotten.

"Come on then..."

"Let me guess, 'this way'," I interject with a grin.

"No, actually." Adam turns away from me and points. "That way."

# Chapter Twenty-Four

## Then

Rose's flip flops smacked against the shiny tiles of the shopping mall floor as she briskly headed to the open plan café in the centre of Cribbs Causeway. She was uncharacteristically late, well just on time, which counted as late in her book. She'd been slower than normal, leaving the house that morning, such was her reluctance to spend an afternoon shopping, but Marco had been so good to her in the last few months, she'd felt that she couldn't deny him this last afternoon together and Cribbs had been his choice.

Arriving at the café area, Rose discovered that, as expected, the ever-tardy Marco wasn't there yet, and she gladly snagged a table slightly shielded from the rest of the Mall by a large potted plant, knowing full well that he would have preferred one right in the centre and in full view of passing shoppers.

It was surprisingly warm for mid-September and people were making the most of the last hit of summer, showing off their tans in shorts, T-shirts and little dresses as they shopped the September sales. Rose was feeling summery too in a navy striped t-shirt dress and a light denim jacket, an outfit that Marco had persuaded her to buy the last time that they'd shopped together.

Just as she was about to get up and order a drink at the counter, she spotted Marco weaving through the crowd towards her. She always got a kick out of watching Marco in crowded places, he moved with such confident assuredness and his suave Italian good looks literally turned heads. He was always impeccably dressed in that European way that many British men struggle to pull off. Today was no exception as he cut a swathe through the shoppers in a crisp white, fitted shirt tucked into tight navy jeans, the outfit emphasising his slim hips, broad shoulders and golden tan. Recently Rose had taken to calling him Black Beauty after his mane of luscious, thick, black hair which he wore swept off his face and curling by his ears.

He smiled broadly as he approached her and she rose to greet him, prepared for the standard over-effusive double cheek kiss and cloud of expensive cologne.

"Ciao, Bella."

"Hi, Marco, was it a good night?"

"I need coffee, then I will tell you all about it," he replied his eyes twinkling. "Latte?"

"Yes, please."

Rose sat back down, smiling to herself as the two girls at the next table watched transfixed while Marco sauntered to the counter.

Meeting Marco was the only good thing that had happened to Rose in months. After her miscarriage, Rose thought she'd never smile again. Adam was gone, the baby was gone, and she had nothing. She sank into a severe depression, dropping out of university and becoming a hermit, barely leaving her dad's flat.

After a couple of months of antidepressants, her dad waded in with some tough love and insisted that she had to at least get a job. He was determined that she needed to get back into the real world and build a life for herself again. He'd called in a favour from the owner of a family-run Italian restaurant in town who was looking for a general kitchen dogsbody.

At first, the wonderfully loud and loveable Italian mama, Sofia, was against the idea of putting a 'pretty young girl' to work in her kitchen but Keith persuaded her that his daughter would be much happier back there doing simple menial tasks and he was right.

Rose's natural diligence meant that she worked hard and efficiently, quickly winning over Sofia who had at first been wary of Rose's pale and quiet demeanour. Being out of the house, mixing with others, doing something new, did help Rose start to feel normal again. Most surprising of all was the friendship that she developed with Marco, Sofia's nephew, over from Italy for a year to work on his English.

Marco worked front of house, effortlessly charming all the customers and increasing his aunt's profits tenfold as he encouraged people to splash out on that extra bottle of fancy wine or treat themselves to a pudding.

He also had all the waitresses eating out of his hand and it hadn't escaped Sofia's notice that they all worked harder and more efficiently when Marco was running the shift, so keen were they to impress him.

Unlike her counterparts who all fawned around Marco, batting their eyes and flirting with him, Rose was her normal, quiet self. Marco clearly found this refreshing as hers was the company he would seek out at the end of the shift or while enjoying a brief break in the alley behind the restaurant where the staff had set up some tables and chairs for themselves. Much to the chagrin of the other girls, who couldn't believe that sombre, weird Rose was the one he was interested in.

Rose knew he wasn't looking at her like that, though, as she had realised during her first shift something that no one else had. Marco was gay. It was so obvious to Rose as she watched him navigate the restaurant that she couldn't believe no one else could see it too, although to be fair the camper aspects of his personality were masked by his 'Europeanness'. But there was no mistaking the flash of desire in his eyes when a good-looking man came in or how, while attentively hosting a couple, his gaze would linger a little longer on the man in the pair.

The first time that they went out for a coffee together after work, (coincidentally, the first time Rose had been out anywhere other than home or work since Christmas), she asked him outright, assuming, correctly, that he may want to talk about it. So relieved to have someone to confide in, he held forth about how hard it was keeping his true self hidden from his intensely Catholic family. It was the start of a lovely friendship.

Although more reticent to discuss her own life, Rose let Marco know enough that he could piece together bits of what had happened to her. She became his project. It was Marco who kindly forced her into a hairdressers for a pixie cut when he declared that he couldn't look at her two-tone hair any longer. Months of not bothering to dye it meant Rose had inches of plain brown before a sharp line of contrast where her bright purple hair had grown into undernourished limp strands.

Still completely uninterested in her appearance, even Rose had to admit that the cropped hair looked good and was much easier to manage. She barely had to do anything to maintain it, which suited her down to the ground.

Marco was the one that she called on the first time that she had gone into Cirencester on her own and a crying baby had been the catalyst for her first panic attack. She'd run to the park and phoned Marco, convinced that she was having a stroke.

In return for his kind friendship, Rose ended up being his alibi when, like the night before, he escaped to the gay clubs of Bristol or Birmingham on his weekends off.

"Here we are," he said, putting the tray carefully down on the table. "I got you a cookie too. I know how much you like your sweets and I think I could make you buy more things if you are happy. I am buttering you in."

"Buttering me up." Rose smiled indulgently. "And thank you."

184

Adam looked at his watch, sighing heavily. The bloke sat opposite him on the weird stool things that they had outside the dressing room gave him a conspiratorial eye roll and smile.

Adam gave him a tight smile back. They'd been in this shop for an age and he was getting bored. He also hadn't made a dent in his own shopping list and there were a few things that he had to get before he went back to Uni.

His first year had been tough but successful as he'd eschewed all socialising and put all his limited energy into his work as the only distraction from thoughts of Rose. He'd ended up with great exam results but few friends or positive memories of the year. He was determined that this next year would be different, and he'd find a happy medium. He didn't want to waste the student experience completely.

Finally, Jenny emerged from the dressing room wearing a very low-cut satin halter top.

"I like everything but I'm not sure about this one. What do you think?"

"I dunno," Adam replied with a shrug.

"Come on, you're supposed to be giving me a bloke's opinion. Do you think he'll like me in this?" She chewed her lip, looking nervous. Jenny was usually so self-assured that it was strange seeing her worry about her clothes or looks. Clearly, this man that she was trying to impress was more than just a passing crush.

"Honestly, you look stunning, it'll definitely catch his attention. But, well..." Adam shifted uncomfortably in his seat. "Is it perhaps a bit too low cut?"

Jenny looked down at where her very impressive chest was straining against the satin fabric, the deep V cut not leaving much to the imagination and causing her breasts to resemble two smuggled basketballs.

"What's wrong with my boobs?" Jenny frowned at him, her hands on her hips.

"Nothing, they're great," Adam squirmed, trying to look everywhere but at his friend's chest. It was quite hard. "Just they're very, you know, there."

"So?" Jenny countered.

"Look, Jen, you look stunning and everything but if you want this bloke to get to know, you know, your personality or hell, even your face, maybe consider something less... distracting."

"OK, fine," she huffed. But she returned to the dressing room smiling.

Five minutes later, the satin top rejected, Jenny paid for her other purchases and they strolled back out into the Mall.

"I just need to go to Boots for some make-up," she murmured.

"Nope. I'm drawing a line. I don't mind giving you opinions on clothes even though it makes me very uncomfortable, but I'm not make-up shopping with you. Besides, if we're going to be in time to meet the others later, I need to get some shopping done myself."

"OK, fair enough, I have been taking the piss, I suppose, especially as I forced you to drive me here in the first place," Jenny replied. "You just make such a good girl."

"Whatever." Adam rolled his eyes good-naturedly. "Shall we meet at Starbucks in an hour?"

"Make it forty-five minutes and then I'll help you choose some new clothes."

"I don't need new clothes."

"You do if you ever want to get laid again," retorted Jenny and then clapped a hand over her mouth. She hadn't said anything that insensitive for a while.

"You're probably right," Adam said with the broadest smile he could muster.

Jenny grinned back, her relief palpable and with a casual wave bounced off in the other direction.

Adam watched her go, feeling pleased. A few months ago, her throwaway comment would have caused sadness to envelop him. He'd had no interest in anyone since Rose disappeared on them all, over nine months ago and any gentle cajoling from Jenny had led to an uncharacteristically harsh response which he couldn't seem to help. So, going against her outspoken nature, Jenny had skirted round the issue and the R-word was never mentioned. No wonder she'd winced just now, but the fact that he'd not minded her 'getting laid' comment was perhaps a sign that he was ready to move on.

He strolled along the upper level of the Mall, glancing down to the lower floor as he turned the corner. Something about a girl in the café below caught his eye and it took a second for his brain to register why - she reminded him of Rose. He stopped in his tracks, causing an irritated huff from a shopper behind him. He had to check, just to be sure.

Adam turned back and leaning slightly over the railing, peered down into the open-plan café below. The girl had her back to him and was talking to some sort of Greek God-looking bloke. It wasn't her. Crushing disappointment mixed with an odd sense of relief.

He could see why his brain had thought it was Rose. She had been on his mind, this girl had a similar frame to Rose and there was something about the way she held herself, her body language, but it couldn't be her. The hair was far too sensible and the clothes were too trendy. Plus the companion was all wrong. Rose would never have the confidence to date someone who looked like a Calvin Klein model.

With a sigh Adam pushed himself away from the railing feeling frustrated. He'd just been congratulating himself on how far he'd come and seconds later, he was gawping at a stranger because her back looked a bit like Rose's. He had to stop. He had to move on. Going back to Uni had to be a fresh start, not just for him but for his family and friends. They had all been so kind and supportive, especially Jenny, even though he knew she was extremely hurt by Rose's disappearing act too, but enough was enough. Picking up his pace he headed towards JD Sports, determined to get some new gear to help his fresh start along.

Rose gripped Marco's hand tightly and felt her heartbeat return to normal.

"Are you OK?" he asked, concern etched into his handsome features.

"Yes, I'm OK."

"Are you sure, you went so pale?"

"That's usual, right?" Rose attempted to joke but it sounded hollow to both of them. "I'm sorry, I just saw someone who reminded me of a person from my old life and it threw me for a bit, that's all."

She'd only glanced up for a second as she'd laughed at something Marco had said and she saw a flash of an afro and a brightly coloured top and for a moment she was so convinced that it was Jenny that she felt her blood run cold and she couldn't focus on anything.

But it was crazy, Jenny wasn't the only black woman in the world, even though natural afros weren't that common. There's no logical reason to assume it would be her, especially there, miles from home.

Still, it had put Rose on edge and made her jittery. She was very glad of Marco's comforting presence. She was going to be so sorry to say goodbye to him the following week, even though the fresh start was greatly needed, and he would be a regular visitor once she was settled.

"Come on, lady," Marco said cheerfully. "let's go shopping. You cannot move to Birmingham with your current wardrobe. I will not allow it. You will be a super stylish student when I am done with you."

"I'm just glad I get to be a student again, I don't care what I look like," Rose said smiling. She was looking forward to studying art again and very grateful that her dad had agreed a fresh start in a new city was what she needed.

With a scrape of chairs, they stood, and Marco casually threw his arm over her shoulders as he led her from the café.

At that same moment, just metres away, Adam crossed the concourse and headed to JD Sports.

# Chapter Twenty-Five

I wasn't wrong about the panda eyes. Looking at myself in the age-spotted mirror above the sink in the teeny café toilet is not comforting. I'm pale and, as I suspected, the night's mascara and eyeliner are smudged around my bloodshot eyes.

I run the tap and splash water on my face. It's quite rejuvenating so I do it a few more times before drying my skin on some paper towels and scrubbing away the last of my make-up. It's tempting to just leave the toilet now, feeling refreshed and ready for breakfast, but I haven't gone out in public without make-up since I was fourteen, so I slap on the basics and brush my hair.

Feeling much more human, I squeeze back out of the little bathroom tucked under the stairs by the kitchen and head back into the café. It's a small, narrow building, with a serving counter at the back of the room, partially blocking the kitchen area. Scrubbed pine tables are dotted about with a variety of chairs and the deep green walls have been decorated with quotes written in an elaborate scrawl and framed black and white pictures of London. It's just the right side of quirky.

I re-join Adam at our table where blessedly there is already a steaming pot of tea, the waitress sticking to her word when she promised me the biggest pot they had. The fact that we had stood outside for ten minutes before they opened at six clearly told her I was serious.

Surprisingly, the little café is already quite busy, seemingly a popular haunt of cabbies and workmen looking for their breakfast fix. I'm not a fan of breakfast, usually only having a slice of toast or a banana as I can't stomach a proper meal first thing in the morning. Today is an exception, though, as I haven't been to bed, this just feels like a second dinner and I've gone for the full English. Adam did the same and I'm confident that his stomach is growling in anticipation like mine, now that the delectable smell of frying bacon is pervading the air.

He smiles as me warmly as I sit back down.

"Feel better?"

"Much, thanks." Although tiredness is making this all seem surreal again.

"It feels a bit weird to be sitting in a normal café, doesn't it?" he says, reading my mind. "Especially when it's still dark outside."

"Yeah, I have no idea what time it is, day it is, year it is," I reply, before taking a long sip of my tea with a small moan of satisfaction.

"I can feel my legs again, though, which is a bonus," Adam adds cheerfully.

Under normal circumstances, I'd probably find the café a bit cold as it's only just opened up and cooking and customers haven't had much chance to heat the air yet. However, to my frozen limbs, it's heaven.

We've taken off our ugly coats and they're currently taking up half of the room as they rest on the backs of our chairs. I've kept my scarf on though, and I'm gripping my mug tightly to absorb some of the heat into my chilled hands. Hopefully, a hot breakfast in my belly will help thaw me out.

As if summoned by my thoughts, the waitress appears with two steaming plates of joy and places them in front of us with a flourish.

"Enjoy, ducks," she says cheerfully before bustling away.

"Definitely a mama bear," I whisper to Adam as I smother my plate in ketchup.

He just smiles at me, his eyes twinkling. He doesn't need to say anything, I know he's pleased that I instigated our old game. We both tuck in.

"So, I've had an idea," says Adam, wiping up the remains of his egg yolk with some toast. I swallow my last mouthful before responding.

"Another one. You're full of them tonight, aren't you? Come on, then, what is it?"

"It's a surprise, but it's up to you. We could just head to the station, I think the trains have started running again."

"I've got time," I smile.

"Good," he smiles back, and our eyes hold for a moment. For once, I don't look away.

"Everything OK here, ducks?" The kindly waitress is back, breaking the moment to clear our plates. We both give our appreciation and Adam asks for the bill as I pour myself a final cup of tea.

"Where we're going doesn't have a loo, so you might want to have a tactical wee before we leave," Adam grins, nodding at the cup on its way to my lips.

"Of course." Like anyone needs to lecture me on tactical weeing. "It's not far though, is it? I don't think I can take much more walking."

"It is too far to walk in time. I thought we could jump in a taxi."

Bundled back up in our layers, we shuffle out into the cold, dark morning, just in time to see one of our fellow diners getting into his taxi and putting the light on. Adam jogs over and speaks to the driver through the window before waving at me to follow, which I do at a much slower pace. My legs feel heavy with exhaustion. I have no idea where Adam is getting his energy from.

He's holding the door open for me but before I get in, I take a deep breath in through my nose, sniffing the air appreciatively.

"It smells like snow," I say, getting into the cab and scooting over.

"Snow doesn't smell," Adam says, sliding in beside me.

"It does," I insist. "I swear the air smells a certain way just before it snows, like sharp and tangy and extra fresh, even here in a city."

"Hmm, I can't say I've ever noticed but the weathermen have predicted snow for Christmas Eve, so maybe you're right."

"Of course! It's Christmas Eve now, isn't it?"

"Yep, Happy Christmas. How do you feel about it now? Still hate it?"

"I don't know," I reply honestly. "It doesn't take a psychologist to realise that my hatred of Christmas has come from that one particularly awful time which I guess has made me bitter about the whole thing. But maybe I have thawed a bit. I mean, this night I've allowed myself to remember good Christmases too; things I did with my parents before they started hating each other. Things I did with you and your family, like the ice skating. I've sort of had that glimmer of Christmas feeling a few times tonight, I must admit."

"So, my de-Grinching has worked a bit then?"

"A little bit perhaps," I admit. "Why are you so bothered about whether or not I like Christmas, anyway?"

"I don't know. I guess because I always think of you at Christmas. You used to love it so much and the two Christmases we spent together were amazing. It just bothers me that you've lost the childlike joy about it that you used to have. Besides, everyone should love Christmas. I mean, ignore the over-commercialised, pressure side of things, which I agree with you about, by the way, and look at the positives. It's the one time of year where we all take the time to let the people that we care about know that we love them or are thankful for them. People spend time together as families, charities receive the bulk of their donations. Goodwill is a real thing, people are just friendlier, more caring. Anyway, imagine how miserable winter would be if we didn't have fairy lights and festive fun to brighten up the dark days of December."

I smile at him softly. It's not like I can argue with what he's saying and turn to look out of the window as the dark London streets pass by. Most windows are black still, but some have lights on, and some shops and cafés are starting to set up for the day. I see the snatches of life that I'm so fond of witnessing as we pass.

The taxi trundles over a bridge but I've no idea where we are going as, away from the central landmarks, my geographical knowledge of London gets a bit sketchy. We pass more houses and blocks of flats, fairy lights, Christmas trees and fake snow abound. As we halt at traffic lights, my eye is drawn to one window where two little girls, twins, I presume, are dancing around their lounge in elf pyjamas, fairy wands in their hands, their bouncy afros tamed into little matching pigtails. Faces alight with joy as they dance about, I swear I can almost hear them giggling. It's beautiful and I feel a little glow in my chest. As the taxi moves on, I crane my neck to continue watching them for as long as I can.

Shifting back around in my seat, I glance over at Adam who is staring out of his window too. I wonder what he is thinking about. Is he as enthralled by others' lives as I am or am I the unusual one?

"Just here's fine, thanks, mate," Adam suddenly says to the driver and we pull up on what seems to be a sort of high street, with an optician, a few cafés, a florist, hairdresser and various other businesses lining the road ahead of us.

Adam pays the driver, waving away my offer to contribute, and hustles me out of the taxi. Jeez, for a few moments, I'd forgotten how bloody cold it is.

"Where are we?"

"You'll see," Adam says mysteriously taking me by the hand and leading me down a dark alley between two tall, red-bricked buildings.

"OK, so this doesn't seem dodgy at all," I joke.

We reach the end of the alley and come up against a large metal gate. Adam taps something into a keypad set in the wall and the gate slides open to reveal a small, empty car park.

"I can't take it anymore: Where the hell are we?"

"My firm's London office," Adam laughs, tugging me into the car park as the gate starts to slide shut behind us.

"Are you telling me that we could have spent the last few hours in a warm office, with wi-fi and a kitchen and possibly a sofa?" I shriek, although mainly for show, as I don't really care.

"No," Adam shushes me. "I know the access code to the car park but because this isn't my actual office, I don't have keys to the building."

"So, what are we doing here?"

"You'll see," he replies cagily.

The concrete of the car park is covered by a glittering layer of frost and our feet leave imprints as we skirt the building. I watch bewildered as Adam drags a Biffa bin from the corner of the car park up to the building wall and starts climbing on it. If he thinks I'm about to do that too, he's mistaken. But suddenly all becomes clear as he pulls a clanking metal ladder down from the fire escape. It slides along runners and hits the ground with a loud clang.

Adam steps off the top of the bin and swings onto the ladder.

"Are you coming?" he asks over his shoulder.

Thoroughly intrigued, I grip tightly to the metal rungs, cold even through my gloves, and nervously follow him up to the first little balcony. Fortunately, all the other steps are narrow but fixed, so I feel a bit safer than I did on the ladder as we crisscross our way up the side of the building.

"This is just like buildings you see in New York in films. I didn't know these sort of fire escapes existed over here," I exclaim.

"I can give you a lecture on the links between the architecture of New York and London, if you like?" Adam's disembodied voice floats down to me from the next floor.

"No, you're OK, thanks," I call back.

Soon Adam is helping me over a brick wall onto a larger, more solid, balcony recessed into the roof. It's bare, except for a narrow metal bin in the corner and a blank, dark green door leading into the building.

"Most people come out here to smoke, well, vape now mainly, but I brought you here for the view."

I turn around and look out over the rooftops, to the black snake of the Thames winding its way through glittering skyscrapers. I can see the top of the Wheel, the Shard, the Gherkin. London is waking up and there are more lights than there were a few hours ago. The whole city twinkles festively like a swathe of giant fairy lights. In the distance, behind Tower Bridge, the faint flush of dawn is stealing over the horizon, causing that corner of the sky to glow faintly.

"I thought you'd like to see the dawn rise on a new day, a new Christmas," Adam says gently. I don't reply, I just take his hand in mine as we stand together against the wall, the city at our feet.

And then I feel the first snowflake hit my nose.

"See, I told you I smelt snow," I say triumphantly as more flakes start to cascade around us.

"Do you want to leave?" Adam asks.

"No, thanks, I'd love to see the sunrise."

With pure white snowflakes slowly dancing around us, we silently watch the sky brighten and the thick clouds turn pink and gold as the dawn streaks across the sky. It's magical and perfect and so Christmassy.

Adam keeps joking about it, but I do feel like The Grinch now; that bit where his heart grows three sizes. I can finally feel it, that joy and sense of love and possibility that I always used to feel at this time of year. I never thought I'd feel it again, but here it is, spreading through my chest and warming my soul.

The snow is starting to settle, coating everything in a fine white powder. I know that, once we're down on the streets, it will quickly be turned into dirty slush but, up here, I can see the London of Dickens' novels.

"OK, you win," I whisper, not taking my eyes from the view. "Christmas can be wonderful."

"Hold on, I'm not done yet."

Adam fiddles with his phone and then pops it back in his coat pocket just as the first strains of a brass band playing, *In the Bleak Midwinter* start pouring from the little speaker. Despite being slightly muffled by the fabric of his coat, it sounds beautiful.

"This is my favourite carol," I murmur, choked with emotion.

"I know, I mean, I remember," Adam says, holding his arms out. I step into his embrace and we start to dance. The snow is falling more heavily now, big fat snowdrops, which stick to my eyelashes and tickle my cheeks. Our steps slow and we draw closer together as if pulled by an invisible force. Eyes locked, I wrap my arms around his neck and then his lips are on mine.

At first, our lips just brush gently a few times and then my knees actually weaken as he pulls me closer and deepens the kiss. It's so achingly, beautifully familiar and yet so sexy and exciting at the same time. My head is in a whirl and I feel like I'm floating along with the snowflakes that swirl around us.

I can feel all my control slipping as I sink into his kiss, into him, my body turning to liquid and my heart pounding in my chest.

Then suddenly the music stops, and a shrill ringing pierces the air. We break apart, both breathing heavily. I don't look at Adam, just turn and walk over to the wall on trembling legs, leaving him to answer his phone.

I can tell he's moved into the more sheltered corner of the balcony to answer the phone, his deep vibrato carrying on the air, despite the softness of the tone. I try to tune out of what he's saying and look out at the view instead.

It suddenly doesn't look as magical and sparkly though, the grey clouds without the glow of dawn to brighten them feel heavy and oppressive as they spit out the swirling blizzard. It's hard to make out the other side of the river now, everything is looking bleak, grey and hazy. I start to shiver and pull my scarf up around my face, burying my hands in my pockets.

To say that I feel unsettled would be an understatement. What the hell was I doing kissing him like that? Yes, it felt amazing, delicious, perfect but I'm sure that's what coeliacs say about tasting chocolate cake just before it makes them ill.

I've been seduced by Christmas and all it stands for and coupled with lack of sleep, it's making me behave out of character and, frankly, like an idiot. It can't happen again. I'm so glad we've had this night and reconnected and put the past to bed, but I can't let myself get sucked in by him again. I can't lose myself again.

Whoever came up with the saying "It's better to have loved and lost than never to have loved at all" was talking bollocks. I think it was Shakespeare, but he clearly didn't know what he was talking about. Really loving someone and losing them is just awful. I'd much rather never have known love. All the failed relationships I've had since Adam and none of them destroyed me, ate me up and spat me out.

It took me years to create a decent life for myself and now Adam's back in it again. I know what happened before wasn't his fault, it wasn't his fault at all that my life blew apart. But the fact is that he has the power to hurt me more than anyone else in the world.

What if we get close again and it goes wrong? What if I start to rely on having him in my life again and then lose him? If that phenomenal kiss is anything to go by, it seems like we're heading down a path towards a relationship, but I don't think I can take that risk. I don't trust myself not to screw it up again, then what would happen? Besides, could he ever properly love me again after what I did? How could he?

The stakes are just too high and I've never been a gambler. I don't want to never see Adam again, not now, but I need to tread carefully. I need to keep him at arm's length until I can work out how to have a friendship with him and still protect myself.

"That was my mum," Adam says, joining me at the wall. "They're going to come and pick me up, she insisted. She said they'll give you a lift anywhere you need to go."

"She knows it's me?" I baulk.

"Yes, I told her straight away, didn't you hear?"

"I wasn't listening."

"Oh, well, I said we met up and have been hanging out and that we had a great night and I'd tell her more later."

"And she'd be OK with seeing me again, after what I did?" I choke out over the lump in my throat. Typical of Karen, still trying to mother me even after all this time and make sure I get home, despite what I've done.

"She always insisted that there was more to it than you just dumping me out of the blue," Adam says softly. "She decided that you'd done it to be noble, that you thought you'd be holding me back if we stayed together. It was a valid theory, given how little you always thought of yourself. She felt better for believing that, anyway. I never told her about seeing your dad."

I don't know how to respond to that, so I just don't. But I do know that I'm not ready to see Karen and Dan again.

"Don't worry about it, I'm happy getting the train," I blurt out instead of acknowledging what he said.

"But why? We could easily drop you at your dad's in Cirencester?"

"I'm just not ready to see your parents, OK?" I snap, and before he has a chance to respond, I continue, "We'd better get down from here. The snow is going to make getting out of London even trickier."

# Chapter Twenty-six

By the time we emerge from the Tube station, the snow has stopped falling and is already turning to brown slush on the streets and pavements. Hopefully, it means the trains will still be able to run.

We were quiet on the Tube ride over. I was able to get a seat while Adam stood chivalrously, and all my energy went into not being lulled to sleep by the hypnotic swaying of the carriages. As we weave our way out of the station, the streets, while busy, aren't as crazy as I'd expected them to be. I suspect that local Londoners are keeping to their districts until the city is empty of stranded train goers like us.

We walk side by side as Adam once again confidently leads the way to the twenty-four-hour shop where our stuff is stored. Even though the snow has stopped, the air is still bitterly cold. My gloves got soaked climbing down the snow-covered fire escape and I've had to take them off, making do with thrusting my hands deep into my pockets to keep them warm.

This has the bonus of stopping Adam from being able to hold my hand which I'm worried he would do if my hands were swinging freely by my sides. And that is the sort of thing I need to stop. I have to start putting some distance between us again, both physically and mentally.

Either he's regretting the kiss too or has sensed my discomfort, or maybe he's just really knackered, because he is being uncharacteristically quiet as we pound the streets once more.

The bright fluorescent lights sting my tired eyes as we enter the shop, so harsh after the muted winter sky outside. I stand back and allow Adam to sort out the paperwork, make polite conversation with the shopkeeper and retrieve our bags from the locker. I can't believe it was a mere twelve hours ago that I stood in this spot, it feels like days have passed.

Once back outside, I pop my heels into my handbag, where they just about fit if I don't zip it up, and I quickly slip into my trusty leather jacket. I hate getting all hot and flustered on crammed buses and trains, it's worse than being cold. The gold monstrosity is just too huge and puffy to wear while navigating London's transport services. I roll it up into a ball and stuff it back into the large brown Primark bag but it's so huge it barely fits, the arms spilling out over the top.

"I thought you'd want to chuck that straight in the bin," Adam observes.

"Nah, I've grown weirdly attached to it. Plus, you never know when a giant, ugly coat might come in handy. Or, you know, I might give it to this homeless charity I know of in Bristol."

Adam just smiles but it doesn't quite reach his eyes. I wonder what he's thinking. I've noticed he's stayed in his giant bogey coat, choosing to put the rest of his belongings into the rucksack.

"I just realised; I haven't asked where you're meeting your parents?"

"Hillingdon. I can get there on the Underground and it's just off the M40 for my folks. Saves them trying to drive right into the city."

"Which line is it on?" I ask as we start heading back towards Oxford Circus.

"I don't know but I'm sure I'll be able to get there from Paddington."

We lapse back into loaded silence as we wind our way to Oxford Street. The morning is well underway and it's positively thronging with people as usual. The traffic crawls past us, pushing the dirty, slushy snow further into the gutters, the ubiquitous red London double-decker buses dotting the road under the arches of Christmas lights. It's like a different place from the quiet street we walked along last night, marvelling at the architecture.

Within minutes we're descending the stone stairs into the Underground, leaving the lights of the city behind us. I feel a slight pang of dismay that I won't see London in its festive glory again until next year, if then. Something that wouldn't have bothered me one little bit twenty-four hours ago.

It's less crowded down here and like a typical tourist, I gravitate straight to the large Tube map on the wall to double-check what line I need and how many stops. Adam stands close behind me; I'm aware of his firm chest against my back and his breath on my hair. I can feel myself start to tremble at his proximity. Damn it.

"Where's Hillingdon?" I croak.

Adam points at the map, his arm over my shoulder pressing closer to me as he does so. I'm so physically aware of him it almost hurts. I could just turn my head a fraction and take his mouth with mine. It would be so easy and feel so wonderful. For a moment.

Is this how my mum feels about wine? But she's just unable to fight that pull, that yearning. Even knowing how she'll feel afterwards, the damage it's doing, that in the long term it's bad for her, she just can't resist that first magical taste. But I'm stronger than her. I can resist. I understand how much relenting could damage me.

I obstinately step slightly away from him under the pretence of scrutinising the map, although now I'm so close to it, it's actually hard to see where all the lines are going.

"It looks like you need the Piccadilly line," I say, tracing it with my finger, "so you're best off getting on the Victoria line from here and changing at Green Park, then you won't have to change again."

"Yeah."

"So, we're going in opposite directions."

"Yes, but I don't mind going with you to Paddington to make sure everything is OK first. It'll just mean a few more changes, that's all."

"By about six. Look, I'm a big girl, I can get the Tube to Paddington on my own," I say crossly, stepping around him so that I'm not as boxed in and there's a bit of space between us again.

"I know you can," he replies quietly. "I just..." he shrugs. I know what he means, he doesn't want it to be over. But it is. It's a new day and the world is back to normal, so we need to be too.

"I appreciate it," I say a bit more gently, "but you'll be late meeting your parents if you go so far out of your way and I'm sure your mum has a busy day planned."

"You're right," he sighs. "They need to pick up my gran too." As he says this he hasn't moved, just stood watching me intently. I'm starting to feel uncomfortable under his focused gaze. It reminds me of the few times I caught him looking at me sternly earlier in the night.

"OK then," I mutter, looking everywhere but at him. People are scurrying antlike towards the ticket barriers, all moving with purpose. There don't seem to be any tourists wandering unsurely; we're the only ones standing still on the edge of the cavernous chamber, barely being glanced at. I direct my gaze back to Adam; he's still watching me intently.

"I guess this is goodbye then?" I say lightly.

"Is it?" He steps towards me so there are only a couple of feet between us. I manage to stop myself stepping back like we're in some weird tango. He's clearly expecting a response but I just shrug, feeling intensely uncomfortable. What does he want me to say?

"When can I see you again?" he asks, softly, reaching out to take my hand. His arm pauses in mid-air as he realises that I'm laden down with my folder and Primark bag and don't have a free hand. I wonder if I did that subconsciously;

I could have held them in the same hand. I think I'm using my baggage as barriers to intimacy. Appropriate really.

"I don't know," I mutter, looking at my feet. Man, my fake Uggs are wrecked; I knew they wouldn't last long.

"Rose, look at me."

I raise my head and determinedly look him straight in the eyes, ignoring the fluttering in my belly.

"Can I please see you again?"

"Yeah, I guess, maybe, in the New Year. Maybe we could meet up again for a drink or something?"

"For a drink or something?' he repeats incredulously. 'That's it?"

"So what do you want?" Christ, I'm behaving like a teenager, but I can't seem to help myself.

"I want you," he says simply, knocking the wind out of me.

He steps closer to me, cupping my face in his hands, his eyes locking onto mine.

"I want to be with you. I want to be us again."

His face tilts towards mine and I know he's going to kiss me. In that split second my body erupts into a fierce internal battle. The feelings-led part of me is desperate to be kissed by him again, to sink into him, to be wrapped in his embrace. But the sensible, intelligent part of me is screaming no, it's too dangerous, get out! For the first time since last night the sensible part of my brain wins, and I step back out of reach.

"We can't," I say firmly.

"What do you mean we can't? Why not?"

"It's not a good idea."

"What? Why? We used to be great together."

"Yes, we used to be, but that was a long time ago. We've both grown-up, we're different people now. We have no idea whether we're compatible any longer."

"But, last night—"

"Yes, last night was amazing," I cut him off, "and I'm so glad we had that time together to sort things out and hopefully we can stay in touch this time, but that's it."

"This is bullshit," he mutters fiercely. "Last night wasn't just about catching up and sorting things out. It's still there, that chemistry between us, I know you felt it too."

"I'm sorry, I shouldn't have kissed you, it was a mistake. Blame Christmas if you want; I was seduced by it all."

"Bollocks. Lie to yourself if you want, but you can't lie to me, I know you, remember? I think you're just scared."

It's strange seeing him angry, it's so rare, he always used to be so unflappable. Proof of what I've been trying to say— we're different people now. I straighten my shoulders and glare at him. I'm not a little girl anymore, I'm a grown-ass woman and I can hold my ground. I say nothing and just look at him as coolly as possible.

"Don't you want to be happy?" he asks, suddenly gentle..

And at that, something in me snaps and I'm overcome by what can only be described as a feeling of pure rage, white-hot and burning.

"How dare you?" I hiss. "How dare you presume I'm not happy. You don't know me anymore, not really. You knew who I was, not who I am. I've spent years moving on, growing up. I've got a gorgeous house, which I own myself, a fabulous job and I'm about to become a published author too. What, you think I've spent the last decade and more just moping around, waiting for a white knight to come and save me? Well, you're wrong. I don't need you, or anyone else, to be happy. I moved on." I'm surprised that steam isn't actually coming out of my ears like in cartoons.

"Good for you," Adam yells suddenly, his voice echoing slightly around the cavernous station and causing a few, less hardcore, Londoners to glance over at us. "But I haven't. I thought about you all the time, wondered where you were, if you were OK. Every girlfriend I had I couldn't help but compare to you and none of them ever measured up. I never felt as complete, as whole, as I did when we were together. And I told myself I was looking back on it with rose-tinted glasses, that it was just puppy love. But then last night, I felt it again, that connection, that sense of completeness. I love you, Rose, I always have."

"But how could you?" I whisper, stunned.

"Because I know you, the real you. And yes, I don't know exactly what you've been up to in the last decade or so, but I know who you are, I know that person you are inside and that's what matters. And I love her." He steps towards me again, taking my wrists. I look down to where his strong, manly, fingers are wrapped around my pale skin, I'm gripping so tightly onto the handles of my bags that my knuckles are almost blue.

I wish I could accept what he's saying, but it's all too much. I can't process it. I can't believe it. How could he possibly love me? It makes no sense. I can feel the panic building, the dread in my shoulders, the weight on my chest. I need to leave. Now.

"I'm sorry," I say, tears springing into my eyes, "but I can't do this." I pull away again and start backing towards the ticket barriers, fumbling as I search in my handbag for my debit card. "I meant it about staying in touch though. I'll email you in the New Year or something."

And then, leaving Adam, the only man I've ever loved, standing statue-like, staring at me as strangers swarm around him, I turn and flee. I push my way through the ticket barriers, blinking away tears and join the masses heading to the platforms. I fight all my instincts to turn and get one more look of him. But as I descend into the depths of the Underground, I don't need to. The image of him standing there is burnt into my retinas, like when you look too long at a bright light and you can still see it when you turn away.

# Chapter Twenty-Seven

## Christmas Eve

For the first time in my life, I have a surly, uncommunicative taxi driver and typically, having previously always wished for one who didn't want to pass on his political feelings or make banal small talk, I feel a little disappointed. I expected lots of questions about my night in London. What happened is splashed over all the papers, radio and TV and is clearly big news, but when I mentioned that I'd got back from London as I climbed into the taxi, all I got was a grunt of acknowledgement. He didn't even ask where I was going, just waited for me to give my address. I actually would have liked to talk about it all with a complete stranger. The further the train got from London, the more it all felt like a weird dream.

I'm at that point of tiredness now where I feel strangely wired and jittery. Although that may partly be due to all the coffee that I've drunk, as well as the lack of sleep. I have to hand it to the transport authorities, they were so well organised, corralling people onto trains or towards coaches with manic efficiency. I only had to wait for an hour until I could board a train, but in that time, I sank two large coffees and rounded things off with a pain au chocolat just for something to do. It's not my fault; I was in line right by The Upper Crust and it smelt too good.

The taxi swings into my street.

"Just here is fine, thanks."

The taxi driver almost imperceptibly tilts his head which I take to be a nod, and the car glides to a stop a few metres from my front door. I swipe my debit card, ignoring the price (getting a taxi felt quite decadent as I live a decent way from the station, but I just didn't have it in me to use public transport as I usually would) and wearily climb out of the car. I've barely shut the door when the driver is off with a blast of exhaust fumes. I think I've found someone even less festive than me.

Making my way to my front door, I stop and look around the street. It's a quiet, Victorian terrace. The houses, all bay windowed, are a mixture of painted, pebble-dashed or the original Victorian red brick. However, the one thing they all have in common is the Christmas decorations. Some have kept it simple with a wreath on the door and a tree in the bay windows, others have strung lights from the roof or wrapped them around the front wall. Some have gone to town and have every possible part of the exterior festooned with lights and tinsel. Mine is, in fact, the only house on the road without a glimmer of Christmas cheer. I still think whoever the anonymous neighbour was who dropped me a note asking me to make an effort was out of order, but I have to admit that my lovely house does look a bit sad. Like the kid in school whose parents forgot that it was a non-uniform day.

I suppose it wouldn't hurt to make my house a bit festive. I always put a pumpkin out on Halloween for trick or treaters and I love seeing the happy little faces of neighbourhood witches, ghosts and frequently spidermen as they ring on my doorbell for treats. Why not make the effort for Christmas too?

Stepping through the front door, I wait for the welcome rush of being home to envelop me. But it doesn't. The house is freezing as I don't have the heating on a timer. It's a cute little house and heats up relatively quickly, especially when I light the fire.

I dump my bags in the hall and slide my boots off, smiling at how wrecked they are. I carry them through the open plan lounge and kitchen and dump them next to the bin outside the back door. In one fluid motion, I flick the kettle on and crank the thermostat up on the wall.

Crossing back into the lounge area, turning on lamps as I go to bring some visual warmth into the room, I kneel down by the fire and light it. Luckily, the perfectionist in me always has a stack of logs and firelighters in the grate ready to go.

I lean back onto my heels and watch the flames start to lick around the logs as the firelighters do their job. In no time, the flames have spread and the fire is raging merrily giving out that comforting smell of woodsmoke that you can only get from a real log fire.

I stand up and look around. The house definitely feels a little more welcoming with the fire crackling in the grate and soft, warm light spilling from the lamps.

I know I'm biased but it is a beautiful room. From the first moment I saw the house, I fell in love with the stripped original floorboards and the exposed brick fireplace. I've made it my own with splurges of rich dark blues on the alcove walls and sofas to stop the white everywhere else from looking too stark. Dotted around are large house plants and, of course, some of my favourite art on the walls.

Naturally, I keep the place spotlessly tidy and friends often remark that it looks like a house out of a catalogue. I always took that as a compliment but today I'm not so sure; do they mean it looks too false, not lived in enough? No heart? Come to think of it, I don't have one single photo on the walls or anything that would suggest that I live here. It could well be a rental house.

Why am I thinking so negatively? Where has all this come from? I love my little house. It's just 'cos I'm tired and edgy. But standing here now, I don't know what to do. I dare not give in to the sleep that my body so desperately craves as it will screw my body clock up even more. A bit like with jet lag, I'm convinced that I just need to power through and then go to bed this evening, just really early this evening.

I stand, floundering for a few minutes. Should I go for a walk? No, too exhausted for that. It's Christmas Eve, all my friends will be busy. I look around the room for inspiration. Of course, Christmas decorations. I can get some for the front and actually it wouldn't kill me to put a few bits up in here too.

I'm almost at the garden centre when I realise that I maybe shouldn't be driving. Is there a rule about driving on only one hour's sleep? If there isn't, there should be. I just couldn't face trudging to a shopping centre and ladening myself down with bags to struggle home with. There's a garden centre a few miles away that I visited with Dad and Jayne once. It's one of those huge places that sells everything so I'm sure they'll have decorations, and I can just park in the car park and load up my car.

I wonder what Adam is doing now. Nope, can't do that. I can't think about him. I spent a very cramped train journey managing not to think about him, I'm not going to start now. Instead, I pop the radio on. It's so rare that I use the radio on my little Clio that I don't have any stations programmed in. When I'm driving to work, I usually listen to music using my phone, but that would involve choosing an album or a playlist or an artist and I just don't feel mentally capable of making any such decisions right now.

I press the search button until it finds Radio Two and I don't bother changing it when unsurprisingly a Christmas song comes on. Instead, I sing away to the Seventies Christmas rock at the top of my voice. How do I still know these words? I haven't consciously listened to this song in years. Maybe these songs have all been played so much, every Christmas, for so long, that they are just living in our collective subconscious now. I wouldn't be surprised if babies are born with the chorus to this song just sitting idle in their brain from a form of mental osmosis, ready to pop out the minute they can talk. A bit like how they grow knees.

Between the cheesy song sing-along, the quiet roads and my over-tired, careful focus I manage to get to the garden centre in one piece and more importantly without thinking about Adam or last night. Car journeys are usually the worst for thinking about stuff that you don't want to think about.

I'm greeted at the entrance by a life-size, mechanical, singing Santa and a lot of fake snow made from bubbles which are blowing out from a machine above the door. The whole centre is covered with tinsel and fairy lights.

Usually, I would have grimaced and tutted at the tacky, garish display but instead, I notice the faces of the brother and sister who are giggling and chasing 'snow' and dancing to the singing Santa, while their parents watch fondly.

I stand to one side watching them for a moment, their joy is so infectious that I can't help smiling, despite the bubbles tickling my nose. I can't believe that, in just one night, my attitude to Christmas can have changed so dramatically. Last year, I'd have barrelled past this little scene, head down, refusing to acknowledge it. Not that I'd have been shopping on Christmas Eve anyway, I'd have sat in my studio, working, out of belligerence or to make some sort of point to God knows whom.

I'm not going to do a Scrooge and start giving out presents and buying giant turkeys or anything, but I have found the joy in Christmas again. I feel like the whole experience with Adam, even freaking out and crying so much, did end up being cathartic. The bitter cloud that I always carried around with me at this time of year has dissipated. Boxing Day will always be a little sad for me, but I can't let that turn me into someone sour and cynical anymore.

It's not like my Christmas Day will be particularly exciting: dinner with Dad and Jayne after a guilt visit to Mum, and charades with Jayne's daughter and her family, but actually it is always a nice day. Jayne's family have always been so welcoming and I've always kept them at arm's length. I don't know why. It's like I refused to even let myself enjoy the day, so convinced I was that Christmas was rubbish that my sucky attitude caused it to be so.

Adam was right, imagine December without Christmas? Without all the lights and good cheer and people giving each other friendly greetings. It would be so miserable. And besides, look at the joy on the kids' faces, that's what Christmas is about. Bringing joy as and where you can.

Feeling determined to keep my new positive attitude, I grab a trolley and stroll into the store, not even bothering to protect my hair from the bubble-snow. One of the staff, dressed as an elf, is handing out mince pies to customers and I take one gratefully. It's still warm and the pastry crumbles deliciously in my mouth, the tangy filling so quintessentially Christmassy. Trying not to make too much mess, I continue munching as I head towards the decorations area.

It's huge! Rows upon rows of decorations all displayed in different sections according to colour. At the end of each aisle stands a fully decorated Christmas tree. I take my time mooching around, examining the different baubles and trinkets from the artful, hand-blown glass ones that seem to glow when I hold them up to the light, to the tacky, plastic Santas and cartoon reindeer. Along with boxes of baubles in all sizes and colours, they have trays part-filled with delicate, glittering snowflakes, bright, shiny stars, little nativity figures made of wood, and robins and snowmen and candy canes.

One aisle is dedicated to displays of mini-houses, churches and railway tracks with little steam trains, all dusted with fake snow. It makes me think of the display I

213

saw with Adam which prompted our night together. Although, from what he's said, I think the talk of Christmas was just a handy excuse and he'd have tried to find some way of us spending time together anyway. Does he really love me? I shake my head and push the thoughts away, refocusing on my mission.

I spend ages examining all the different wreaths that they sell before settling on a very realistic looking fake one, covered in pinecones and tartan ribbon with fairy lights embedded in it. That'll look nice on my front door. I grab a few boxes of fairy lights from their depleted shelves in the lighting section and then go back to the wreaths section and pick up a garland that I'd seen and rejected at first. Like the wreath, it has lights in among the fake pine needles but is also covered in little silver, glittery baubles. It will look lovely on my mantelpiece. I'm going for things I can just chuck up with little effort. I may have had a mini epiphany, but I don't want to spend hours on this stuff.

I'm about to go to the tills when I pass through the forest of fake Christmas trees. They range from a foot high, to giant-like proportions. Some look real, some are silver or white. Some come covered in fake snow. I suppose a little tree could look quite nice in my bay window.

I choose a three-foot-high dark green one, with a dusting of fake snow on the tips of the branches. Then I swing back to the baubles section, selecting a box of small, silver ones and a box that contains a mixture of balls in an array of blue shades.

Finally satisfied with my selections I push my laden trolley towards the tills, humming along to the carols being piped out from hidden speakers around the building.

Once home I do admit to feeling a bit of giddy delight at the thought of decorating my little house so that it can shine like the rest. The heating and the now dwindled fire have done

214

their job and the place is toasty warm when I step inside. It feels ever so quiet though.

"Alexa, play some Christmas carols," I instruct loudly into the silent space.

"Playing Christmas carols," replies the artificial voice.

"Well, you can't decorate a house without carols, can you?" I say out loud, not that I'm expecting an answer.

I have a fun half an hour setting up the garland along the mantelpiece, stringing fairy lights up my stairs and setting up and decorating the Christmas tree, making sure that everything is just so. I have a cup of tea on the go and sing along to the carols that I know.

I allow myself to remember Christmases when I was a kid and how I'd go with Dad to choose a tree and then decorate it with Mum, although she always insisted on the cheesy pop tunes rather than carols. I also allow myself to remember decorating Adam's house with his family and how, like most of their events, Karen would get her disco light out and it would end up in a living room dance party.

For once, despite the mild melancholy it's nice to remember the good times. It's ridiculous really, now that I think about it. I'm so bloody stubborn that I refused to let myself think of any of that stuff before. Or join in with Christmas in any way. I did the mental equivalent of putting my fingers in my ears and shouting 'lalala'.

Finally, I go out to my front door and hang the wreath on the knocker, making sure that the lights are switched on. Then I cross the road to admire my handiwork. The tree, which I'd placed on my coffee table in the bay window, twinkles merrily and the wreath looks nice too, brightening up my dark blue front door. I've still got the original brick façade on my house and I'm glad I went for the more traditional green tree, rather than silver, as it looks nice against the brickwork. Maybe next year I'll put some lights up around the roof like some of my neighbours have done.

Before crossing back, I take a deep sniff of the air. It smells like snow again, even more noticeably in the clearer air of the Bristol suburbs than this morning in London. I look up and sure enough, thick, heavy clouds cover the sky, hiding any blue. I'm sure it's going to snow.

I skip back across the road and into the house, shivering as I lock the door behind me. A wave of exhaustion washes over me. I check the clock in the hall; it's just coming up to three o'clock. Is that all? If feels like it should be at least eight! Just a few more hours and I can go to bed. I allow myself a moment to imagine slipping under the soft duvet and snuggling against the pillow.

The huge breakfast I had, along with a couple of snacks, has seen me through the day but I'm feeling a bit peckish now so, after re-lighting the fire, I make myself a mug of soup and settle down on my sofa, flicking the TV on. I'm sure there'll be some action-packed film on Netflix that I haven't seen yet and will keep my attention.

# Chapter Twenty-Eight

## Christmas Day

The room is eerily dark when I wake up, except for the twinkling of the Christmas lights in the window and over the fireplace. I shiver slightly, the fire having long since died out. Pushing myself up from my slumped position on the sofa, I look at the clock on the wall in the dim light. It's four o'clock in the morning. I can only remember the first twenty minutes of the film that I put on, which means I've been asleep for about twelve hours. How on earth did I sleep on the sofa for twelve hours straight? I must've been more tired than I realised. I guess the days of being able to pull an all-nighter and still function are behind me. It's strangely light outside for so early in the morning, though.

I stagger to my feet, feeling thoroughly out of sorts and pad over to the window. Sure enough, the whole street is covered in a blanket of pure, white snow, reflecting the streetlights and brightening the navy sky. Fat snowflakes are falling lazily from the sky as if the clouds are giving up and this is their last, half-hearted effort. It's beautiful and I feel the sense of childlike wonder deep in my chest as I stare out at the silent, still, frozen night.

I wonder if any other households are awake yet. I wonder how many excitable children have woken up their parents this early, desperate to know if Santa has been. Would parents play along and just get up despite the time, or send their children back to bed for a few more hours?

Well, there's no point going back to bed for me now. Besides, I feel gross. I'm still in the same clothes that I wore to London nearly forty-eight hours ago. I'll have a shower and then go for a walk and enjoy the snow before it all gets ruined.

The heat of the shower feels amazing and I take my time, washing my hair and cleansing London off my skin. I wish it was as easy to cleanse my mind, though.

I can't stop thinking of Adam, picturing his face, hearing his laugh, the rich timbre of his voice. Every time I try not to think of him, images from our night together play like a montage in my mind. On the one hand, it's novel to be trying to ignore new thoughts and memories of him rather than the old memories that would randomly resurface and catch me unawares sometimes. However, these super HD images are harder to shrug off and ignore.

I somehow managed to ignore them yesterday, for the most part. Possibly because I was so exhausted my brain could only concentrate on whatever task I was doing. Now though, after a long sleep, fuelled by dreams of him, my brain is firing on all cylinders and I can't power it down. As the water rushes over my face, I shut my eyes and give in to it. I allow myself to remember every second of our kiss and how wonderful it felt. Why was I so desperate for it not to happen again?

The sense of fear and panic that I felt after we kissed has diminished and is slowly being replaced by a feeling of such acute, agonising longing. Obviously, I'm aware of the term 'yearning' but I've never understood it before, never felt it. Now though, I realise that is exactly what I'm feeling. Every cell in my body is yearning to be near him, to touch him, to talk with him.

As I turn off the water and step out onto the shower mat, a wave of dread washes over me again. But this isn't like before, it's not a fear of what could happen, it's a fear that I may have really fucked up.

I swiftly dress in jeans and a soft polo neck jumper and go through the motions of blow-drying my hair on autopilot, my mind in a constant whirr as I try to untangle my knotted emotions.

Then, going purely on instinct, I climb the stairs into the loft conversion which I use as my studio. To make up for a lack of loft storage space, large cupboards have been built into the eaves which house suitcases, boxes of old drawings and my art folders from college and Uni. But not much else, thanks to my fastidiousness and inability to hoard anything. Except for one plastic box, tucked right up into the corner of the space. I've carried it through all my house moves, always tucking it away, out of sight, on top of a wardrobe or in a barely used cupboard somewhere. But I've never opened it, not since I packed it away over a decade ago.

The stars are shining brightly in the inky patches of sky that I can see through gaps in the snow which has settled on the skylights. The clouds have finally given up and disappeared. It feels a bit like a secret den up here, under the snow and the stars. I can't bring myself to turn on the main light and ruin it, so I just switch on my small desk lamp.

I find the box easily and drag it out, dust motes floating in the dim light. The brittle plastic lid opens with a pop and I gingerly start lifting out the items inside: a small jewellery box containing the silver necklace which Adam bought me for my seventeenth birthday and I wore every day right up until that awful time. The hoody that I accidentally stole from his flat that fateful night and didn't realise I was still wearing until later that day but couldn't bear to throw away. I pull off my jumper and slip his on. It's not as baggy on me as it used to be but it still fits. His scent is gone, though, and it's a bit musty. I keep it on.

Removing the hoody from the box revealed a treasure trove of stuff. Some of it is silly bits of tat from days out that we took and some of it gifts he gave me over the years. There are piles of cinema tickets and concert tickets and receipts from every date we ever went on. I look at each one and allow myself to remember, when I can.

Finally, at the bottom, underneath the teeny boppers from our first Christmas together, is my Adam photo album. A plain, burgundy photo album over which I'd written our names in black permanent pen using swirly, romantic, writing. I'd forgotten that I'd done that silly, childish, sentimental thing, quite out of character for me, even then. It shows how smitten I was.

Feeling strangely nervous, I flip the album open and start flicking through. It follows our relationship from early days through to the day he left for Uni. I still remember his dad taking the photo of us outside his Halls; despite my smile, you can see the sadness in my eyes. Looking closely, I realise Adam has the same expression. We're holding each other tightly, our bodies turned in towards each other, clearly so besotted, clearly so loath to say goodbye.

I start at the beginning again and slowly this time examine each photo as the months pass and our faces change and my hair goes through every colour of the rainbow. But I don't see any of that, I see the expression on my face, the happiness radiating from it in every picture. Even ones where I'm pretending to pout at something, there is a clear twinkle in my eye. I see the way that we look at each other, the adoration in our eyes. It's there in Adam's too.

I'd always assumed that I loved him more than he loved me. I could never quite believe that he could feel the same way that I did. That I was deserving of the same level of love and devotion. Was that why I was so quick to believe that he'd met someone else? Was that why I was so quick to dismiss the thought of a relationship with him again? All that therapy I had and I'm still following the same patterns that I did as a teenager, believing I'm not worthy of being loved, that I'm somehow broken.

I think back to his last words to me at the train station yesterday. He said he loved me and always had. And I still didn't believe him. What the hell is wrong with me? Why didn't I leap into his arms right then? Instead, I ran, like I always do. I'm so scared of being hurt, of opening my heart again that I closed it off, shut it down. But I know that Adam would never hurt me, he'd never hurt anyone. And, if I'm honest with myself, I know that he isn't the sort of person to say 'I love you' unless he truly means it.

God, I'm an idiot. He loves me. And I love him. Of course I bloody do. I've always loved him. Even when I hated him, even when I was thoroughly broken, I still loved him. I got all stroppy because he accused me of not being happy but is that because he hit a nerve? Am I actually happy? I'm content. I have a nice life, it's pleasant. But I look at the face of the girl in these pictures and I never feel happiness like that anymore. I don't feel pure unadulterated joy. I haven't since I lost so much all those years ago. I've never felt happiness like I did back then.

I want to feel that way again. I want to laugh till my sides hurt. I want to dance with abandon. I want to have amazing sex. And I want to cuddle all night long. I want to have someone I can turn to and rely on when I'm fed up with being strong. I want to share my life with someone special, someone I can be myself with, my true self, without wondering if I'm good enough. I want to love and be loved with all my soul.

I want Adam.

I grab the teeny boppers and, uncharacteristically leaving the contents of the box strewn around the floor, dart down the stairs. Adrenaline coursing through me, I hurry into the kitchen and rummage in my 'everything drawer' for batteries. With trembling hands, I take the old ones out of the teeny boppers and replace them. I flick the switch and do a little skip of joy when the lights come on.

Still trembling, I dash to the hall and yank the hideous gold coat, that I'm now very fond of, out of its bag and rustle myself into it. Then I stuff the teeny boppers along with a hat and gloves into my handbag, shove on my flat boots and grab my car keys.

I crunch my way down the path and out onto the street and then stop. I need to calm down. There's no need to rush; it's five in the morning; he's not going anywhere.

I take a deep breath and take in my surroundings. Once again, I feel like the world has paused and I'm the only one awake. The air is so still and so silent, I can't even hear the usual thrum of distant traffic. The sky has cleared and the stars are shining brightly, despite the glare from the snow which blankets the street in undisturbed, brilliant white. It looks fake in its perfection, like something off a movie set or postcard. It's almost a shame to ruin it with my footsteps and tyre tracks, but I'm a woman on a mission and snow isn't going to stop me.

All the cars look similar, shrouded by snow, but luckily, my little Clio is easy to spot. I start the engine and put the heaters on full, then get out and scrape the snow off the roof and windows, my fingers turning numb in the process. I also use my snow scraper to clear the snow off the road just in front of each of my tyres to help me get going.

Eventually, I cautiously ease the car out of its space and slide down the road. I can feel the lack of control in the wheels and grip the steering wheel tightly, cruising as slowly as I can and praying that the car doesn't slide into another one and dent it. Fortunately, living quite close to a main road. it's only a few nerve-wracking minutes until I'm pulling onto the recently cleared and gritted A-Road.

# Chapter Twenty-Nine

## Christmas Day

It's a gruelling hour and a half later that I enter Cheltenham, the icy roads ensuring that I kept my speed to a minimum. It had felt strangely eerie driving along the almost deserted M5, the sparkling white, enveloped landscape almost unrecognisable and only the occasional lorry or gritter providing any other signs of life. Once again, Radio Two kept me company. The cheesy Christmas tunes and the cheerful voice of the DJ were nicely grounding.

I'm too nervous to attempt driving along snow-covered side streets again, so just pull into the first space that I see on the main road near to where Adam lives. I'm pretty sure that I should have a permit to park here, but at this stage, I'm willing to risk a parking fine.

I crunch along the quiet streets, towards Adam's square. I remember us spending a summer's day there once, picnicking and playing frisbee so I know where he lives, just not which flat. Some of the buildings already have lights on; the world is waking up to Christmas Day, although, outside on the suburban streets, it's still and quiet. And bloody freezing.

Without breaking my stride, I pull my gloves on and yank my bobble hat down over my head as I turn into Clarence Square. I stop for a moment, my eyes sweeping the buildings. Somewhere behind these walls, Adam is fast asleep. He told me he'd be sleeping at his flat over Christmas as his auntie and gran are at his parents and he didn't want to sleep on the sofa at their house for the sake of a few minutes' walk in the mornings.

Clarence Square is a set of cream-painted, period, four-storey townhouses built in a square around a small park. They're charming buildings with wrought iron railings and steps up to the front doors and down to the basements. Most of the windows are in darkness, save for three which have soft yellow light spilling out onto the snow. I can totally see Adam living here. Just in which one?

Most of the houses have been converted into flats and he said that he had a view of the park, so that discounts the basement flats. I start from the beginning and climb the steps of the first building, holding tightly onto the handrail as my feet slip slightly on the soft snow. I scan the list of names next to the intercom. Nope, not here. One of them is blank though, what if Adam hasn't put his name on his flat? I'll never find him. Oh well, I'll cross that bridge if I come to it.

Methodically, I make my way around the square, up and down the steps, my footprints in the snow a trail of my disappointment. Finally, about a third of the way round, I see it.

*A Curtis. Flat 4.*

My finger hovers over the buzzer, butterflies raging in my stomach, but I don't press it. I'd been so intent on getting here, on seeing him, that I didn't think this through. I don't even know what I'm going to say. I guess 'I love you' would be the obvious choice. But to just wake him up and declare 'I love you' feels a bit ambushy. I know I'd be a bit thrown if that happened to me. I turn back to the square, which looks magical in the snow and I have an idea.

I carefully make my way back down the steps and cross the road to the park. The entrance gate is on the corner and, as I enter, I stick close to the edge of the fence so as not to disturb the snow. There are a couple of large trees in the centre of the square, but Adam's flat directly overlooks the large area of grass currently obliterated by a pure white, glittering canvas.

Swinging my arms to help my projection, I leap into the middle of the snow, landing gymnast-like with my arms aloft for balance. I then shuffle my feet round in the snow spelling out the letters.

It's harder than I imagined and I'm quite warm by the time I finish shuffling round. I leap back over to the fence and turn to study my handiwork:

*Merry Christmas*

It looks good. A few more apartment lights came on as I was writing and I like the idea of children looking out of their windows, seeing the snow and my message. Adam's windows are still in darkness though, so time for part two of my plan.

I pull my teeny boppers out of my handbag, switch them on and, pulling my bobble hat off, place them on my head. Then I scoop up a handful of snow, pat it into a ball and launch it at the top window of Adam's building. It misses and hits the wall with a soft thud. The ball hovers for a moment against the paintwork before sliding down the building. Unperturbed, I make another ball and try again. Yes! A direct hit.

I keep throwing. Four hits and three misses later, the light finally comes on. Thank God! I was beginning to worry that perhaps he had stayed at his parents' after all. I already have a snowball in my hand, so I launch that one too. I watch it arc gracefully through the air and hit the glass with a pleasing splat.

A second later, the sash window is pulled up and Adam's dishevelled head and bare shoulders appear. He still sleeps naked then. A shiver of lust runs through me at the thought. Even from this distance, I can see the confusion on his face as he takes in the scene and then I see his features break into a smile.

"Rose, what are you doing here?" he calls incredulously.

I pause for a moment. Now would be the perfect time to say, 'I love you'. However, I might have taken big strides this morning, but declaring love from a beautiful, snow-covered park on Christmas Day is just too Rom-Com for me.

"It snowed," I say instead, stating the obvious. "I thought you might like to build a snowman?"

Great! Instead of Rom-Com, I seem to be channelling a Disney character.

Adam doesn't seem to notice, though as, smiling again, he shuts the window, disappearing out of sight.

As I wait, I stamp my feet and blow on my frozen hands. My gloves, soggy from all the snowy handrails and snowballs, are not doing much to keep my fingers warm. I look around the square. It really is lovely and so close to town too; I can see why Adam chose it. He was lucky to find a flat here, they must be in high demand. It almost looks too pretty; the old-fashioned street lamps casting a golden glow over the white snow and cream buildings and silhouetting the sparkling branches of the majestic trees. Once again, I wish I was a photographer and could accurately capture it all.

I feel so excited, so elated, it's like I've taken something, like my whole body is vibrating. I also feel incredibly, inexplicably nervous. I'm really doing this. Taking the plunge. Putting my heart out there. I've never made the first move before, not that this is technically the first move, but it's a big gesture. Adam deserves a big gesture.

So, I guess he'll come out, we'll build the snowman, have a giggle, then maybe go back into his flat and have a coffee. And then I can apologise for running away in London and ask if he still wants us to be a couple again. Sorted.

If only he'd hurry up, he's taking a while to just throw some clothes on. Unless, well, he didn't actually say he was coming down. What if I misread the smile? He was far away and the light was poor. What if it was more of a grimace? What if I really blew it in London and he decided I'm not worth the drama?

Oh, for God's sake, I'm doing it again, assuming the worst, not listening to rationality. Even if he had changed his mind, Adam has integrity, he would still come out here and tell me to my face.

Suddenly the door to his building swings open and Adam appears, the shy smile he bestows on me alleviating my fears a bit. He's dressed in his ugly coat too which makes me grin, despite the feeling of a hundred fluttering birds in my chest. As he walks closer, I can see the expression on his face is slightly wary. I'm not surprised, he must be wondering if I've finally cracked up completely.

"Hi," he says softly as he enters the gate, a few feet from where I'm standing, and his eyes scan my message again.

"Sorry I ran off in London and I get you're probably mad at me," I blurt out.

"What makes you think I'm mad at you?" he interjects blankly.

"Well, why wouldn't you be? And, you know, you took ages coming out, I thought maybe you..." I trail off, this isn't going how I pictured. Seeing him there in front of me is jumbling my thoughts. Before I can continue blathering, he cuts in again.

"You don't need to apologise for the Tube station. You'd not slept, and it had been an emotional night, to say the least. Of course, you'd need time to process everything, I shouldn't have pressured you like that, it wasn't the time. And as for why I took so long to come out, I was trying to find batteries."

"Batteries?" I ask, confused.

"Yeah, for these." And he whips his pair of teeny boppers out from his pocket, flicks the light on and pops them on his head with a smile.

He kept them, after all these years, he kept them. All my plans for what I was going to say and do disappear in an instant and before I know what I'm doing, I'm flying at him, throwing my arms around his neck and kissing him fiercely.

I feel him stumble momentarily as I leap at him, but then he steadies himself and his arms are around my waist holding me tightly and he's kissing me back. It's not a sweet, gentle, romantic kiss; it's wild and passionate with all the crazy emotion of the last twenty-four hours poured into it. The nervous birds in my stomach are quickly replaced by bolts of desire ricocheting through my whole system as the kiss intensifies. I feel like I'm floating. I feel like fireworks are exploding. I feel like I may actually burst. I feel all those things that I used to think were contrived cliches. I feel alive.

Eventually, Adam breaks our kiss, stepping back from me slightly and taking both my hands in his. We stand for a moment, staring at each other, both of us breathing heavily, my whole body trembling. Again, this would be the moment to say something, but I can't gather my senses enough after that phenomenal kiss.

"Not that I'm complaining," Adam says gently, breaking the silence, "but that's not how you build a snowman. You know that, right?"

A giggle escapes me at his deadpan expression and his face breaks into a warm, gorgeous smile in response.

"Sorry, I just couldn't help myself," I say, biting my lip.

"It's the bogey coat, right? It's just too sexy."

"Actually," I say, stepping closer to him again and softly touching the teeny boppers, "it was these. I can't believe you kept them, after all these years."

"Of course I did," he says so matter of fact that emotion swells in my chest, as I trail my hand down his face, stroking his cheek. "I have a box of stuff that I keep under my bed."

"You have a Rose box?" I whisper, incredulously.

"I have a Rose box. And, in case you're wondering, only a Rose box."

"I have an Adam box," I reply, unzipping my coat to reveal what's underneath.

"Is that my old hoody?"

"Yep."

"I thought someone stole it the night of that party. I was gutted."

"Well, technically someone did," I smile, relieved that talking about that night doesn't come with crushing guilt or feeling of panic. What happened, happened, but we're here now and we have a second chance and that's all that matters.

"So, why would you have an Adam box?" he asks gently, brushing a lock of hair off my forehead and looking deep into my eyes. For once, I don't get uncomfortable or look away. I stare back into his handsome face and finally say, "Because I've always loved you. I still love you. I will always love you."

"Good. Because I love you too. Always have, always will."

"Merry Christmas," I whisper.

"Merry Christmas," Adam whispers back before kissing me tenderly.

# Acknowledgements

A huge thank you to all you lovely people who have bought this book. I hope you enjoyed reading it as much as I enjoyed writing it.

Seeing my book come to fruition has been a dream come true and I would like to thank the team at Saron for making that happen.

This book would not have been possible were it not for the devotion of my loving parents, Peter and Julie McGowan. They have always encouraged our family to strive to achieve our dreams and they support us through everything. They have always believed in me when I didn't believe in myself. My mum is a brilliant writer (I thoroughly recommend you check out her books!) and I doubt my book would have attracted a publisher without her insight and edits.

I'm eternally grateful to come from such a close family and want to thank all my siblings and their spouses for their love and support. In particular Susan and Titch for being the first people I ever allowed to read my work and for their continuous, enthusiastic, encouragement. I'm also very grateful that you all provided me with beautiful nieces and a gorgeous nephew to direct all my excess maternal love towards!

To all my wonderful friends, you know who you are, thank you for enriching my life. In particular, Beth, for being my long-time bestie and always having my back, no matter what.

Jo and Karen for all the giggles. Our adventures around London spawned the idea for this book.

Helene and Lisa for always being on hand with practical and emotional support... and often a glass of vodka. As always, Aly is never far from my thoughts. She would have got a real kick out of me doing this.

40Fest gang for generally being awesome and always making me smile. You're more like family and I love that our friendships have not only endured but flourished throughout adulthood. Spending time with all of you feels like it recharges my soul.

My mum friends: Amy, Amy, Emily, Jess, Rach. I'm very thankful to be part of our little crew. I would have gone mad during the last few years had it not been for our walks, chats, laughs and just being there for each other. Cheaper than any therapist!

Dave, thank you for making me feel like the lead in my own romantic story. I feel very lucky to have found you.

Finally, I want to thank my two beautiful children who bring so much joy and sunshine into my life. You are my reason for being and I love you more than words could ever express.

# Meet the Author

Cat was born in Surrey and moved around before finally settling in Wales with her two adorable but rambunctious children and their fluffy Cocker Spaniel. She put her theatre degree to good use while co-running a successful theatre company for several years. She wrote all the plays they performed and continues to write productions for a children's drama group in her town. Writing novels is her new passion and she hopes many more will follow *Under a Christmas Sky*. Cat loves to travel and, when she can't, she relies on books to transport her to different places. Her free time is spent with her kids, climbing trees, doing arts and crafts or eating cake. Otherwise, you can find Cat stomping around the hiking trails of Monmouthshire.

You can follow Cat on Facebook, Instagram or via Twitter at @Cmcgowan_writer.

Milton Keynes UK
Ingram Content Group UK Ltd.
UKHW052342251024
450203UK00012B/27